John Hawksworth lives in Liverpool with his wife and son. He worked in the pensions and life insurance business as a compliance officer for 20 years. He has climbed the three peaks, canoed down Ben Nevis and jumped out of three perfectly serviceable airplanes for reasons best known to himself. He is considering a new fitness regime, for which he has downloaded the 'couch to 5K' app. Whether he will do anything further remains to be seen. He is a committed Christian and attends his local church as often as work and life allow.

For my family, and all those making the journey.

John Hawksworth

THE IMPOSSIBLE MAN

Book I of The Judean Chronicles

AUSTIN MACAULEY PUBLISHERS™

LONDON • CAMBRIDGE • NEW YORK • SHARJAH

A CIP catalogue record for this title is available from the British Library.

ISBN 9781398435490 (Paperback)
ISBN 9781398435506 (ePub e-book)

www.austinmacauley.com

First Published 2023
Austin Macauley Publishers Ltd®
1 Canada Square
Canary Wharf
London
E14 5AA

Writing is the best job I have ever done. Even though it is a strangely isolated process, it cannot be achieved without the help and support of others. First of these are my wife and son. For the last two years they have been largely ignored. Their unspoken acceptance of my lunacy is always a surprise and always appreciated. I also want to thank Harris. He is the manager of Domino's Pizza in Allerton, Liverpool and one of the best bosses I have had the privilege to work for, and has always managed to give me the time I needed. There is also the amazing team at Austin Macauley that have held my hand and guided me through this process. Thanks must also go to the congregation of St Andrews church in Clubmoor, Tuebrook. In particular four people. Amanda and Blair, who's constant enquiries about 'the book' have helped push it to its final conclusion. The other two are Mark and Brenda, thank you for bringing me back. I finally want to thank all those who elected to follow my Facebook page, bought the first book and left such kind remarks on Amazon.

Prologue

Judea was in turmoil, again.

It was the usual, meaningless, regular disturbance. Judea, like the Germanics, Gaul's and Britons before them, wanted their independence. One of the last three bastions of the Roman Empire, they were fighting for their freedom, freedom from their Roman aggressors.

For three months, Judea had been battling with the Roman army. It had started without any warning. Suddenly, out of nowhere the revolutionary forces had attacked and wiped out the garrison of soldiers at Madena.

This had followed with further successes. The twenty first legion had been surprised at the border crossing with Egypt two days later, losing nearly half their contingent.

A week later, the famed tenth legion had met with an embarrassing rout on the outskirts of Ma'ale Gilboa.

Rome had been humiliated by this rag tag band of Judeans. That shame had been reported around the world, capturing the interest of all the major news outlets.

The fervour of revolution had swept through the nation, inspiring the people. Thousands had rallied to the cause. At long last, after almost two thousand years of oppression and brutality, freedom seemed tantalisingly close.

Why not?

The Britons had been enjoying self-governing independence since the twelfth century. Although, this was mainly due to Rome abandoning their interest rather than through revolution. With the necessity of a sea crossing, Emperor Victus III had decided to leave the troublesome Britons to their own devices. He had assumed that the land would descend into tribal warfare; but it hadn't.

Yes, at first there had been a number of internal squabbles and power struggles. Then the King in the north had united the country. As a consequence,

Britannia had remained relatively peaceful, and it had flourished. The Britons were now a force in the world, leading the technological advancement and developing the third strongest economy.

More recently, as near as the eighteen hundreds, across western Europa, the Gauls had united. After six years of war, they had finally thrown out their Roman oppressors.

In the early nineteen hundred the Germanic tribes had achieved the same.

So, why shouldn't the Roman province of Judea achieve their freedom?

Unfortunately, the Judean revolutionary leader, Ishmael Barabbas was little more than a street fighter. He lacked the skills and finesse to succeed.

Those early achievements had not been repeated. The Roman army had regrouped, licked its wounds and hit back ruthlessly. The Judean forces had never had a chance of winning the war. They called themselves an army, but the truth was that they were just a disorganised rabble. They never stood a chance against the might of the Roman army. Rome was better equipped, more experienced and highly organised.

Barabbas had been out classed, and out manoeuvred by the superiority of the Roman military machine.

The Judean revolution was over, along with their dreams of independence.

It was not just the hearts of the people the revolution had wooed. It had also captured the headlines of the world press. Something George Ambrose, languishing in a cell, knew better than most. As one of the most respected reporters based with the London Times, he had been writing about the conflict since day one. Until two weeks ago, when the Judean forces had snatched him. Now they held him prisoner, convinced he was in the pay of Rome's intelligence bureau.

Therefore, the fact that the war was in its last days did not bring him much comfort. In fact, he suspected this made his situation even more precarious. He had insisted all along that he was just a reporter. They were not inclined to believe him, and had taken the last two weeks trying to extract a confession.

To begin with, he had thought he had been taken for ransom. That they knew who he was, and connected that knowledge to who his father was. A connection he had kept quiet throughout his working life. That his father was a high-ranking functionary inside his majesty's government.

However, once the interrogations began, it was soon obvious they had no idea who it was they held. Various methods, both ancient and modern, had been employed to gain a confession of his supposed crime.

It had started with beatings. His hands would be shackled behind him, they would drench him in ice cold water prior to beginning. A variety of implements were employed, besides their fists. Wooden bats, plastic straps and metal rods. He was punched, slapped and kicked. Sometimes by a lone assailant, sometimes more than one. They would take turns, careful not to take it too far and end up killing him.

When this proved less than successful, they changed their approach to include the use of cattle prods. Now, while they beat him, they administered sudden, sharp electric shocks. Not strong enough to kill, just a low current, high voltage shock. Strong enough to inflict a significant level of pain.

This addition to the daily punishment ritual also proved unsuccessful. It had surprised his captors. It only served to add to their conviction that they had the right man. Surely, if he was just a reporter he would have cracked by now. Only someone who had received specialist training could resist this level of punishment. The contradiction of this never entered their minds. Such was the belief they held that they had the right man.

So, they took it up a level. Torture. A method colloquially known as the helicopter. Georges hands and feet would be tied behind his back, then he would be suspended in the air. Sometimes they would leave him hanging there for hours. It was during one of these sessions that his shoulder had dislocated.

Then all of a sudden, after what George judged to be about ten days, it stopped.

Had they given up?

Where they finally convinced he was not what they thought?

Through the fog of his pain, George did not think so. They had been very persistent, and the distant sound of gunfire hinted at an end to the hostilities. He had also overheard snatches of conversations between the guards. Not much, but enough to know the war was not going well. There had been talk of abandoning their station, but the commander had told them all he would execute anyone who tried to leave as deserters. This didn't stop the discussions, they wanted to get out of this madness alive while they still had the chance.

The sound of fighting had been getting closer. George could sense that the end was near. He could hear the fighting from outside, in the compound. It would either be rescue by the Roman forces, or a bullet from his captors. At this moment, he was not sure which he preferred. After ten days of brutal treatment, he just wanted it to end. To be free of pain. Along with the shoulder, he was fairly sure a couple of his ribs were broken.

The door to his cell was suddenly thrust open, one of the senior members of the Judean revolutionaries rushed in. Raising the pistol in his hand he spoke, "At least I get to finish you." As soon as he spoke, George managed to role himself off his bed, landing on the floor and shouting out in pain. He was not quite quick enough, as the bullet left the barrel of the gun and entered the thigh of his right leg.

A further salvo of shots rang out, making his attacker perform some macabre dance as the bullets punctured his body.

George looked at the man who followed. He just made out the form of Colonel Vespian of the Roman Army before he passed out.

Vespian rushed over, calling for a medic as he went. Reaching George, he grabbed him saying, "It's ok, old friend. I've got you." Seconds later the doctor was at his side, strapping a pressure pad against the wound in his leg. Completed, he turned his attention to the rest of George.

"Hospital, now," he stated brusquely.

Vespian barked out orders, two soldiers appeared. They gently supported George, carrying him out to a waiting ambulance. They settled him down on the stretcher. The doctor jumped aboard, the doors where slammed shut and, sirens blaring, the vehicle rushed away.

The Colonel watched as it left, then turned back to the business at hand. A lieutenant came up to him, saluted and confirmed they had them all, except some of the ring leaders. Vespian swore under his breath, yet again Barabbas had escaped.

"What are your orders, sir?" Lieutenant Aurelias asked.

"Gather the senior member of their so-called army, have them shipped back to the barrack cells for questioning."

"And the others?"

"They are enemies of Rome, deal with them."

"Yes, sir."

"Well, get on with it, and send Isaak over."

The Colonel swept the compound with his eyes. The clean-up was already taking place. The injured soldiers were being attended to, the fallen placed in body bags, to be returned to their families for burial. The bodies of their enemies were being piled up, they would be burnt later. As usual, everything was being carried out efficiently by those under his command.

Isaak had arrived, turning to address him the Colonel spoke, "I am reliably informed you are the best tracker in all Judea."

"Colonel?"

"I have a job for you. Ishmael Barabbas has escaped. Find him, and bring him back to us." The Colonel called three privates over. "Take these with you." He turned to speak directly to the men. "You are to give any assistance, bring Barabbas back to me. Alive." The soldiers nodded, turning back to Isaak he continued, "And I will ensure your usual terms are agreed."

"Thank you, Colonel. I am grateful."

"Just make sure you find him."

"I will not fail."

"Make sure you don't. I want him alive, understood?"

"Yes, clearly."

"Anyone who helps him in any way, they are enemies of Rome and are to be dealt with accordingly." All four men nodded their understanding of what they were being told. "Good, take one of the jeeps." All four left to begin their task.

The Colonel called the Lieutenant. The officer appeared at one of the doorways. The Colonel shouted over, "Carry on with the clean-up, I'm heading to the hospital." Not waiting for a response, he walked over to his driver, instructing him and climbing into the passenger seat.

The journey to the military hospital took twenty minutes. After some preliminary enquiries he was directed by one of the nurses to room four hundred and nine.

The room was empty, he assumed George was in surgery. As that occurred to him, he heard a trolley being pushed along the corridor containing the man he sought.

Without being asked, the doctor spoke, "He is slightly malnourished, so we will provide a protein drip. Blood pressure is a little high, heart rate fast. Nothing I wouldn't expect under the circumstances. He also has three cracked ribs, I had to reset the left shoulder and his body is covered in bruises and contusions. Whoever administered the beating knew what they were doing. Inflict the maximum damage without actually killing him. The bullet has been removed from his leg, it was a clean entry and exit through the flesh, so no serious damage caused. He will eventually make a full, physical recovery. Mentally, I can't say. Not my area. I have passed the details over too one of my colleagues, an expert in those things."

"How long?"

"About six months. He should be able to return home in two."

"Thank you, doctor."

At that moment alarms went off, shrilling loudly. The doctor rushed over to his patient, hitting the red alarm button next to the wall.

Part One
Thursday

Chapter One
Return

As usual, George Ambrose woke up with a hangover. Not the normal head banging, stomach turning one. This time he just had the dull, throbbing sensation behind the eyes. Added to this, his shoulder was painful, increasing his discomfort. Forcing himself to get up, he ambled through to the bathroom. After turning the shower on to warm, he opened the wall cabinet. Reaching for the pain killers he kept there, he popped the cap open and shook two out onto the palm of his hand. He tossed them into his mouth, through his head back and swallowed. Stripping out of his shorts, he stood under the shower, letting the water wash over him.

He had slept sporadically. For the first time in a week the nightmares had returned. Terrifying visions from his ordeal in Judea eighteen months earlier. After the initial recovery period at the military medical station, he had been flown back to London. There he continued his recuperation for another two months, including three weeks of intensive physiotherapy. His shoulder had still not fully regained its mobility, standing still at an eighty-five per-cent return in use.

Then came the therapy sessions. The directors of the paper had agreed to pay the bill, had engaged one of the finest psychologists in the field. George had attended when required. At first, they had been useful, but in the later weeks he had come to dread these appointments. The doctor had wanted him to talk through what had happened, and do so in endless detail. All George wanted to do was forget, put it all behind him. As far as he was concerned, all these talks did was to remind him, add to his trauma. Making him relive it all over and over again. How was he supposed to 'move on' as they put it if they just kept on insisting on hearing it all? So he stopped going, telling the board he was fine now.

When he had first returned, his editor in chief, and oldest friend, Charles Harcourt-DeVere had ensured he only had light duties. No big story to cover, nothing that might add to his stress. Small, local interest stories. As a result, he had travelled the length and breadth of the country. He had seen more of it in the last four months than he had in his lifetime. Through the stress, his work had suffered as well. That legendary quality that had seen him awarded two prestigious journalism awards. The talent that had catapulted him to fame in the close-knit journalistic world. That ability had seemingly decided not to return from Judea with him.

In those early days of his return to work, he had been sought out by other reporters. Hailed as a hero. It didn't last long, it soon became obvious that he was not the writer he used to be. No longer the star he was, a spent force.

Now they rarely spoke to him, avoided him. It was as if they considered him infectious, guilty by association. The younger reporters no longer asked for his advice. The majority of his colleagues no longer thought if, but rather when he would be let go.

His personal life had suffered as well. Those few friends he had, he'd pushed away. Tired of their sympathy, their false platitudes. Their attempts to understand, as if they could relate to what he had been through. Only Charles remained. Faithful to the last.

George had initially had trouble sleeping. The nightmares had been frequent, eventually occurring less often. The problem though was that they did not just come in the night. There were times when something would occur that triggered a memory. These flashbacks were so vivid, he felt like he was living through it all again in real time. Back there, in that cold, dank cell.

George knew it was only his mind playing tricks with him. That knowledge, however did not stop the emotional and physical sensations that came flooding back. Filling his mind and body. The fear, the sweating and the smells of his incarceration. They still felt very real. These occurrences, like the nightmares, had lessened over the months, but that did not make it any less frightening.

George fought back, by trying to keep as busy as possible. Taking on jobs that should have gone to the younger, less experienced reporters.

What he found really exhausting though, was this inability to be able to fully relax. Constantly on his guard. Always alert to any imagined danger. Living in this perpetual state of hyper-sensitivity was over whelming at times.

As he dressed, George heard his mobile ringing from the other room. Buttoning up his white shirt, he walked over and picked it up. Noticing the caller ID, he swept his finger to accept the call.

"Charles, this is unexpected,"

"Are you on your way in?"

"About to leave, be there in half an hour."

"Good. Try and make it sooner. Pack a bag and bring your passport, something's come up."

"What?"

"I'll tell you when you get here." Charles responded, then hung up. Brief, and to the point as normal George thought. George put the phone in his shirt pocket and finished dressing. He grabbed his go bag, lit a cigarette and grabbed some toiletries from the bathroom.

George was not particularly concerned by the call. Charles knew what he was going through, better than anyone. If he needed to send him off somewhere he would have a very good reason for doing so. George was well aware that Charles had been protecting him from the board, protecting his position on the paper. It was possible that the board had finally lost patience and given an ultimatum.

Picking up the keys to his flat, he headed out the door. He decided to take the stairs rather than wait for the lift. Descending the three flights, he exited through the rear entrance of the apartment block. Walking through the resident's gardens he reached the gate, opened it and turned left down Hatton Gardens. At the end of the road, he negotiated the crossing where five roads all met together. Continuing down New Fetter Lane, he made another left-hand turn onto Fleet Street. The office of the London Times was about a third of the way along.

As he walked, he observed the local café's dealing with the breakfast rush. As had become habit since returning, he entered the Cock Tavern to purchase his morning coffee and a bacon sandwich. He liked this establishment. Their coffee had a strong, smoky flavour to it. It was also the only place he knew near the paper that served their bacon between slices of toasted Irish sourdough bread. He shared a joke with the girl serving him, paid and continued on his way.

Within a couple of minutes, he was entering the famed offices of the London Times newspaper. Founded in seventeen eighty-five, its original name had been The Daily Universal Register. On the first of January seventeen eighty-eight it was changed to The Times. Forty-three years later The Sunday Times arrived in eighteen twenty-one. Both papers remained separate entities, complete with their own staff. It was founded by John Walter after the insurance company he worked for went into bankruptcy. He took on the role as editor, even being convicted and spending sixteen months in Newgate Prison for libel. However, his innovative work to obtain world and domestic news helped to build the paper's global reputation. Those early pioneering efforts to gather international news made it the most read newspaper for politicians and financiers. This was also due to his use of experts, rather than just a reporter, in the fields of politics, art, literature, and finance.

It was in those early days, that the profits were huge for the eighteenth century, while any competition was virtually non-existent. This meant it could pay more for information than its rivals. In eighteen seventeen, a new general editor, Thomas Barnes, was appointed. In that same year, the long-standing printer James Lewson died, passing on the business to his son John. John developed startling new processes in printing, and their collaboration drove the reputation of the paper to new heights.

The paper gained a nickname, The Thunderer. This was due in no small part to the work of two of its journalists. Peter Fraser and Edward Sterling. Their articles pushing for social and political reform increased the paper's circulation as well as its reputation and influence.

Circulation was further improved with the arrival of steam locomotion, enabling distribution further afield.

The paper was the first to employ what would later become known as war correspondents. Sending their reporters into danger zones all over the world to bring up to date reports from the battlefields.

The paper was now in the position of enjoying a five million circulation figure and a reputation envied throughout the industry. The Times, and by association the journalists, became a name you could trust. If it was printed in the times, it must be true. The current board guarded that reputation jealously.

Arriving at the paper, George waved to the receptionist before pressing the button to call a lift. Once it arrived, he entered pressing the for the top floor and dropping his bag at his feet. Other journalists got in and out on his journey, few even acknowledged his presence. George could remember a time when they would have made a point to talk to him.

Arriving, he exited, turned right and headed down the corridor to Charles's office at the bottom. He passed portraits of the long dead former proprietors and former editors that decorated the walls. As he entered the office of the editor in chief, he greeted Jean, his secretary with a cheerful good morning. She was on a call, but she indicated that he could go straight through to the editor's inner sanctum.

Charles was also in the middle of a call, giving some poor individual the benefit of his wrath. George sat down as he finished the call.

"…and tell him from me, if he does anything that stupid again, the next thing he will be working on will be his C.V." Charles Harcourt-DeVere replaced the receiver. Looking over at George he said, "Even in a fresh suit you still look like shit."

"Thanks. You look good too."

Charles passed over some papers. "This came in through the overnight bag yesterday. The board have been made aware of its content, and they have taken the usual stance should the worst scenario be realised."

"The 'we do not negotiate with terrorists' stance?"

"That's the one. A bit premature in my opinion. Well, read it and you will see what I mean."

George began to read the information he had been passed. After the usual platitudes the next paragraph sent chills through his body:

'We gave this assignment to James Henry Abbott. In the beginning his reports were well balanced and objective in content, as one would expect.

'In the last couple of days these reports have changed dramatically. The objectivity has gone. We now suspect he is being held against his will, forced to write what they want.

'The writing has become very one sided, some would say even fanciful. It is as though they are using him to write their manifesto; one that will be used to found a new political party, one that will dispute all that the current council stands for.

'I would not ask this if I did not think it was essential. Especially after what he went through. However, George still has a lot of contacts out here, people that could help us.

'We need George and his contacts.

'James is a good journalist, he has a natural instinct for a story. Either one of two things has happened.

'Firstly, they are holding him against his will in order to get their message out to the public.

'Or, he has fallen under the spell of their charismatic leader, Joseph Bartholomew. Has become one of his followers.

'Whichever one it is, we need to help him.

'So, if you can spare him and he is willing, can we have George Ambrose back?'

George handed the papers back. "I see why you wanted be to pack a bag. Does Derek know?"

"No."

"Does the board?"

"No-one knows. As you both requested, no-one on the paper knows James is your son." Charles paused. "Speaking of the board, do you know what they said when they saw that?" He nodded towards the papers on his desk.

"Apart from the obvious, no. Enlighten me."

"They said, and I'm quoting here, 'send him, He's been no effing use to us for months.' They also said that if you refuse, I am under strict instruction to kick your sorry arse out the door. As far as they are concerned, this is your ultimatum. I assume you will go?"

"Of course. He's my son, and probably the only reason I would go back."

"The board also asked me to let you know this is your final chance at redemption."

"Redemption?"

"Their exact words. You never know, this could be a good thing."

"In what way?"

"Facing down your demons. Your worst nightmares. I don't know."

"Sounds like the claptrap the psychologists used to come out with. I can tell you, that's not what it feels like."

"Well, whatever. I will be glad to see the back of you for a couple of days. Because, quite frankly, you have been a huge pain in the arse."

"Thanks."

"You're welcome, and I notice you didn't disagree. With any luck you will discover that old spark that won you the Arthur Koestler award and brought down a government." Charles stopped, looking fondly at his old friend. "Everyone here thinks you are about two steps away from becoming a washed-up hack. One of the also rans."

"Is that what you think?"

"Not by a long way. I believe the journalist I know is still in there somewhere. It just needs the right spark to get the engines going again."

"And this might just be it?"

"I hope so, old friend, because I'm running out of excuses to give the board."

"When's my flight?"

"There is a driver and car waiting to take you to the airfield now, they are letting you have use of the company jet."

"They really do want me gone," George joked as he stood up, picked up his bag and said his goodbyes.

Charles watched as George left with a mixture of hope and dread. The hope that he would be finally able to put the ghosts of the past to rest. The Dread that going back might be that one step to far. Charles believed if he could get through these coming days, he would arrive at the other side a better journalist than he had ever been.

When George reappeared on the ground floor, he saw the driver in his uniform stood by the reception desk. He walked over and introduced himself, the driver checked his order slip. "George Ambrose, transfer to Queen Victoria airfield," he confirmed. "This way, sir."

"Lead the way." George commented and followed him out through the front entrance. The driver opened the rear door of the black Bentley Mulsanne. George threw his bag in, then climbed in after it. The driver closed the door and walked round to take his position in the driver's seat.

It was a short, forty-five-minute drive to the airfield, where the companies Lear Jet waited on the tarmac. Checks completed, and ten minutes later they were taxing towards the runway.

Once airborne, George released his safety belt, asked the steward for a coffee and settled back for the six-hour flight.

He had never wanted to make this journey ever again. He had decided that part of the world belonged to his past. However, as soon as he read that it concerned his son, the decision to return was already made. James was the one, good, last thing he had left. Whatever it took to protect him, it would be done.

It was a long and boring flight, he tried to catch up on some sleep, but was too restless. In the end, as he had nothing to do as the only passenger he asked if the steward played chess. He did, so they spent the rest of the flight competing across the board. George was a reasonable player, above average anyway. The steward, it turned out was something of a grand master. George had his arse kicked, then handed back to him. During the remainder of the flight, they managed three games, George lost them all. He was relieved when the seat belt light came on as the plane began its descent. Looking out of his small window, George could see the city of Jerusalem in the distance.

Safely on the ground, bag in hand he made his way off the plane. As soon as he left its air-conditioned comfort, the heat hit him with an intense ferocity. It surprised him, he had forgotten how suffocating the heat could be in this part of the world. It was all encompassing, like a slap in the face as it hit him. There was no escape from it, other than to get inside. By the time he had walked across the tarmac into the customs terminal he could already feel the sweat prickling his back. As the only customer, and only the one handheld piece of luggage he was cleared quickly.

Following the signs to the main concourse, he was surprised to see Colonel Vespian waiting. They shook hands warmly, Vespian talking.

"It is good to see you again, my friend."

"How did you know I was coming?"

"I have a new role since you were last here. Senior adviser to the governor. As a consequence, all flights are approved through my office, I saw your name on the flight manifest. So, as you had not bothered to tell me, I thought I would come and meet you."

"Sorry, I would have called you but it was something of a sudden decision."

"Anything I should be concerned with?"

"Definitely not, just some minor problem with the paper out here. They decided I was the best person to deal with it."

"Then I am pleased they made that choice. May I commandeer you for dinner this evening?"

"You can. I need to ensure I am contactable, perhaps we could eat at my hotel? I'm staying at the King David."

"Their restaurant is excellent. Shall we say seven-thirty?"

"Perfect, and this meal is on me. In return you could bring me up to date?"

"A fair exchange. Please, I have some further business here, so allow my driver to drop you off."

"That's very kind, but really not necessary."

"I insist. We Romans do not have many friends in the international press, so we must look after those we do have."

"In that case, thank you."

As they talked, they had been walking and had reached the main doors. Vespian signalled to a man stood outside, who came running forward. "Take Mr Ambrose to his hotel, then come back for me."

"Yes, sir," the soldier replied.

Turning to shake George's hand once more, he spoke again, "Until this evening." They parted company as George left with the driver. It was a short journey to the Hotel, while being driven George was thinking. Vespian had access to flight approval, manifests and was on the advisory staff. This meant that he was part of the intelligence community. He suspected Vespian may have been playing down the position, he was a full Colonel. A decorated soldier.

He was looking forward to dinner. George had been out of the area for well over a year. That was a lifetime, things changed rapidly due to the complicated political set up of the region. Power struggles within the Jewish Council, the unsettled relationship between them and the Roman governor. The constant stream of ever-changing governors also added to the restlessness. Each successive governor always tried to stamp their authority over the council upon arrival. It would be useful to get up to date with the current situation. He wanted to see his son, but had no idea where he might be. He would ring the paper once he was in the hotel, arrange to meet him later. Or with the editor, Derek Watling.

George became aware that they had come to a stop, the soldier had already opened the door for him. As he got out, the driver wished him a good day and even saluted. George hoped that last action had been done out of habit.

He thanked him, then looked up at the King David Hilton Hotel. He had always found the building, from the outside anyway, indescribably ugly. A modern building dumped between the ancient, it looked completely out of place. Once inside, however, it was very different. The main lobby had been decorated tastefully, giving a welcoming feel to the whole building. George walked up to the receptionist; a young man dressed in the company uniform of a pale blue suit with the traditional gold 'H' on the collars.

After completing the registration forms, the gentleman behind the counter passed him a brown envelope. "This was left for you earlier today, and a Mr Watling left you a message, Mr Ambrose. If convenient, he will meet you in the bar at ten this evening." Handing over a telephone message slip. "All the details are here."

"Thank you."

"Enjoy your stay with us, sir."

George headed to the lifts, getting out on the fifth floor. His room was no different to other hotels, although being the Hilton the furniture was of a slightly better quality. The usual double bed with more pillows than any one man could possibly require. A wardrobe, desk and chair to work from if needed. There was a small coffee table in the room, accompanied by two armchairs. A large flat screen TV hung on the wall, the controls sat in a box next to it. A kettle, with tea and coffee sat on a corner table.

George dropped the door pass, brown envelope and the contents of his pocket on the desk. He picked up his mobile phone and called the paper. He left a message for Derek to let him know ten that night was fine, although he might be delayed slightly. These things done, he adjusted his watch to local time, stripped off and headed into the bathroom for a shower.

It was a little after seven thirty when he finished. Picking up his mobile, cigarettes and the brown envelope he headed out the room and down to the restaurant. It only took a moment to locate the Colonel, and walk over to join him.

"What would you like to drink?" The Colonel asked him as a waiter appeared as if by magic.

"Scotch. Glengoyne, two ice cubes, please," George announced.

While they waited, George looked over the menu, asking, "What would you recommend?"

"The shakhouka, it's the best in the city here. Have it with their lofa bread, you won't be disappointed." The waiter appeared with George's drink, asking if they were ready to order. George followed Vespian's recommendation. Jotting it down on is order pad, the waiter turned to his dinner companion.

"Make that two, and bring a side order of your excellent tabbouleh salad."

"Would you like to see the wine waiter?"

George replied, "Do you have any Chateau Muser left in the cellar?"

"Yes, sir."

"Bring a bottle of that, please." The waiter finished writing, then taking the menu's away he left to deal with their request. George could see Vespian examining him, closely.

"I'm impressed with how well you seem to be coping with the after effects. There are still some small signs, but on the whole, I would say you are making good progress."

"What do you mean?"

"My new, modern medics are calling it Post Traumatic Stress. It's how they classify the stress, the after effects of going through a devastating event."

"Never heard of it."

"Like I said, it's the new thing. I am guessing that it is what we used to call battle fatigue, but the new batch of medics coming through don't like that phrase. So, they came up with a new name for it. There is some enormous evidence that backs up what they say, and I can see some of the indicators in you."

"Such as?"

"Constantly looking for something to do with your hands."

"I'm a smoker, we all do that, most of the time."

"You also bounce your left foot on its sole, and your eyes keep darting to the entrance whenever someone new comes in, as though you are expecting trouble."

"I've been sat here for less than five minutes, and you noticed all that?"

"It is what I am trained for. Besides, I've seen similar in some of my men. If it helps, no-one would dare touch you while you are with me."

"So, I just need to be concerned when you aren't around?"

"You have no reason to be concerned, but it is pointless to say so. You have been through hell, it takes time for the mind to heal. A lot longer than the body. However, I do have some news that may help. Ishmael Barabbas was captured this morning. He is currently languishing in one of my cells awaiting execution."

"How did you find him?"

"We had a tracker on him, but in the end one of his own gave him up. Also, to put your mind at rest, it is a lot calmer here these days, and with the arrest of the last of their revolutionary leaders they are a broken force." Vespian stopped talking as the waiter brought them their food. The wine waiter followed close behind, George told him to just pour it. Once they had left them, Vespian continued, "So, what brings the illustrious George Ambrose to Judea?"

"Nothing important. They just needed someone with a bit more knowledge of the region. I don't expect to be here long."

"Anything in particular?"

"Joseph Bartholomew."

"The prophet?"

"The what?"

"The prophet, that's what the locals are calling him. He has been antagonising the Jewish Council since he arrived last Sunday. It has been fun, to be honest, to watch from the side-lines. Seeing the council become more and more frustrated with everything he says and does."

"I think I like him already." George joked. "What about you? Has he caused any problems for Rome?"

"No, it's a purely local matter. Nothing to do with Rome, the governor or the emperor. Besides, I'm a soldier not a politician. Those problems lie with the new governor."

"Another one? What happened to Gratus?"

"Recalled to Rome," Vespian said, ominously.

"Who's the new one?"

"Pontius Aquinous Pilate. He arrived the same day you left. A personal appointment of Emperor Tiberius himself."

"What sort of person is he?"

Vespian considered the question before answering. "Cleverer than his predecessor, which wasn't difficult. He is smarter than most of those before him. Something people have a habit of underestimating. He can seem bullish, and he has a fiery temper. However, he is much shrewder than Gratus ever was."

"How?"

"Gratus was a bully, essentially. Like all bullies, he was an idiot. Upon arrival he tried to impose Roman will on the Jews. He misjudged them, because he didn't understand them, as a result he made a huge error in judgement."

"In what way?"

"He thought he ruled here, when in reality it is the council. He did not take them seriously, he considered them beneath him, answerable to him alone; when we all know they only answer to their God. He also forgot that Caiaphas, the leader of the council, has a close, personal relationship with the emperor. They are in constant communication with each other. Caiaphas was more than happy to pass everything he knew about Gratus to Rome."

"What sort of information?" George asked, more for something to say than out of any genuine interest.

"His sexual indiscretions with the young men in the city, and under his command. That was enough to have him recalled. It wasn't just that, Caiaphas used the information he had as a means to get rid of him. He knew it was only a matter of time before Gratus came after him as he had the others before him. Gratus would not leave them alone, he constantly interfered with their leadership.

"In the few years he was here, the council leadership changed five times. It caused unsettlement, it was one of the causes of the disturbance that you got caught up in. First there was Ananas, he was removed because he refused to cancel one of their religious festivals. He was followed by Ishmael Ben Fabus, he had him arrested for crimes against Rome when he refused to recognise Tiberius's birthday celebrations. Eleazar followed him, I can't prove it but I am sure Gratus had him assassinated. The next two, Simon and Annas I don't know the reasons behind their removal. I know the current high priest, Caiaphas is the son in law of Annas. I'm also sure he had a hand in his removal."

"Fun and games. What happened to Gratus?"

"He lives in disgrace, stripped of all rights of citizenship. He lives as a pariah in the northern reaches of the empire. He was stupid, he forgot Tiberius's maxim."

"Which is?"

"That he considers the Jews as a sacred trust, and they are to be treated as such." Vespian paused as he finished his food, taking a sip of wine he continued, "Pilate arrived two days later, and immediately confirmed Caiaphas as the new high priest and head of the council. It has not been perfect, Pilate has made mistakes. The difference is that he has learned from every one of them. There is now an uneasy truce between the governor and council offices. Pilate stays out of their business, and they keep out of his. It works, in a fashion. It is more often the idiot who occupies the royal palace that causes most of the problems."

"King Herod?"

"The puppet king. Appointed by the late Ceaser Augustus to have sovereignty over the area. He causes most of our problems."

"How? I wouldn't have thought he had any power to cause you issues."

"He doesn't. However, he was an over indulged, privileged child that has grown into the same as an adult. He may have been born here, but he is more Roman than Judean. He was sent to Rome as a child to be educated. Now, he has an obsession with the Roman way, the empire of the emperors. There has been a slow building outrage towards Rome. The people are convinced that we are responsible for the crippling taxes imposed on them. The rebuilding of the city, Seppharis spiralled out of control. Herod taxed the people to pay for it.

"Thousands of the people, his people remember, have lost their livelihoods, have had to sell their children into indentured service to pay back taxes." George remained silent, Herod's extravagances were well known. He decided to change the subject, if only slightly.

"Who is this Joseph Bartholomew that my paper is so curious about?"

"If you believe what the people have been saying, he is their saviour. The long-awaited messiah."

"Another one?" George asked with sarcasm.

"Indeed. This one seems a cut above the normal, run of the mill preachers they get with a mundane regularity out here. By all accountants, he is not well educated but seems a very intelligent individual."

"You referred to him earlier as The Prophet?"

"Yes, it's what the people, and his followers call him. It started in Galilee about, what? Two or three years ago." The waiter appeared to clear away the dinner plates. Both men declined the offer of desert. Vespian continued the conversation, "I suspect the council have already made plans to deal with him."

"Why, when did preaching become a crime?"

"When you use it to criticise the council's authority to govern. Anyway, as I said, it's not my problem. It is theirs to deal with. If my sources are correct, he has already been betrayed. The council have someone in his inner circle. I don't know who, just that he has agreed to give him up."

George glanced at his watch, it had just turned ten o'clock. He finished his glass of wine. "I have to go. I'm meeting a colleague and I'm already late." They both shook hands, and Vespian watched George leave, then signalled to a man sat at another table. The man stood up and quickly came over.

"Well?" Vespian enquired.

"Nothing, sir. We searched his room thoroughly. Nothing of any significance."

"You are sure?"

"Yes, sir."

"Maybe he is here for the reasons he stated."

"What do you suspect him of?"

"Nothing."

"I don't understand."

"As well as being a formidable investigative reporter, George Ambrose also used to do the odd job for his country's intelligence services..." After stating this, Vespian headed out of the hotel.

George turned left after he exited the restaurant and entered the bar. He spotted Derek easily, sat on a stool at the counter. He sat next to him, ordering a beer he turned to face him.

"So, Derek. You want to tell me what the hell is going on?"

Chapter Two

The Testimony of James Henry Abbott

George was back in his room. The conversation with Derek had confirmed two suspicions. The first, that James had not been snatched, was not been held under duress. The fact that Vespian had not made any reference to the possibility had raised the initial doubts in his mind. It was implausible the man responsible for Rome's security in the region would not know. If such a thing had occurred, Vespian would have known that was the reason for George's arrival. He may be many things, but he was no fool.

Therefore, if James was not being held against his will, this left only one further possibility. The conversation with Derek had confirmed that reality. His son had, it appeared, fallen under the spell of this Joseph Bartholomew. He had become a convert.

A number of the other things he had been told during their meeting together were beyond belief. Most of what Derek told had come from second-hand sources. Other bits had been told to him by people who claimed to have been there, had witnessed these events.

George had no reason to doubt what he was being told. Derek was an excellent editor in chief, and had been a superb reporter in his day. One that never allowed his own emotions or opinions to cloud the story.

More importantly, connecting the lines between what Derek had said, together with Vespian's information, meant that his son was in more danger than he knew. There was a good chance that James could become a wanted man. George was well aware of the pettiness of the Jewish council. Everything he had learned so far pointed to the fact that they would not let this go. They wanted Bartholomew.

George had never understood why this part of the world spawned these prophets with alarming regularity. Never having been particularly religious, he found it a constant mystery. The spell they all cast over the people. In his experience, religion was more often used as an excuse for peoples' actions. Some of those behaviours carried out on a horrendous scale. All committed in the name of one God or another.

Organised religion was no better. From the Romans with their numerous deities, the pagan religions practised in his own country and the Jews with their one, true god as they claimed. His observations had only confirmed that the authorities used it as a means to control the people through fear. As a means to fill their already overflowing treasure chests.

Reaching into his pocket for his cigarettes, he pulled out the forgotten brown envelope. He opened it as he walked out onto the room's balcony to smoke. As he unfolded the pages, he recognised his son's handwriting. Skipping through the opening greetings, he leaned against the balcony rail and began to read...

"I know you won't believe any of the things I am going to tell you in these pages, but every word is true.

"In order to appreciate these things, I need to explain some of the Jewish heritage. For thousands of years, they have been promised a messiah.

"This premise is scattered throughout their religious texts, their holy scriptures. A person who will come to save them as God's chosen people. It is an accepted fact, as important to them as the laws of Moses. A founding block of their belief structure.

"A saviour given by God, personified in flesh on earth. A direct descendent of King David, that he would be greater even than that revered sovereign. The messiah would be born in Bethlehem, and be a ruler of Israel. The Jewish scholars have always maintained that he would reveal himself as a great warrior. One that would sweep aside all enemies, and restore the nation of Israel to its rightful place. He will bring the people out of oppression. At long last the people would remain undisturbed, safe from their enemies. Bring peace, and establish a Jewish dynasty that will last a millennia.

"I have met a man, Joseph Bartholomew, who has the capacity to change the world forever. If he survives.

"Stories and tall tales had been circulating for some time before his arrival in Jerusalem. At first, I treated these tales with scepticism. People talked of miraculous healings. Enabling the blind to see, the crippled to walk. One of these tell of the curing of ten men of leprosy – a disease that is still prevalent in this area. The greatest of these is that he raised a man, Lazarus, from the dead.

33

"As I write this, I can imagine the look on your face, can see you rolling your eyes in disbelief.

"You haven't met him.

"I have.

"Prior to his arrival, the anticipation had been building for weeks. It reached a feverous peak six days ago. When he entered the city, people came out of the homes, the hotels, restaurants and bars to welcome him. Some of them brought palm branches to line the road with, something normally reserved for royal visits.

"Everyone assumed he would arrive in a grand show. He didn't. No fanfare, no huge entourage. Just him, riding into the great city on the back of a donkey, in humility.

"Everyone wanted to catch a look, no matter how fleeting. The people shouted their approval, calling out 'praise God for the son of David' The city was in uproar. I was there to cover the arrival for the paper. I've reported on celebrity arrivals before, but I have never seen a reaction like this man received. This unassuming figure, sat astride a donkey. This prophet from Galilee. I couldn't understand the people's reaction, it lay beyond me at that moment.

"It was expected that, as tradition dictates, that he would present himself to the council immediately. That is not what he did. His first point of call was to go straight to the temple, intent on attending morning prayer. When he reached his destination, and saw the stalls and bankers trading, he lost it. Completely. Kicking over chairs, overturning tables, scattering livestock, goods and money everywhere. He was like a madman. Standing on the temple steps, he faced them all down shouting, 'My temple will be a called a house of prayer, but you have turned it into a den of thieves.'

"It was really something to behold. It certainly made for a headline story. The Jewish Council condemned his actions, even though they had bemoaned these activities for years. Had complained about the traders using the temple as a market place, yet never taking any action. Now, here was this man, in the city for less than an hour, doing what they had never dared.

"I returned to the office in order to write the story. I wish I had stayed with him, because the stories started to circulate later that day. How he had cured the sick and disabled in the temple.

"When I caught up with him again, on the following day, he was being questioned by some of the council members in the town square. It was clear from their manner they hoped to catch him out.

"The examination was in respect to an obscure, archaic law. It was about how, if a man dies without any children his brother should marry the widow. To have a child, to ensure the continuation of the brother's name. The council members tried to confuse the issue. They said there were seven brothers, all of whom dies without children, each having married the widow in turn. Then, the woman died. They asked him, 'whose wife will she be at the resurrection?' Joseph looked at them, then told them they had misunderstood the scriptures. That God is for the living, not the dead.

"It was, I can tell you, a rare thing to see and hear. This man, who could only have received a modest education, telling the council scholars that they do not understand the scriptures!

"It was at this point that I realised I needed to stay in his company, to be better able to give a fair report. To be able to witness first hand his mission.

"I'm glad I did, because this wasn't the only time the council levelled questions at him. They asked him about taxes. He looked at them squarely, asking whose image was stamped on the coins. Naturally, they told him Ceaser's. His response? 'Give to Ceaser what belongs to Ceaser, and give to God what belongs to God'

"After again failing to trip him up, they tried another approach. 'Which of Moses commandments is the greatest?' they asked of him. 'To love your God with all your heart, all your soul and all your mind' he told them, then added 'there is a second commandment, equally as important' In their eagerness to find some fault, they asked him what it was. 'To love your neighbour as yourself. The entire law, and all the prophets demands, are based on these two commandments.'

"Over the following days, he said many things. I remember most of it. There was one thing he said that set the wheels in motion. One story that made the council decide his fate. I relate it now in full.

"A landowner planted a vineyard, built a wall around it, dug a pit for pressing out the grape juice, and built a lookout tower. Then, he leased the vineyard out to tenant farmers and moved away to another country. At the time of the harvest, the landowner sent some of his servants to collect his share of the crop. However, the tenant farmers seized his servants. They beat one, killed another and stoned the third. So, the landowner sent another, larger group of servants. The results were the same. Finally, the landowner sent his son, thinking they will, surely, respect my son.

"When the tenant farmers saw his son coming, they said to one another; 'here comes the heir to the estate. Come on, let's kill him and get the estate for ourselves.' So, they grabbed the son, dragged him from the vineyard and killed him.

"At the end of this telling, it was clear the council understood the reference; the hidden meaning was there to be seen in their shocked faces.

"To explain, the landowner represented God, the vineyard was the nation of Israel. The Jewish Council were the tenant farmers. The servants sent represented the few prophets and priests that had remained faithful to God. The landowner's son was the Messiah. It was a testament to how the council had corrupted themselves and the word of God.

"If there had not been so many people present, I swear they would have arrested him there and then. It was after this that he became less subtle on his condemnation of the council leaders. Here is a list of just some of the things he said about them;

- "Their hunger for power, money and status has made them lose sight of God. Their blindness has infected the people and has driven a wedge between them and God.
- "The laws they make for the people to follow, they themselves do not obey. They are hypocrites.
- "All that they do is for show, it does not glorify God, that it is for their own self-glorification.
- "Their actions are preventing the people from entering the kingdom of God.
- "They place the law of man above God's, moving the people away from Him, leading them to follow man made traditions instead of the word of God.
- "Involving themselves in every aspect of the people's lives, but fail to deal with what is important: Justice, poverty and faith.
- "They make sure they put on a good show of religious piety, yet their private lives are corrupt.

"The council has been plotting his downfall ever since. They see him as a threat to their power, to their hold over the people and their life of comfort. They have even tried to convince the Roman authorities that he represents a threat to their continued rule.

"I also suspect that the council have an informant among us, his followers. I have not been able to discover their identity, at least not at the time of writing this.

"Father, I cannot explain any of this. I have never met a man like this before. He is fearless. I have never felt like this before. I use words for a living, but I cannot find the words to describe what or how I feel. I don't even understand how this happened.

"I know one thing, I feel as though a huge weight has been lifted from my shoulders. A sense of peace and contentment has filled my soul. It is as if I have been reborn, I can't think of another way to describe it.

"I know you have friends, contacts and a modicum of influence with others in this city. If there is anything you can do, I beg you to do it. Help me to save him.

"I only hope and pray it is not already too late."

George folded the pages, put them back in the envelope. Virtually everything James had told him confirmed Derek's version of events. It also confirmed his fears that his son had become a devotee of this Joseph. Instead of remaining an impartial bystander, reporting the facts objectively, James had become part of the story.

George could not understand, grasp the reasoning of it.

People are not suddenly cured of lifelong disabilities, or receive miraculous cures for debilitating illnesses.

And, people definitely did not come back from the dead.

This Joseph was not the first, the history of Judea was littered with similar characters. Nor would he be the last. Someone the people would latch onto, claim as their saviour. Admittedly, from the little he knew this man appeared to be more intelligent than the usual run of the mill. Certainly, none had previously had the courage to face down the council.

George recalled another, not long before he had been snatched. That one, he remembered, had spent all his time urging the people to repent. Those that took him up on his offer, he baptised in the river. Hence the nickname of The Baptist. Now that he gave it more thought, the people had never hailed him as the Messiah. Some had asked, and he had denied it. He wasn't around anymore. Having got on the wrong side of the King, Herod had had him arrested.

Bringing his thoughts back to the letter, George realised that James considered himself part of the company that stayed with Joseph. That he was determined, regardless of any risk to himself, to save this Joseph from the council. It was just as obvious that same council was just as determined to bring an end to him. For reasons George couldn't grasp, this Joseph frightened them.

The council had tendered in the past to humour these so-called prophets, made then seem comical. A joke. However, this one had the brains to get the measure of the council. Maybe that was what frightened them. That and his challenges to their right to any authority over the people. Even to question the validity of their very existence. If he represented a threat to their continued reality, their continued comfortable lives, their wealth, there was no length they would not go to. They would do whatever was necessary to ensure their own self-preservation.

What was really bizarre though, if Joseph had been born in different circumstances, had been given access to better education, there was a good chance he would have ended up a council member himself.

If the council where indeed conniving with the Roman authorities, it was likely Joseph Bartholomew was heading towards a very nasty end. A determined, public example. A statement to the people, this is what happens when you don't follow our rules.

However, as far as George was concerned, none of that mattered. All that was important right now, was that his son was heading into trouble. George had to stop him, convince him somehow that he had fallen for an elaborate confidence trickster.

George started to open drawers in the room, finally finding the tourist map they always left for visitors. Opening it out, he started to search for the place Derek had mentioned earlier. He found it, and it did not look to be that far.

It was already late, sunset had been an hour ago. With a mounting sense of foreboding, George put the map in his back pocket and headed out the door.

Chapter Three
In the Midnight Garden

James Henry Abbott was having doubts. Not about the man he had decided to follow. No, that was the one thing he was certain about.

His doubts were about the wisdom of writing the missive to his parent. James expected his father to treat most of what he had written with scepticism at best. However, he was hard pushed to know what else he could have done. His incentive was to do whatever he could in order to save, to protect, Joseph Bartholomew.

In less than one week, James's whole world had changed from knowing where he was going in life, to a complete uncertainty. It had been easy before. Spend the next couple of years working in Judea, gaining a reputation as a reporter on the city desk here. Then, apply for a move to another country, he had always fancied a tour of duty in the Americas. After a few years there, consolidating his reputation, apply for a move over to the editorial team.

Now, because of this man, none of that mattered anymore.

James had grasped the opportunity with both hands when his editor had offered him the assignment. The rumours about Bartholomew had been flowing into Jerusalem for a couple of months. Stories about a young preacher, travelling the land and captivating the hearts of the people. James could not help himself; he was intrigued before he was even offered this chance.

What surprised him now was how his opinion had changed in just a few days. Curiosity mixed up with a modicum of suspicion had become admiration. Then he became captivated by this fearless man as he continued to berate the authorities, until this final devotion. One he could not explain or had expected.

He knew what his father would say. That he had been seduced by his words, drawn in by the charisma of the man.

James knew it was more than that.

It was a belief, a commitment to the man and his ideas.

It had only been six days since he had arrived in triumph. There was no other way to describe it. James had been there, seen the reaction from the crowds. Nothing like it had ever been seen before, and that included the visits made by some of the greatest emperors Rome had produced.

Over the next couple of days, James had watched as the council questioned him. Bombarded him with words in an attempt to embarrass him, show him up as a fool. Their questions phrased in such a way as to try and trip him up. He had proved to be more than a match for them, turning their arguments on their head, then verbally throwing them back.

The thing James had begun to realise over the time in his company, Joseph had never acted or spoken out of malice. Rather, it was done with a sense of sadness, that these people could not see the fault in what they said or in their actions. It was done in the hope they would see their own hypocrisy, that they would change their behaviour. It hadn't worked, instead they had just become more antagonistic, more determined.

James had been stationed in Judea for four and a half years, had watched the authorities on both sides. Whereas Rome was the occupying force, it was akin to a policing action. The decisions in regard to the people were made by the ruling Jewish Council. He considered this group of people to be both morally and politically corrupt. They were all powerful when it came to Jewish matters within the city. They could have used that power to improve the lives of the citizens. Instead, they stood by and watched as they were taxed into oblivion. Used their power to line their own pockets. To keep the people in their place.

The Jewish authorities oppressed the people just as much as the Romans did. Increasing their own personal authority and wealth rather than improving the lives of the people; and now someone had turned up and pointed these things out to the people. Joseph Bartholomew represented a threat to their comfortable lives and their positions.

James was willing to accept that not all of the council was corrupt. However, those few decent members, and their voices of reason, where drowned by the louder majority. Those few good men held little power within the confines of the council, so nothing changed.

Some were even willing to hear what Joseph had to say, open to his words. Again, the larger force within the council had the final say, and the plot to bring down Joseph had begun.

James looked around the gardens. Like himself, all of them had made sacrifices great and small to be here. To become a disciple of Joseph. Taking them all in, he realised someone was missing. Including himself, there should be twelve, but he could only see ten others.

There was Peter, John and the other James sat together in silence under an olive tree.

Andrew was stood by the entrance to the gardens, and that was Nathanial walking over to join him.

Philip was sat alone under another of the olive trees.

Matthew and Thaddaeus were sat together, chatting quietly.

Thomas was further over, pacing back and forth.

Finally, he spotted Simon sat with his back against the wall.

That left Judas. James scanned the area again, but could still not find him. He assumed he must just be out of sight, although he had a sense of unease. James had got to know each of them more as he spent his time in their company. Judas was a scholar of small reputation, coming from a privileged background, or at least compared with the others. His father had been a moderately successful businessman, so he could afford to provide a better level of education for his son. As a result, Judas had qualified and been able to attend a reasonable university. James had spoken to him a couple of times, never in great detail, but each time he sensed that he was holding back. A sense of some deep secret, a hidden, smouldering anger below the surface.

While he had not found out how Judas had joined, the conversations with the others had been much more open and forthcoming. James, John and Andrew had all been fishermen by trade, until they had fallen in with a man he knew as John the Baptist. It had been the Baptist who had instructed them to follow Joseph. It was fortunate that they heeded his advice, because the next day Herod had ordered his arrest.

It was partly due to Andrew that Peter, his brother, had become a follower. Peter had been happy to share the circumstances of his first meeting with Joseph.

Having spent the day fishing as usual, Peter had returned to the shore with the days catch. A pathetic haul for the nine or so hours they had been out on the water. Barely enough to cover the days wages and associated expenses of doing business. He was not in a good frame of mind, angry with everyone and everything. This had been the fourth day his team had only just been able to cover their costs. Therefore, when his brother turned up with yet another of those preachers he kept falling in with, he was in no mood to be sociable. Roaring at Andrew about all these so-called prophets he had followed over the years with benign complicity, and at the injustices of the world in general. Andrew had continued to urge Peter to meet Joseph, eventually getting him to relent and agree.

When Joseph suggested they go back out, initially Peter had refused. The day had already been a long and tiring one. Again, it had been at Andrews urging that he had finally given in and agreed, taking Joseph with them. Peter had told him, what happened next was nothing short of a miracle. When they returned to shore, it was with the largest haul of fish they had ever seen. Peter could not understand, the fish had not been there just an hour earlier. He could not explain where they had come from. Yet his nets were bursting with livestock.

It had not just been that one thing, Peter had said, as if that wasn't enough. That same night, something happened, and it had involved Matthew.

Before he joined Joseph, Matthew had been a much-reviled member of society. As a tax inspector, it had been his job to ensure that payments were collected. To ensure that the high levels of tax were imposed. Matthew had carte blanch in the area to do whatever was necessary to recover whatever was owed. This he did, and relished the authority given to him. Peter was one of those who had fallen behind in his payments. When Matthew heard of his good fortune, he headed over to his house to collect. Words were exchanged, tempers flared, threats and insults were swapped. Then Joseph had stepped in, calming them he sat them both down. He proposed to tell those gathered a story, as he spoke it was obvious these words were for Matthew and Peter in particular.

They had both retold the tale to James, both calling it by the same name. The unforgiven debt. The effect of the words on both men had been profound, From the moment the tale was finished, they had put their differences to one side, settled their arguments and come together as the friends they had once been. Matthew had left all that he had been behind, following Joseph from that night.

Over those early days, others had joined. First came Philip, who had brought Nathanial with him. Both had regaled James with tales of miraculous healings. Nathanial said he had seen Joseph cast out demons from a teenage boy. When he heard this James had been transported back to the dark ages. Tales of demonic possessions belonged in the uneducated, unenlightened past. Stories with which to frighten little children. Philip had added that the religious leaders in the area had accused Joseph of being in league with the devil. As far as they were concerned only servants of demons could drive out demons.

Then Philip had taken up the narrative, telling another anecdote. James had considered this one as implausible as the others. Joseph had been preaching, a huge crowd had gathered to hear him. Philip, and the others had urged Joseph to send the crowd home, it was becoming late and they would soon become hungry. Joseph told them, 'You feed them.' All of them announced this was not possible, the only food they had was a small quantity of bread and fish. It would be barely enough to feed themselves.

Joseph gave them instructions. They were to gather the people into small groups, divide the supplies between the baskets. Then he sent them out into the crowds. Everyone had been able to eat their fill that afternoon, with twelve baskets filled with left-over food at the end.

James had, in those first days, assumed the stories were being embellished. What he was being told by them was farcical. There had to be another, more realistic explanation. Except, as he talked to them, they all had similar stories to tell. From curing various diseases, illness, crippling disabilities to turning water into wine at a wedding they all attended.

Simon, he was a curious man. He had been part of the revolutionary forces, had killed Roman and Jew alike in the name of his cause. Yet here he was, welcomed by Joseph as one of them.

Then there was Thomas, who refused to believe anything he had not seen with his own eyes. Again, here he was, a firm believer. A disciple of this strange, enigmatic man.

The last to join them had been Thaddaeus. The oldest, he had been a major force in the retail and cotton trade. A man who regularly mis-trusted people's real intentions, convinced they were trying to somehow put one over him. It was the way business worked, he had told his three sons. He had lived a life of relative comfort, slowly building his little empire to hand over to his heirs. Then, one day he just left it all behind to follow. Now, he slept were ever Joseph slept, ate whatever he was given. This former captain of industry happy to carry out any menial task he was given.

Over the last week, James had observed the dynamics of the group. The subtle relationships. He discovered that everyone got on with each other, there was no competition between them, no jealousies. He had noticed that three of them seemed to have been singled out by Joseph. What for was not clear. Peter,

James and his brother John. Peter in particularly held some special place with Joseph, he definitely had some unspoken, special task for him.

In the beginning James had been cynical, even when he spoke with Joseph. Joseph, for his part had treated James with courtesy and patience. He had time for everyone.

That was the other astonishing fact. Joseph's willingness to give his time to all; but especially to the poor, the abandoned of the city. Most of the time he surrounded himself with the outcasts from society.

He was unlike anyone James had ever met. There was no self-serving purpose in what he said and did. He did it because it needed to be done. His mission from God, he called it. He was here to do his Father's bidding only.

That was another startling observation. He spoke of God as though he was a living, breathing person. When he spoke, or read from the scriptures it was as if they had come to life. Lifted from the dry, dusty pages to become a living thing. He brought a depth and clarity to those ancient words.

James had been with them now for just four days. In that time he had changed. He had heard and seen things that had altered his outlook on the world around him. He had been witness to stunning, unbelievable events. Or they would have been if he had not seen it with his own eyes.

The first was outside the temple gates. A man was sat begging, holding out his bowl, acting in such a way that it was obvious he was blind. Joseph had approached him, crouched down to speak with him. Then, Joseph had reached out, taking the man's head in his hands and pressing his thumbs into his eyes. The beggar had begun to protest, then shouting that his eyes were burning. Joseph had asked for water, then had washed his eyes. Moments later, the man was crying with joy, saying he could see again.

Immediately the guards began shouting, backed up by some council members. "This man is well known to us. He is a charlatan, a professional beggar. He was never blind."

If that had been it, a one-off isolated incident, James would have been inclined to side with the guards. Only it wasn't. That was just the first of many.

A deaf boy hearing his parents' voices for the first time.

A crippled man throws his crutches in the river.

A disabled woman stands up and walks, leaving her wheelchair behind.

Now, here he was sat in the olive gardens of Gethsemane. A firm believer. A disciple.

James looked up from his deliberations, there was a disturbance at the entrance. Andrew and Nathanial were exchanging words with someone he could not see clearly. James started to head over with the others, recognising him as he came closer.

His father pushed the others to one side, walking over to him.

"Do you know him?" Matthew asked James.

"Yes, I know him. It's fine, he isn't here to cause us problems." More of them were coming over, intent on seeing who this interloper on their gathering was. Matthew waved them back, indicating it was safe to let him through. Turning back to James he asked another question.

"Why is he here?"

"I asked him to help. He knows people of influence, men who may speak for Joseph."

George had reached them both, ignoring Matthew, he spoke to James, "You have to come with me, now. It's not safe here."

"What do you mean? I can't leave him while there is a chance to save him."

"There isn't. It's too late."

Matthew spoke, "How do you know that?"

"I passed them on my way. The council are on their way, they are bringing the temple guards, accompanied by Roman soldiers."

"We must warn him, get him away from here," James stated, making to move away, only to be stopped by his father's hand gripping him by the arm.

"James, it's too late. The decision has already been made."

"I have to try," James responded, shaking himself free. He headed off towards a smaller grove on the right. George chased after him. As he did, a man emerged from the grove. As James rushed up to speak with him, George assumed this was Joseph Bartholomew. When he caught up with them, Joseph was saying something to James he couldn't hear. Bartholomew looked up, raising his voice to he heard he said, "You must all leave now."

No one moved, they just stood and stared.

George sensed movement behind him, turning he watched as a young man entering the gardens. He walked straight up to Joseph, bending to kiss him on the cheeks. As soon as this happened, the gardens were lit up as the guards and soldiers turned their torches on.

The only person George recognised was the presence of Colonel Vespian. He was accompanied by a weasel face man. Vespian appeared completely uninterested in the events, while this little man had a look of supreme triumph.

Joseph spoke, "Who is it you want?"

It was the weasel faced man who stepped forward to answer. "We have an arrest warrant for Joseph Bartholomew. We are here for him, hand him over."

"Then you have him," Joseph said. "Leave these others, they have done nothing wrong. I am the one you want, they are not important."

The man nodded to the temple guards, who swiftly moved forward, seized him and led him away. Vespian made his way over to were George and his son stood. The others had already scattered.

"May I ask what brings you here?"

"A reporter's curiosity, nothing more." George said.

"And you?" Vespian asked, turning his attention to James.

George quickly answered, "This is James Abbott, he is a colleague of mine. He asked if I would accompany him, to get another perspective." James did not contradict him, and the Colonel seemed to accept the explanation.

The relative quiet of the gardens was suddenly shattered as a scream filled the air. As Vespian walked towards the sound, George told his son to leave then followed the Colonel. When he caught up with him, a soldier was on his knees, Joseph stood over him. George heard the fragment of a conversation, unsure of what was said. The soldier's moans of obvious pain ceased.

The Colonel checked his soldier over, berated him then told the rest to get on with their duties. Joseph was once again led away by the temple guards. Vespian re-joined George. "It was nothing. He was unharmed." The two of them headed towards the entrance. "Where did your young friend go?"

"Back to the paper. What happens now?"

"He will be questioned by the council, they will find him guilty. something severe enough to ensure his death."

"You seem sure?"

"I am. Micah, the man you saw, is determined to ensure the outcome." As an afterthought, Vespian turned to George. "Would you like to attend? In a purely observational role, for the paper?"

"You can arrange that?"

"Yes, I think so."

"Then yes, thank you."

"Good, it will achieve two aims. I will have someone who will provide me with impartial information, as well as annoying Micah. Something I do enjoy." George had assumed there would be a cost, and he had no problem passing any information to Vespian.

"Will he agree?"

"Not at first. A token objection will be made, but he knows I can insist on having an observer present. He won't like the fact that it is you, though."

"Why, we've never met?"

"You're a journalist. He has a deep, let's call it distrust of the press."

When they reached Micah, he was berating one of the temple guards. As soon as he had finished, Vespian called out to him. He headed over to them, speaking as he walked.

"What is it, Colonel? I am needed back at the council chambers."

"This will only take a moment, let me introduce you to Mr Ambrose. He works for…"

"I am well aware of who and what he is," Micah spat.

"Good, then you will understand his interest in the proceedings. He will be attending as…"

"He will not. This is a council matter, it is nobody's business but ours."

"That's the second time you have interrupted me, Micah. Don't do it again." Micah looked stunned by the hidden threat. "Mr Ambrose will be attending the proceedings as my observer."

"The high priest, Caiaphas will never allow it."

"Nice try, but as we both know it is you who makes these decisions. The governor's office is entitled to send an observer to any council meetings, as you are well aware."

Micah seemed to give this some thought. "Very well, under the condition that he makes no notes, does not interfere or ask questions during the proceedings. He is strictly an observer." Micah turned to leave, George spoke which made him stop.

"What time?"

"The council meets in one hour," he said without turning, then continued on his way.

Vespian spoke again, "I enjoyed that. I like annoying that jumped up, pompous little shit."

"You don't like him?"

"I have no feelings either way. But, even by the standards of the council members, Micah is an exceptionally gifted, conniving little bastard. His eyes, and ambitions are firmly fixed on Caiaphas's position. He will do anything, sacrifice anything, to achieve that. And, he will destroy anyone he perceives to be a threat to his goal."

George asked another question, "Why the urgency?"

"They want to be able to have this decided before the sabbath. They are also aware that we have executions taking place, they want to include him."

"Execution for what? I know I don't know much about this Joseph Bartholomew, but what I do know seems inoffensive. He appeared to be just telling everyone to be nicer to each other."

"Things have changed while you were away. Micah is determined to ensure the council's power is all pervading. He is using Bartholomew as an example of that power.

"Caiaphas inherited the title from his father-in-law. Annas is officially retired. In truth, he had no choice. Certain financial irregularities, under the counter payments to the revolutionaries, which were then used to purchase arms. The Roman governor gave him a choice, arrest and execution or retire. Caiaphas became high priest, and Micah moved up to council leader, one step away from his ambition. What Caiaphas and Annas don't know, is that the evidence was given to the governor by Micah. Now, he is on a mission to ensure that the people know their place. There will be no further contributions to their revolutionary causes.

"I'm telling you all this as background, so you are aware of the type of man you are dealing with. A man who will do anything to hold on to the second most powerful post a Jew can hold in Judea."

"I get the idea."

"Good, and just to reiterate; Annas has grown more and more bitter at his, perceived unfair treatment. He blames the people. Four months ago, with the help of Micah, they invoked their ancient law of crucifixion. Convinced the council to put it back on the statute books. They still need the governor's agreement to carry it out, but the people know it is there. That is the fate that awaits Bartholomew."

"Why? He's just a preacher, what has he done to deserve that?"

"Nothing, that's the point. The council don't care, he insulted them, questioned their right to lead. By association, he has called into question the morals of Caiaphas. His fate was decided within twenty-four hours of his arrival. For Micah, and Caiaphas, the question was never if, but when he would die. From that moment, everything they have done has been to reach that point. I heard from a very reliable source that Caiaphas called the council to order. Some of them had supported the idea of giving Bartholomew a chance to speak with them, even suggested that he was harmless. Caiaphas told them they had no idea what they were talking about. They had no understanding of the danger this man represented. Better for one man to die than a nation be destroyed. Or some such thing.

"Joseph Bartholomew frightens them, because deep down they know he speaks the truth. He threatens their continued power and hold over the people. Therefore, they see his death as a necessity."

"As you said, though, the governor has to approve the sentence of death. Surely he won't agree to it?"

"Pilate's position here is weak. He is currently out of favour with Tiberius. Caiaphas and Micah both know this, they will use that to apply further pressure."

"So, I am attending a show trial," George stated simply.

"You are, when they have finished with him, they will send him to the governor. I would appreciate it if you could let me know how the proceeding go, so I can advise the governor."

"Of course."

The two men had reached the administrative buildings, where they parted company. Vespian to the left and towards his office, George off to the right to the Council Chambers.

Part Two
Friday

Chapter Four

Witness to a Travesty

George arrived at the council chambers. He hoped that he would be allowed to find his own way to the proceedings. That was not to be, two of the temple guards were waiting for him. They escorted him through to Micah's office. He greeted George with a level of contempt he had rarely experienced.

"I want to be clear, I object strongly to your presence here," he said immediately.

"Yet, you hide it so well."

"Sarcasm may be your stock in trade, Ambrose, but it will not be tolerated here. You will treat these chambers with some respect."

"I apologise, but this is a news story. I just want to be sure of the facts before we decide whether to write anything."

"This is a small local matter. I doubt it will have any interest outside of Jerusalem. Now, these are closed proceedings, a private matter for the council to decide."

"At the moment, perhaps, but you never can tell how these small local things can escalate."

"If that happens, it will be due to you and your paper's sensationalist treatment. I have experience with the international press. The constant lies you write in regard to the work this council carries out for the welfare of the people. I am well aware of how you people view this council. Therefore, before you print anything it is to be approved by this office."

"If we decide to report, you will be provided with a copy for a comment. But that's all."

"And this office will reserve the right to make any changes to ensure the version of events reflects the truth. Do not underestimate us, you aren't in London anymore, where your weak authorities allow the press to publish whatever they please. That is not how it works here." Micah considered the subject now closed. George was unmoved, he could demand whatever he liked, there was no way he would give up approval of anything he wrote to an outsider.

Micah assumed this lack response meant agreement, and continued speaking. "The initial questioning will be carried out by Annas."

"Why? My understanding is that he was retired, that he had no active part on the council anymore. I was expecting the questioning to be conducted my yourself." There was a subtle change in Micah's demeanour. George thought he had hit a sore point.

"Annas was high priest. It is a role normally taken for life. Due to circumstances that do not concern you, he felt he had to resign. However, Caiaphas has kept him on to perform some minor functions." All of this was delivered in a brusque manner, Micha's feelings on the matter obvious. "As I was saying, Annas will conduct the preliminary enquiries, then decide if this needs to be referred over to the Lord Caiaphas. Please remember, you are here as an observer only."

"I promise, I won't interfere in any way with the proceedings. However, I may need to ask some questions, to provide some further clarification in regard to the legalities. Who would I direct those questions to?"

"You may submit them through me, I will arrange for one of our lawyers to respond." Of course you will, George thought, and I can imagine how long that will take, but he said nothing. "Good, now if you follow me. Proceeding are about to start." They walked across the office and through a side door. George followed him, Micah directed him to a small seating area off to the left.

This was the lower chamber, the domain of Annas. As soon as he entered, it was obvious he liked his comfort, enjoyed showing off his wealth. The room was elaborately decorated, expensive tapestries depicting scenes from their scripture hung from the walls. To George they looked to have been specially commissioned, they were too large and intricate not to have been created by an expert in the field. There were four in total, and George had to admit they were beautiful.

The first showed the creation of the world, the Garden of Eden and the temptation of man. The second, the destruction of that world, the ark and Noah.

On the opposite wall hung a larger piece showing Joseph at the walls of Jericho, ready for battle.

The final one took pride of place, hanging on the wall behind the seat Annas would occupy to oversee his duties. It was huge, at least forty square foot, it showed Moses at the foot of Mount Sinai in receipt of the ten commandments. On the opposite wall hung some items from Annas's private art collection. George was no expert, but even he recognised a number of the paintings. If they were originals, there value would feed the hungry of Judea for several years.

Annas sat in his seat, raised on a platform the Moses tapestry behind him. The comparison was there for all to see, Moses the recipient of God's law, Annas the practitioner of those laws. This was his personal throne, and he wanted to make sure everyone understood that. He was a small man, no more than five foot, bald with a full, perfectly groomed beard. George was aware that Annas was in his early seventies, but you would not know it to look at him. He had not lost any of that force of nature that had propelled him to the highest office in the land. He had served as high priest for nine years before his fall from grace. Allowed to retire, he had grudgingly accepted this lesser role from his son-in-law, Caiaphas.

Council members were beginning to fill the room, with nowhere to sit they stood in groups. They surged inside, a little to eagerly, holding their ceremonial robes off the ground. They scrambled across each other, trying to get a decent spot to see from. Taking another look around, George could see other bodies in shadows of the balcony that lined the room. Micah's confidence that this was a private matter lost. Word had got out, it was possibly only within Annas's household servants, but it wouldn't remain that way, word would spread, by the morning the news would be everywhere. It was inevitable.

Two of the councillors had decide to occupy the available seats in front of George. There was an element of surprise in their conversation. It seemed that after all the amazing things this Joseph had reportedly done, there had been some trepidation around his arrest. "Who would have thought," one of them was saying, "that he would turn out to be such an ordinary man. Such a large force to arrest him was not needed, one man could have achieved the same result." George privately agreed, the size of the force at the gardens to arrest one man had seemed excessive.

There was a change in the atmosphere of those gathered, a sudden heightened expectancy. The doors at the end of the room had opened, all eyes were looking in that direction as two guards brought in the object of their attention. This was the first chance George had to really see Joseph Bartholomew. As he was brought to stand before Annas, he did not see anything remarkable about him. George was surprised to find a sense of disappointment, he was no different to any other man. A little over six foot, possibly. A slight frame. His hands were bound behind him, a plain face with a short goatee beard. It was the eyes that drew George's attention. Piercingly blue, there was a steeliness in them, and, yes George thought, a sadness. For what, George could not say.

He wasn't the only one. Annas was also closely examining him. Maybe this was the first time they had met also. Joseph Bartholomew appeared quite normal. What had motivated this nobody, this son of a Nazareth carpenter, to take on the authority of the all-powerful council?

Annas had no intention of spending all night questioning this man. He knew what was expected of him, a quick assessment then pass him off to Caiaphas. Looking around the room, he realised that virtually the full membership of the council was here. He needed a minimum of twenty-three, a third. There was more than that present. Micah, as usual had carried out his duties with his usual efficiency. Caiaphas disliked Micah, but he was forced to admit that he was very good at his job.

Despite himself, Annas had been intrigued by this man stood before him. By all accounts he was clever. He must have known the council would eventually want to question him, especially if the claims made of him where true. Normally, the likelihood of being questioned would relate to how popular a preacher became, and this one had been astonishingly so. Reports of thousands gathering to hear him speak. His popularity caused other problems, especially as it was well known that much of what he said was a direct criticism of the councillors gathered here tonight. It was important they escaped the accusation of being petty and vindictive.

Annas admitted to himself that the charge of blasphemy he faced could easily be dealt with. However, his actions on that first day in the temple, they could not so easily be dismissed. Both he and Caiaphas had lost a small fortune that day, and neither of them was willing to forgive that.

The council were growing restless, eager to start. He leaned forward in his seat, and asked his opening question.

"Do you understand why you have been brought here?"

This query was met with a stony silence. This surprised Annas. Most people bought before him took the first opportunity granted them to splutter their apologies, to grovel and plead for mercy. Not this one, he stubbornly met Annas's stare, and there was a self-confidence in those eyes.

Annas tried again. "I am told you are considered a great scholar of the Torah. Where did you receive your education, where did you study?"

Again the silence.

"Well, what do you teach? Who are these followers of yours? Haw many are there?" To his surprise, this time he received a response.

"I have only ever spoken openly. In synagogues and temples, never behind closed doors. I did nothing in secret, so why ask me? Ask those who heard my words, they will know what I said."

A temple guard came forward and slapped him across the face. "This is no way to speak to your superiors."

Joseph shook his head, saying, "If I have said something wrong, tell me what it is. If I spoke the truth, then why did you strike me?" The guard drew his hand back to strike again.

"Enough!" shouted Annas, stopping the guard in mid flow.

Watching all this from his seat, George was fascinated. It was as if the prisoner had already accepted his fate. As though he knew the verdict of this council was a foregone conclusion. George knew it was, but he had been expecting some show of defence; it looked as though Joseph had decided there was no point in trying to prove his innocence.

Annas continued to stare at this strange man. He did not think he was going to achieve anything further, or achieve anything at all. He stood and addressed the council members, "Take him to Caiaphas, how can I make a judgement if the accused refuses to answer? Perhaps he may be more forthcoming in the presence of the High Priest." He motioned to the temple guards, who came forward to take custody of the prisoner.

George was sure that Annas was well aware of the laws that he had broken in the short time he had spent questioning Joseph. The laws, some of which Annas himself had written, that dictate the process of these trials. George estimated they had broken at least three in the space of the thirty minutes he had been here. Numbers two, four and five he reckoned.

Rule two stated that no steps in the criminal prosecution can take place after sunset. Bartholomew had been arrested a few minutes before midnight, just an hour ago. The sun had definitely not been out.

Rule four: No trial is permitted to take place before the morning prayer and sacrifices. It was a new day, the ceremonies would not be carried out for another eight hours.

Finally, rule five required that all stages of trials must be held publicly. No part can be held privately or in secret.

George was finding it difficult to remain completely detached by what was being done. How many more of their laws would they break in order to satisfy their zeal to be rid of this man? He was also ill at ease, uncomfortable with the memories being brought back. He had experienced a brief flashback to his own incarceration when the guard had struck Bartholomew across the face.

These thoughts had passed through his mind as they all made their way across the concourse to the council chambers. George saw one of the page boys running ahead, presumably to inform Caiaphas of their imminent arrival. He doubted that was necessary, which was proven when they entered the chambers, Caiaphas was already sat in his place.

The members found their places on the seating arranged down each of the side walls. George found a seat, and looked over at the High Priest. He had not even bothered to pretend that this was unexpected, he was dressed in the full regalia of his office. It would have taken time to dress. He gave the prisoner a scornful, cursory glance then ordered the witnesses to brought forward.

There goes rule seven, George mentally noted. The defence is given priority to speak before any accusations can be made.

Witness after witness were brought forward. It was obvious from the lack of any conviction in the way they presented their evidence that they had been schooled in what to say. At least two witnesses had to agree on what they had seen or heard. It took a while to achieve this minimum requirement as they were paraded in front of the council.

Two men claimed they had heard the defendant say he could tear down the temple and rebuild it in three days. Several members of the council openly scoffed at such a suggestion. It had taken many years to build the temple of Jerusalem. The chamber reverberated with their laughter.

The integrity of the witnesses was examined, both of them stood by their words. Both confirmed that it was the man stood before them that had made this claim.

Caiaphas seemed lost in thought. Standing up he approached the accused, saying, "Are you not going to answer?"

Bartholomew said nothing, just looked at Caiaphas.

"You have nothing to say in regard to the testimony you have just heard?"

Still, no response.

His continued silence was a mystery to George. Joseph did not exactly breath charisma, however he had seduced thousands with his words. Convinced men to give up everything to follow him, if he was such a powerful speaker, why did he remain silent?

Caiaphas had returned to his seat, deep in thought. Finally, leaning forward, the elbow of his right arm resting on his knee he pointed directly at the prisoner. In a calm, almost reverential voice, he spoke to Joseph Bartholomew.

"Many things have been said here. Many things have been heard, your reputation as a prophet has been brought into question. So, tell us all this one thing, under oath by the living God," at this he pointed his finger towards the heavens, "Tell us, are you the Messiah promised to us, the living son of God?"

There was a moment of silence, no-one expected him to reply to such a question. The words that they all heard him speak where, perhaps, made all the more shocking because of that expectation.

"The words are your own. Whatever your concept of the Messiah is – I am He. I tell you this, one day you will see the son of man at the right hand of power, coming on the clouds of heaven."

There was a stunned silence. Then Caiaphas cried out in horror, tore his clothes and slumped in his seat.

It was a good act, George thought, but he had seen the gleam of triumph in his eyes. He continued to watch as Caiaphas made a show of regaining his composure. When he spoke again, he made a show of how difficult it was to control his emotions. "He has spoken blasphemy!" He exclaimed. Surveying the council members, he addressed them, "Do you, or I need to hear anymore? How can further witnesses help when he condemns himself with his own words?

"I know, fellow councillors, the normal procedure would be to deliberate for another day. I see no need for this, you have all heard his words and the Sabbath will soon be upon us. I see no reason for any further delay. Are we all in agreement?"

The shouts of agreement came from all areas of the chamber.

"Then I call on the clerks to take your ruling and your considerations of the sentence."

The two clerks stood, taking it in turn to call out the names of the individual members. Every member declared him guilty, when asked for their sentence, death was the only word heard.

Once completed, Caiaphas stood again to address them.

"I accept the decision of this council. The prisoner will be taken before the Roman Governor, where our case will be pleaded. This council meeting is dismissed, I thank you for your work." Caiaphas sat down again.

As they left the chamber, the councillors walked past the condemned man. Some of them slapped his face, some punched him and others openly spat in his face. One of the guards produced a length of cloth and blindfolded the prisoner. Hitting him they would then shout out, "Come on then prophet – who hit you?"

George was revolted by their behaviour. He was also disturbed, his palms were sweating. Memories where flooding back, he closed his eyes and concentrated. Eventually the noise in the chamber died down and he was able to gain some control over his emotions. He looked up over to wear Caiaphas sat. That look of triumph was back. He had achieved what he had set out to do he had got Joseph Bartholomew to condemn himself with his own words.

Micah was suddenly at his side, George had not even heard him approach, so deep in his own turmoil. The little man spoke, "Well, that is that. I will have you shown out."

"I don't think so. The council's decision has to be ratified by the governor. Only he can confirm your sentence."

"A mere formality."

"Really? What crime has he committed against Rome?"

"I assure you, the agreement of the governor will be secured."

"We will see."

"I will, certainly. However, your role as an observer is over. I can permit you access to our proceedings, but I have no authority to grant you access to the governor's office." With a satisfied, smug look Micah continued, "You can, of course, make a formal application through the relevant department – they open in a couple of hours. Goodbye, Mr Ambrose." Micah beckoned two temple guards. "These gentlemen will see you out, I have my duties to perform. I doubt we will meet again. I do have a piece of advice for you, if you want it?"

"What would that be?"

"Stay out of our affairs." With that parting statement, Micah walked away.

George left with the guards. Once outside, he reached into his pocket and pulled out his mobile. He dialled the number, it was answered almost immediately. George spoke, "I'm on my way, should be with you in ten minutes."

Vespian responded down the line. "Excellent. I assume you will want to be here for the proceedings later this morning?"

"Definitely." George finished the call and continued the short walk to the governors' offices.

Micah had watched George leave the chambers. He doubted he had heard the last from that quarter. It had annoyed him that the Colonel had forced him to accept his presence. Micah found the whole of the international press abhorrent. They had an arrogance about them, thought their job entitled them to print whatever they liked. When he had assumed this position, he had taken steps to ensure the journalistic community were locked out. Now, he had been forced to let one of their number in again. As he entered his office, he called over one of his guards and spoke to him, "George Ambrose is a reporter with the London Times. He is staying at the King David. I want him followed, I want to know everyone he meets, no matter who they are. Do you understand?"

"Yes, sir."

Micah dismissed the guard, taking his seat behind his desk. There was no point in sleeping, Bartholomew would appear before Pilate in the next two hours. He would need to spend the time to ensure their case was ready to present. Despite his show of confidence earlier, he knew that the reporter had a point. It was not a foregone conclusion, even with the pressure Caiaphas would apply. The governor could be a pig-headed idiot if he was not handled right. There had been a number of occasions when he had refused to fall in with the council's needs. Sitting at his desk, resting his chin on his steepled hands, deep in thought. Which was how his secretary found him later. The governor was ready to see them.

Across the city, Governor Pontius Aquinous Pilate was annoyed. It was seven in the morning, and he was sat in his office. He had only returned from a Roman outpost five hours earlier. Looking forward to a long sleep and a late start, he had been told the council had this appointment. His head of security, Colonel Vespian had brought him the news. It was a matter of urgency, apparently. Pilate was dubious, everything the council brought to him was a matter of great importance.

Pilate had little enough patience for the locals even without the council and their never-ending demands. Pilate tolerated their stream of festivals and celebrations with a resigned indifference. All of them were just religious mumbo jumbo wrapped up with a constant begging for forgiveness.

The governor knew he walked a fine line. If the populace revolted, which was not out of the realms of probability, he would be blamed by Rome. If he then took a tougher stance, he could be recalled to Rome, a phrase that still sent a chill through one's body. Pilate had been made governor relatively recently, spending most of his time mediating local disputes, keeping the peace between Roman and Jew. This was no easy task, especially with the countless amount of Jewish rules and laws. How the people remembered them all was beyond him.

Pilate had been ignorant of these regulations when he had arrived, a confrontation was inevitable. It came within three months of his arrival. For convenience he decided to move his headquarters from Caesarea into new accommodation here in Jerusalem. Included within his household and army effects was the usual collection of busts of the Emperor Tiberius. As a show of his loyalty, Pilate had arranged for them to be displayed in his new quarters, and around the public gardens. These actions, however, were in violation of Jewish law forbidding the making and displaying of images. There had been some unrest, mutterings from the locals and the council. Pilate felt he needed to show his authority, and refused to remove them. Further unrest followed, culminating in a very verbal protest. Pilate called out the guard, threatened them with violence if they did not disperse. To his astonishment, they refused. They would rather die than see their laws flouted. He was left with no choice, the statues were removed from the gardens. They were not so important as to warrant the deaths of hundreds.

To further humiliate him, Caiaphas had written to Tiberius. Pilate had received a sever reprimand and a reminder that the Jews were a sacred trust.

Things had not improved. While he had a working relationship with Caiaphas, the rest of the council seemed determined to thwart him at every opportunity. Pilate had suggested the building of a new water system, which would have improved the supply to the city tenfold. When he proposed the costs be shared there was outrage at the suggestion that their sacred funds should be used. At the next public festival, the people had hurled insults and curses at him. So, yet another project was brought to a halt.

Slowly, over time, the two parties had come to an understanding. A relationship that worked. He may be the governor, the Emperors chosen representative, the authority of Rome, but it was Caiaphas and the council who ruled. Unspoken agreements were met upon, so Pilate kept his position and Caiaphas continued to increase his grip on the council, and his wealth.

Few people, or council members, knew of the high priest's private friendship with the immoral, degenerate Emperor Tiberius.

Now, the council needed him to condemn one of their own.

A page boy had arrived in the early hours. Vespian had passed over the charge sheet, and given an outline of what had occurred. He had even introduced the source of that information, a journalist whose name he could not now recall. He did remember agreeing to the reporter being present when he met with the council.

Pilate decided he had kept them waiting long enough, standing up and making his way outside, another thing that frustrated him, their refusal to enter the governor's residence. As he arrived, he was surprised to see the whole of the council in attendance, and some members of the public. He had been expecting a small delegation of council members, yet here they all were dressed in their ceremonial clothing. The people it seems had heard something was happening. Pilate scanned the crowd, spotting Micah stood off to one side. He did not look happy, quite the opposite. Micah was looking off at something to the left, behind Pilate. He turned to see what was the object of his disapproval, saw the journalist stood next to Vespian. If this was the effect that just the man's appearance had on Micah, Pilate decided they were going to get along.

Pilate took his seat as the prisoner was brought in. He took in the man before him. He did not seem a dangerous criminal. He looked ordinary. His lips were swollen, the cheeks discoloured, there where flecks of blood on his shirt and he was filthy.

The council members stood with Micah were deferential in their manner, yet seemed nervous. Further back, more people had begun to arrive. They filled up the archways, some were hanging onto the wall light fittings. The noise levels made normal conversation difficult. Pilate raised his hand, slowly the chattering subsided. With this signal, two Roman soldiers had replaced the temple guards on either side of the accused. Joseph Bartholomew was now a prisoner of Rome.

"What charges are you bringing against this man?" Pilate demanded.

Micah took a step forward. He was concerned by the question. He knew Pilate had been provided with a copy of the charges. This was an unnecessary query, so why ask it? He had also assumed that, due to the presence of the ever-troublesome reporter, he had been told in detail about the hearing. Maybe that was why, the reporter had probably given a one-sided account, so Pilate needed to satisfy himself. He had another concern, if Pilate decided to have the prisoner re-tried by the Roman court. If this happened, he would be cleared. Bartholomew had not committed any crime against Rome. Micah Spoke, choosing his words carefully.

"If he were not a criminal, we would not have brought him to you," Micah was disappointed, he could hear the frustration in his voice. Taking a deep breath, he continued, "He has been found guilty of blasphemy, of breaking our most sacred laws."

"What is that to me? Jewish laws, not Roman. Take him back, judge him by your own laws."

Several of the councillors began to protest. Pilate heard one of them saying, "…we have no right to execute…" the rest of the words were lost in the general outcry.

Micah brought them back to order, turning to address Pilate again. "Under our laws, the charges against this man carry a death sentence. We have tried him and found him guilty. We, as you are aware, have no authority to put a man to death. Just recently, your administration removed our legal rights under the laws of Moses for stoning. Therefore, we have no other option than to bring him before you."

"Blasphemy is a Jewish law, he has not broken any laws under Rome. This is your own internal problem, not mine."

"Except, your honour, he has placed himself above the emperor, as he claims to be the rightful king of the Jews."

Pilate allowed himself to be impressed. He had heard Micah was clever, that he used his words as power. Should he become high priest, he would prove a formidable opponent. Micah was correct, of course. By claiming to be their rightful ruler he had placed himself in direct conflict with Rome. However, strictly speaking he still had not broken any Roman laws. Pilate realised that Micah had been speaking, Pilate asked him to repeat himself.

Micah inwardly sighed, thinking that once he was high priest, Pilate would have to go. "I said, he has subverted our laws, and therefore our nation. He opposes the payment of taxes, passes himself off as the Messiah, the saviour of our people. That places this man as a threat to Rome."

The council had tried this man, found him guilty under their laws. As far as they were concerned, they had fulfilled their duties. Now they wanted to pass this local problem onto Pilate. Claiming this man was a menace and a real threat to Rome and the emperor.

Pilate could not defend this man, that wasn't his job. He was uneasy, though. There was more to this than appeared. Something else was going on below the surface. Standing, he made his way down the few steps to face the prisoner.

"So, are you? Are you the king of the Jews?"

"The words are yours. Is the question your own? Or have others told you about me?"

Pilate's attitude softened a little. "Am I a Jew?" Some of the soldiers laughed at this. "Your own people, and their leaders have handed you over to me. What have you done?" Pilate knew the truth of the matter. Bartholomew's arrival had not gone unnoticed by the Roman authorities. Vespian had dispatched spies, reports had been received. Pilate knew this man had never feigned to be their spectral saviour, had never courted it. He also knew the truth about the taxes, the coin and Ceaser's image. He was giving this man the chance to openly deny it. To save his own life.

Joseph was speaking again. The words were strange, considered. "My kingdom is not of this world. If it were, my servants would have fought to save me, to prevent my arrest; but my kingdom is not of this world." Joseph paused, looking directly at Pilate. "You all say that I am king. I was born into this world to testify. Anyone who is on the side of truth will here me."

"And what is that truth?"

"Simply that I am the way, the truth and life."

Pilate gave up, in exasperation he went back to his seat. He addressed those assembled. They watched him, waiting. "I find no basis for a charge against this man."

There was a stunned silence, then everyone attempted to speak at the same time. Micah stared back in disbelief. He turned to the crowds, arms extended to heaven, calling on God to help. This had the effect he wanted, the crowd grew more restless. The Roman soldier, in fear of their governor's life, placed their hands on their sidearms.

Micha was both angry and confused. Angry at the smug smile on the reporters face as he looked on. Confused, because he could not fathom what Pilate was doing, what his ulterior motive was for his decision. The councillors had joined the people in voicing their disapproval.

Micah was about to speak, but Pilate raised his hand, pointing at someone. He motioned for him to step forward, calling for silence as he did so. Micah watched as Shamon, a young initiate into the council emerged from the crowd.

"What did you say?" Pilate demanded.

"I mentioned that he stirs the people up with his words," the young man nervously repeated. "You can see the effect he has, just look around. He came here from Galilee just to undermine everything we have achieved. This man..." Pilate interrupted him.

"Why Galilee?"

"That is where he is from."

"If he is from Galilee, that is not in my jurisdiction. Take him to Herod, he has the authority over that province. This is for his consideration." Pilate motioned for the soldiers to carry out his orders.

As they handed the prisoner back over to the temple guards, Micah was struggling to hide his frustrations. Pilate knew everything about this Bartholomew. If he knew it was a matter of jurisdiction, he could have said so from the beginning. No, for some reason Pilate was trying to get out of making any decision in this matter.

Pilate, on the other hand, was pleased with himself. There had been a minor falling out between himself and Herod. Sending this prisoner to him was a gesture, a mark of respect. A signal that he, Pilate, recognised his authority. At least that was the way he hoped the puppet king would see it. In truth, involving Herod in the process, no matter what the outcome, would seal their friendship anew. The king could not very well make a complaint to the emperor if he had been involved in the process. With one decision, Pilate had effectively removed himself from a contentious situation.

As a bonus, the decision would place both Micah and Caiaphas in a difficult position. If either of them decided to make a formal complaint to Tiberius, Pilate could call on Herod to clear up any dispute. This in turn would damage the relationship the two of them had with the emperor. Thus, giving Pilate the upper hand in the region.

Pilate reached the stop of the steps, walking into his office accompanied by Vespian and George.

"Brilliantly handled, governor," the Colonel complimented.

"Thank you, but I doubt that will be an end to the matter." He turned to face George. "Micah doesn't appear to like you."

"The feeling is mutual. I don't suppose there is any chance I can get inside Herod's palace?"

"None, I'm afraid," Pilate answered. "Herod has complete control over who comes and goes. He does not like the press, and he dislikes strangers even more. It is mostly paranoia, he is convinced someone will assassinate him."

"I would be the same had I been raised with that family."

"I won't argue with that. Tell me, Mr Ambrose. Do you play chess?"

"Yes, I do."

"Then might I suggest we play a game, while we wait for Herods's response?"

"It would be a pleasure," George responded truthfully.

Colonel Vespian spoke, "Then I will leave you to it, I still have one or two things to attend to." He saluted the governor, and they parted ways to their own offices.

Left with no other choice, Micah had followed the rest of the councillors as they made their way to the Palace. As he walked, Micah called on of the page's that served the council, a boy of around fourteen. Speaking to him quickly, he sent him on ahead to inform Herod of their impending arrival. The boy was delighted to have been given the job. Herod was known to reward messengers by allowing them access to his personal brothel. The stories of what went on there were legendary.

Micah watched the boy go. The inner members of the council continued to argue amongst themselves. Micah was furious, the sun had been up for a couple of hours now. The whole city would be aware that something was going on. It was now nine-thirty in the morning. What was meant to be a quickly dealt with case was beginning to spiral out of control. Attracting too much attention. He needed this to be sorted before sundown. The prisoner had to be executed before the end of the day. If not, the Sabbath would be upon them, God's holy day could not be defiled by an execution.

There could be no more delays. If it was not completed today, then it would be eight days before anything could be done. After the Sabbath, the Passover festival was due to begin. By the time it was over, the followers of Bartholomew could rally thousands to their cause, against the authority of the council. It would likely end in bloodshed as a result, perhaps even a revolt across the whole nation.

The palace of Herod was vast, stretching a thousand feet north to south, and a hundred and eighty east to west. The Two main palace wings sat at either end, surrounding a central courtyard. Herod had built three towers to fortify the palaces, and to provide a place of safety in times of danger.

The largest of these towers rose to one hundred and forty-five feet. He had named it Phasal, after his brother. The middle tower was a modest hundred and thirty feet high, named Hippicus after his mother. The third and final of these towers of vanity was a paltry seventy-four feet in height. This last building was also the most attractive. Named after his wife Marianme, who he had executed. Herod had declared that as this tower was named after a woman he had loved that it should be the most beautiful.

Each of the towers had been constructed out of white marble. Such was the skill of the stone masons, it is said that they appeared to have been carved from one rock.

When the page had arrived at the palace, the boy had been escorted through the gardens. These too were spectacular, lush and green. Canals ran through the grounds, several groves of trees allowed for long walks. Tame doves and pigeons lived within. Shown through the main doorway the page was presented to the king in the main throne room. He quickly delivered his message, then waited in the hopes of been sent to paradise. He was to be disappointed, as the King dismissed him once the message had been relayed.

Herod was quietly pleased that Pilate had insisted that his authority should be recognised in this matter. He understood what Pilate wanted. Herod would question man, then send him back to Herod in a show of solidarity. This would cause embarrassment for the council, an authority they had both clashed with in the past.

While the king waited, he took the opportunity to discuss the matter with his advisers. Speaking to them, he said, "Unless there is a good reason for me to pass judgement, my intention is to merely question this man, then send him back to Pilate."

One of the advisers spoke, "A wise decision, Majesty."

Another, spoke up. "As usual, you have seen straight into the heart of the matter. Why antagonise the people of Galilee? Let the responsibility of this case rest on the shoulders of Pilate. It clearly falls into the parameters of the council, let them argue their case to Pilate."

"My thoughts exactly," the King continued. "The charges against this man, and all the evidence rest in Jerusalem. Let him be brought before us, out of respect for our Roman friends. We will speak with him, then send him back to the Jerusalem authorities as we all agree."

The king was pleased. He would be able to fulfil his desire to meet this prophet, but without any of the blame for his fate resting with him. He had heard many things about him, he reminded him of the Baptist. Surly, if he spared his life, it would atone for the death of the other?

He could hear the councillors arriving. Sitting back on his throne as they pushed the accused to the front. Herod watched the man look around at his surroundings. It was obvious he was not impressed by the opulence of the palace. As with all these preachers, he probably thought it should be sold and the money distributed amongst the poor. They never understood the need for him to keep up appearances, after all was said and done, he was a king.

Herod addressed the prisoner with politeness. He admitted he had heard many things about him. Joseph just stared back at him. This man had murdered his cousin, the Baptist. He had stolen his brother's wife, was in an adulterous relationship as dictated by their laws. He was a coward at heart, loyal to no one. This ruler would do nothing.

The King was speaking again, "From what I have been told of you, we all hoped to see some evidence of your powers. A small thing perhaps? Make water pour from the walls. Or a role of thunder?" The walls remained dry, the skies silent. "It might help you if you were more cooperative."

Micah moved forward, wanting to move the farce along he began to list the charges. Herod commanded him to be silent. He was not interested in the legalities. He had no intention of getting in the middle of their dispute. The last thing he wanted was the blood of another possible holy man on his hands.

He tried again, holding up a pewter plate, saying, "Turn this into gold." The plate remained unchanged. "Do you hear me?"

Silence.

The king's temper, always close to the surface, was growing. How dare this little man defy his royal prestige. "Very well, if you are a king, you need a kingly robe." He spoke to one of his advisers, who left the room, returning moments later. He handed over a red, dusty, moth-eaten robe. The king made a great show of shaking it out, then throwing it around Joseph's shoulders. It was all done in a comical manner, all those present laughed sycophantically.

"Take him back to Pilate," he commanded.

Pilate was angry when he heard they were back at his door. The fool Herod had failed to remove this matter from his desk. It was now plain that he would have to deal with it himself. Here they all stood, gathered before him with nothing but revenge in their minds. He had tried to do everything he could in order to get Joseph Bartholomew released. He had been blocked at every turn. Worse still, word of this had spread. Over a thousand people were gathered in the grounds, all watching and waiting.

Pilate sat, looking at those gathered, all wanting this man dead. While Vespian spoke into his ear. Pilate looked startled at what he was being told. "Are you sure?"

"Yes, it is an ancient custom, but it still remains in the province of the governor's office."

"Do we have any other prisoners?"

"Three, all sentenced to death."

"Their crimes?"

"Two petty thieves, they killed a man during a robbery. The other is the Zealot and terrorist, Ishmael Barabbas."

"Bring up Barabbas."

"Governor, surely you aren't serious?"

"I am. They would never choose him over this supposed holy man."

Vespian wasn't so sure, but he gave the order.

Pilate stood to address the crowds. "This man was brought before me, accused of blasphemy. I have examined him personally, and in the presence of your council. I have found nothing to deserve the sentence they have passed on him." The crowd became restless.

Micah was now apoplectic as he realised what was about to happen. He quickly spoke to the council members, sending them all out into the crowd. He only hoped it would be enough.

Pilate was speaking again, "Under the ancient customs of Rome, as a show of clemency for your Passover festival, I can release one prisoner sentenced to death. We have two such prisoners. This Bartholomew, who has committed no crime, and the butcher Barabbas. The choice is yours, who goes free?"

The crowds went into a frenzy, screaming one name over and over. Pilate realised he was beaten. His one last chance to save this man was snatched away from him. Vespian was speaking to him.

"You can't release him, he is one of the most dangerous men we have hunted."

"The people have spoken. I have no choice." Pilate changed his stance to look at Bartholomew. "I wander, Colonel who is really the more dangerous."

Pilate faced the crowd again, one last hope he thought. Pointing at Bartholomew he asked them, "What would you have me do with him?"

As one, the crowd answered.

Micah was triumphant. Everything he and Caiaphas had hoped for had been achieved.

Pilate was disappointed.

Vespian was horrified at the release of Barabbas.

George Ambrose felt physically sick.

Chapter Five
Food for Thought

George Ambrose had returned to his hotel as soon as it was all over. He had exchanged farewells with both Pilate and Vespian. The Colonel had urgent matters to attend to. The recapture of Barabbas for one, as well as organising the execution of three men. George had asked him about that, having assumed it was only Joseph Bartholomew. The Colonel had informed him, the council had insisted that the two petty thieves should meet the same fate. George had not understood why at first, then he realised if three men where crucified there was less chance of any accusations of revenge.

He had made copious notes at first, then lay on the bed to sleep. Considering that he had just witnessed the release of the man responsible for his incarceration and torture, he had the best night's sleep in months. No nightmares.

When he awoke, it was just after noon and he was hungry. He had not eaten since the meal with Vespian the night before. He showered and dressed. He tried to call his son, with no success, the phone going straight to his son's voicemail. He left him a message. Leaving the hotel he headed to a restaurant he had known from his previous time in Judea. It was only a short walk from the hotel, an old family run establishment. Going back four generations, he remembered it as one of the best in the city.

For old times' sake, he ordered the matzah ball soup, followed by lamb cholent, a hearty, spicy stew. He was not disappointed, the food was as good as he remembered. Even so, it could not divert his thoughts from what was happening at the fields of Calvary. Although that name was inaccurate, as it was actually a building built on the original fields. It had been a place of execution for centuries. It had seating for the general public, accommodating up to five thousand. That was on the right of the building, the official seating was on the left. Every member of the council is required to attend. The execution had already begun, scheduled as always to begin at noon.

History assessed there to be three forms of execution considered as the most brutal. Number three in this hit list was being burned alive, number two was decapitation.

The top spot was held for crucifixion. It deserved its place. Throughout the world it had been universally condemned. Only one place still had it on the law books, Rome. However, even they had shied away from its use. The last crucifixion had taken place over three hundred years ago. Only Judea, and its council considered it an acceptable punishment for the unforgivable crimes, as they called them. Crimes against their god.

Crucifixion is an ancient form of punishment, it had originated with the Carthaginians, who used it against their defeated enemies. Once the battle was won, all surviving officers and one in ten of the soldiers would be crucified. Its popularity spread through Persia, Macedonia and eventually into Rome.

Even Greece, recognised as an advanced civilisation, the home of democracy, had employed its use. After the Phoenician war, Alexander had ordered two thousand survivors to be crucified.

In those ancient days it was a common form of punishment. Rome had used it throughout their empire. For the execution of slaves, pirates and enemies of the state.

The Roman senator, Crassus crucified six thousand men after the rebellion led by Spartacus. It was reported in the histories that the crosses stretched all the way from Capua to Rome. A distance of one hundred and two miles. They hung there until long after their death, a warning to others. This is the fate that awaits you if you stand against Rome.

As a rule, Roman citizens were exempt from this form of punishment. It was considered to be a disgraceful way for a Roman to die. There were exceptions, but these were rare and the crime would have been extremely severe.

By the time Rome had adopted it, crucifixion had developed into a much more sophisticated process since those early days in Carthage.

In the first instances, the victim would only be fastened to a single upright pole. They would be attached with barbed thongs wrapped around their body. This method was improved upon by the introduction of impalement. Now the upright would be thrust through the body, entering via the anus and up out of the at the nape of the neck. Naturally, impalement was extremely painful, but relief came quicker through a faster death. The other manner meant a much slower, agonising death. Expiration would come as a result of a combination of factors. Constant exposure to the elements, exhaustion, torments inflicted by other people. If they were fastened low enough, they would be eaten alive by wild animals.

From those early experiments, improvements were made which included the addition of a cross beam. Now the outstretched arms of the victim could be tethered with ropes, and eventually nailed into position. The full weight of the arms would prevent the muscles of the lungs from working correctly. The condemned would die from asphyxiation within a short period of time. In order to prolong the agony, a foot support was added to lift the body making breathing easier. The feet would be nailed into position.

It was after the slave revolt of fifteen thirty-six, when over three thousand were crucified, that a movement started. The people had been horrified and sickened by the sight and the stench of the dead. People began to object to its continued use. Even within the senate, objections were being made.

The great orator, Cicero, made an impassioned speech for its abolition at that time. Describing the process as 'A most cruel and disgusting punishment, the very mention of which should be far removed from the Roman citizenry, from his mind, his eyes, his ears and from his very soul'

It was as a result of this speech that the movement gathered real momentum. With the support of Cicero and other senior senators, pressure was applied to the ruling classes.

It took many years to achieve, mainly due to the ever-changing emperors. Some would be sympathetic, others hostile. It was not until the early eighteenth century that the practice finally stopped. The last crucifixion by Rome took place on Wednesday, July twenty third eighteen thirty-two. It was the first in thirty-three years. Emperor Caligula III passed the sentence against Senator Piso. A cruel and vicious emperor, it had simply amused him to have Piso crucified.

While Rome had ceased to use it, the allowance for it was still written into their laws. It was because of this, Caiaphas was able to get it back into the Jewish law; and so the council were able to achieve their aim. To ensure the complete, public humiliation of Joseph Bartholomew. Because that is what it is. Not just an horrific death. It was a humiliation that made the condemned man as vulnerable as possible. Like everyone else, George had never seen a crucifixion, nor did he have any desire to. That wouldn't stop every single seat in Calvary being occupied. The nature of the beast, the human spectacle to watch the suffering of others.

There is a precise process to be followed, and it would be excruciating; a word that is derived from the act of crucifixion. First comes the scourging. Bartholomew would be whipped, it would not be performed with an everyday whip. It would be done using an implement that is inset with either nails, bones or broken glass. With each delivery of the lash, it would latch onto the skin. When pulled back, the skin would be ripped from the back, exposing the raw flesh and bone beneath. If he was lucky, he would not survive this scourging.

If not, he would be tied to the cross beam and forced to walk through the city to the place of execution. It was a myth that the condemned were made to carry their cross. The weight of a full cross was over four hundred pounds, whereas the cross beam was a mere hundred and thirty pounds.

While he was paraded through the streets, it was very likely he would be subjected to further abuse. People will line the streets, some throwing objects, other spitting at him. The least that can be expected is a torrent of verbal abuse. The walk itself would be agonising, after the scourging. The weight of the crossbeam against his back would reopen the wounds, leaving a trail of blood in the streets.

The execution team, consisting of four soldiers and a captain will keep the spectators at bay. Should Joseph stumble, they are under strict instructions not to assist him in any way.

Following behind the condemned man walks the whole of the Jewish council. Under their own rules they are required to observe every stage of the execution. George hoped that at least some of them would have a sense of shame and disgust. He doubted it, it had been plain to see at the trial that they all wanted their vengeance.

Once they reached the site, Joseph would be kept waiting while all the officials took their seats. During this time he would be left standing for all to see. A further delay will be made as a representative of the council confirms the charges and the sentence.

Only after all this does the execution squad begin its grisly task. He will be stripped naked, as a further humiliation. If he needed to urinate, or defecate, he would have to do so in full view of the public. This will bring further discomfort through the attraction of insects.

The securing of the victim to the cross beam begins next. The soldiers will split into two teams, one for each arm. One will hold it in position, while the other will drive a metal spike through the wrist. This needs to be done with precision, entering between the two bones, radius and ulna. This action will destroy the median nerve, creating intense pain.

Ropes are now looped around the cross beam and, then hoisted up and secured to the upright. If the soldiers have made any errors in earlier process, it is at this point that they will discover the fact. It is possible that one, or both, of the arms can rip free and the victim either fall, or remain hanging from the one arm. If so, the whole process will have to be repeated.

The feet will be placed one over the other on the support. A further metal spike will be driven into the top, through the metatarsal bones of both feet. This will destroy peroneal and planter nerves, creating further, intense pain.

Once all this is completed, the condemned will be left hanging there, dying a slow and unimaginable death.

The council have no further responsibilities at this point. Once the physicality of the process is completed, so are their duties. Some may stay, for whatever reason. The public would slowly drift away, becoming bored with the spectacle of a man just hanging there. With no further excitement, they would leave for their homes.

The Roman soldiers did not have that luxury. These men would have to stay until the end. Hoping for a quick death so they too can return to their homes. The council too would want it over quickly. The next day was the Sabbath, with the Passover festival beginning the day after. They would not want bodies ruining the festivities. With this in mind, they may request the soldiers finish it.

This can be achieved in one of two ways. Firstly, the captain can order his men to use a sledgehammer to smash the bones on the legs. Without their support, breathing will become difficult and death would follow quickly through suffocation. The second method is quicker. Using the long spear, it is thrust into the side, just above the third rib and into the heart. Death is swift.

All of this pain, this torment, because Joseph had allegedly offended their God. The God of the Jews, it seemed, was a touchy deity.

George's deliberations were interrupted. There was an ominous rumbling from below the ground, working its way up. He knew what those sounds and vibrations meant, an earthquake was coming. This knowledge was confirmed within seconds. The tables began to shake, cutlery smashed onto the floor, bottles were shaking off the shelves and various items bounced across the tables. If was over almost as soon as it started, no more than minute.

It passed, only to be replaced by sudden darkening of the skies, accompanied by a roll of thunder and then a downpour of rain. George had never seen a storm gather so quickly, and certainly not in this part of the world. The skies boomed with thunder, lightning lit up the heavens. He had finished his food, but decided he would sit and wait out the weather, ordering another coffee he settled back in his chair.

His mind wandered back to his thoughts. The Jews only had one God to follow. Even if he was a touch sensitive, and the rules ridiculously complicated. At least according to the council.

The Romans, on the other hand had a dozen, thirteen if you accepted that Tiberius, as emperor, was a living God. It baffled George. The Romans had built a vast empire, the largest the world had ever seen. More impressively, they had also managed to hold on to it for two thousand years. They had achieved all this, yet they still held on to this outdated, ancient belief structure.

Twelve God's. Chief of which was Jupiter, king of the Gods. The God of the skies, thunder and the patron of Rome. Standing alongside him was his wife and sister, Juno. Protector of Rome's women, patroness of Rome. If the stories coming out of that city were even half true, she wasn't doing a very good job protection wise.

Then they had, ironically, Minerva, Goddess of wisdom. A gift that seemed in short supply in Rome these days. She was also the goddess of the arts, trade and strategy. Whereas, Jupiter's brother, Neptune had command over the waters, earthquakes, hurricanes and, oddly, horses.

The others all followed, Venus the mother of the Roman people, goddess of love, beauty, fertility, sex and desire.

Apollo, God of music, healing, light and truth.

Diane, Goddess of the hunt, the moon and birth.

Vulcan, God of fire, volcanoes, metalwork, the forge, and, naturally blacksmiths.

So they went on, until you came to the last of them, Mars. The God of war. The mythology of Rome begins here, with Mars. Legend, and some of the brightest of Rome's scholars, would contend that Mars was the father of Romulus. The founder of Rome. These same scholars also maintain that he, along with his brother Remus, were suckled and raised by wolves. When they got older, they had a falling out that resulted in the murder of Remus.

After this dispute, Romulus renamed the small province he ruled as Rome. Seeking to increase his powerbase, he allowed all men, free and slave, to come to the city. All men, distinguished or not were welcome. They came, seeking a new life and prosperity.

However, Romulus faced another problem. These men, the first citizens of Rome would need wives. In order to achieve this he invited the neighbouring villages to a great festival. While they were there, he kidnapped their women.

War followed. Once Romulus had secured victory, he invited King Titus of the Sabine nation into a shared kingship. Agreement of terms was completed, then he handpicked one hundred of the noblest men. This first senate would act as advisors to the king.

In these early days of Rome, there were three main peoples inhabiting the areas. Rome, ruled by Romulus; The Sabine, co-ruled by Titus and Romulus; And the Etruscans, who had their own ruler.

Rome continued to grow under the rule of the Senate and Romulus. It was not until after his death that the Etruscans decided to make their move. Slowly, bit by bit they became the dominant force, eventually seizing power of the area from Rome. The last three kings where all Etruscan, managing to hold onto power for the next seven years.

Rome had been reduced back to the small province it had started as. During the seven years of Etruscan rule, Rome made agreements with the other Latin cities. Defending them against a number of Sabine incursions. A final victory at the battle of Lake Regillus and Rome was once again the dominant power. They began to expand, eventually conquering all the surrounding areas, including their Etruscan neighbours.

Rome controlled all of Italy.

Not content, they turned their eyes further afield. Over the next seven centuries they expanded their power base. By the end of the seven century wars, they controlled Greece, Egypt, the Middle East, North Africa, French and Spanish Gaul, Germany, Briton, Netherlands, Portugal and Belgium. It was an empire never before seen, and their power was absolute.

A citizen of Rome could travel across the known world in complete confidence. Secure in the knowledge that should they be assaulted, robbed, or murdered the country responsible would face the full wrath of Rome. Such was the power of the words, 'I am a citizen of Rome'

During all these wars, invasions and subjugations, Rome continued with its own internal power struggles. The expansion of the empire provided huge opportunities. Especially for those hungry for power and wealth. The growth of the empire had produced a different set of problems. A set of unique demands that the old republican political structure could not solve.

A young man found himself in the middle of one of these power struggles. The current dictator, Sulla was an enemy of this fatherless eighteen-year-olds uncle Marius, and of his father-in-law, Cinna. In order to avoid being dragged into their argument, he joins the army. He does not return to Rome until Sulla is dead; but when he does, Gaius Julius Ceaser returns as a hero.

With the help of his friends, his new found allies, the great Pompey and the phenomenally wealthy Crassus, he rises through the ranks of Roman government. He proves to be an excellent, inspiring speaker that the people come to love and admire. Eventually he rises to the highest office when he is appointed Consul of Rome.

Consuls only serve for one year. At the end of his term, Ceaser is appointed governor over the unruly French Gauls. He proves to be an inspired choice. He brings them to heel, eventually conquering all the remaining provinces to control the whole of the French region. He now stands shoulder to shoulder with Pompey as one of Rome's greatest generals.

However, back in Rome the political landscape had become increasingly hostile. Many of the leaders had grown Jealous of Ceaser's success. Chief among them is Pompey. Where Ceaser had the support of the people, Pompey had the aristocrats.

When Ceaser announces his intention to run for Consul again, the senate under the influence of Pompey, insist he must relinquish his command of the army. Realising this is a strategy to weaken his position, he refuses, crosses the Rubicon, marches on Rome and seizes power.

The next eighteen months are spent in fighting Pompey. Chasing him across the world into Egypt. Here, as a gesture of friendship, the young Pharaoh Ptolemy VIII presents Ceaser with Pompey's head.

Returning to Rome, Ceaser is now the most powerful man in the world. The senate immediately appoints him dictator for life.

Gaius Julius Ceaser rules as though he is one of the kings of old. A contingent within the senate grow weary of his behaviour. Fearing he intends to replace the republic with a monarchy, he is assassinated.

Ceaser's nominated successor, Octavian, is out of the country. When he hears of his uncle's murder, he returns immediately. Together with Marc Anthony and Lepidus they hunt his assassins down. At the end, they come to an agreement to rule Rome in partnership, as a triumvirate.

All goes well at first, but it is not long before fractures appear in the relationship. A power struggle begins, which leads to all-out war for supreme power.

Lepidus is defeated by the armies of Marcus Agrippa, Octavian's closest friend and ally.

Marc Anthony has aligned himself with his Egyptian lover, Queen Cleopatra. Everything comes to a violent climax at the battle of Actium. Each knows that the winner will control Rome.

Octavian wins the day.

The senate congratulates him, and appoint his as supreme ruler, Emperor of Rome. The republic is finished. Octavian adopts the name of Augustus.

While the basic government of the republic, the senate, remains in place it is Augustus who rules. He will have ultimate power, the final word. He is the first of the emperors, the founder of the Julian dynasty.

His rule brings two hundred years of peace. He is a beloved and brilliant ruler. Sadly, those that follow him are not of the same standard.

Over the next thousand years there are those emperors whose only concern is the wellbeing of the people they rule. There are those who are completely ineffective, incapable of making a decision. There are those who rule in name only, delegating the real work to others.

Then, there are the ones who are just mad, psychopathic lunatics. Men who use their position to settle old, schoolboy squabbles from childhood. Men who have grown into cruel, vindictive adults.

Added to these, there are those who use the position to indulge in their own set of perversions.

It is only in the last two or three hundred years that there has been some reasonable consistency in the emperors, and the governing of the empire.

There are still occasional acts of spite, of cruelty. However, time moves on and the expense of running such a vast empire is becoming prohibitive. It is placing a huge strain on manpower, equipment, finances and their struggling economy. Technological advances had left them isolated, in a precarious position as they refuse to leave the old ways behind them, to welcome these advances.

That is until the arrival of Emperor Victus IX. Finally, they had a ruler who was willing to embrace this new world of the late eighteen hundreds. A ruler who told the people they must join this new world, or die with the old one. A ten-year plan was drawn up and applied with ruthless efficiency. New businesses were developed, experts were brought in from around the world. Automotive, aviation and medical advances implemented.

Within the ten years, Rome was dragged into the modern age. Rome again has a strong economy and powerbase to work from. Emperor Victus begins negotiations with the furthest reaches of the empire, giving some of the powers of government back to them. Eventually, he negotiates a complete withdrawal of Rome from these provinces. It is not always achieved peacefully, violence is inevitable.

Other emperors follow his example. Emperors who had been educated in the sciences, economics and technology. From its vast size it is now continues to hold power in three areas. The Middle East, including Judea, North Africa and Egypt, its oldest ally.

Emperor Augustus X begins talks with Egypt to grant them independence, the withdrawal of Rome. To work to a peaceful solution. Unfortunately, he dies before they can be completed. It is assumed that they will continue under the new emperor. This does not happen.

Augustus X is succeeded by his corrupt, debauched and power-hungry stepson, Tiberius XII. All hopes of an Egyptian independence died with Augustus.

Tiberius is a different ruler than those who came before him, he is a throwback to the ancient emperors. A cruel man, consumed by paranoia. Convinced he will be assassinated, he has retired to his mountain fortress on the Isle of Capri. Delegating virtually all decisions, all responsibility to his trusted adviser Sejanus. It is he who holds the power in Rome.

Meanwhile, free from the scrutiny of Rome, Tiberius is free to indulge his ever-growing perversions. When not working at the few tasks he retains, he likes to be amused. To be entertained in a very particular way.

Dozens of handpicked young boys and girls. Picked for their looks alone will perform sexual acts on each other. All for his own perverted satisfaction.

Occasionally, he will demand that they dress as mythical spirits of nature. Should any of them lack the necessary experience, sex manuals are provided for their education. Some nights, if all goes well, and he has been sufficiently entertained, he may join in. Selecting one of the teenage boys or girls, or both, to fulfil his own gratification.

All of these youngsters believe they will be allowed to leave afterwards. Tiberius, terrified news of his behaviour will reach Rome, has other plans.

The house in Capri has been built on the edge of the cliff face overlooking the Mediterranean Sea. It has become known as 'Tiberius leap.' After the initial outcrop. It is a thousand-foot drop.

Each of the of the young entertainers will be thrown from it once the festivities are completed. None will survive. This action is not just to ensure their silence, Tiberius enjoys their screams of terror as they realise their fate.

Tiberius is a man with no sense of morality, devoid of any human capacity.

George had finished his coffee, and the weather had finally cleared up. He stood, intent on catching up with his son. As he was stood at the counter, settling his bill Vespian walked past. Seeing George, he waved and stepped inside.

"You didn't go to the execution?" It was more of a statement than a question.

"No. I've seen enough horrors in my lifetime, I don't need to add another to the list," George answered.

"Well, yes. I can understand that. It was pretty ghastly."

"You went?"

"Ordered to by Pilate. To ensure there was no trouble."

"Was he expecting any?"

"I don't think so, not really. It was just a precaution."

"It's all over then?"

"Yes. The bodies are being removed."

"I thought it was the custom to leave them there, as a warning to others."

"Normally, yes, I believe I read that somewhere. The Passover festival starts next week, the council thought a couple of bodies hanging around might put a bit of a dampener on the celebrations."

"What will be done with his body?"

"It should be disposed of, thrown in the body pits reserved for those executed. The other two will end up there, for the wildlife to deal with. Pilate has released Joseph back to his family." Vespian paused. "Curiously, a local business man has provided funds for the purchase of a tomb."

"Who?"

"Joseph Arimathea. He is well known for his acts of philanthropy." Both men were stood on the pavement, outside the restaurant. "What about you? Will you continue with the story?"

"Maybe. If I can find some of his followers to speak to, but as he's dead." George accompanied this statement with a shrug of his shoulders.

"For now."

"Pardon?"

"You haven't heard? Apparently, he has promised to come back from the dead. On Sunday to be precise."

"You are joking?"

"No. Seriously. That is what I am told, anyway."

George could not think of anything else to say to this ridiculous statement. "What about Barabbas?"

"He won't get far. I expect to have him back in the cells within twenty-four hours."

"You seem very confident."

"I am. I have issued a shoot on sight order, and promised a significant reward for any information that leads us to him."

"What about Joseph's followers, what are the councils' intentions towards them?"

"Nothing, as far as I know. The council have got what they wanted. It would be a mistake to continue their persecution of his followers. It will serve no purpose, and only prove to the people that they acted out of malice."

"I hope you're right."

"The council will leave them to wallow in their own self-pity. I doubt that any of his disciples, as they are being called, will do anything. Not now they have seen the consequences. He is dead, if he had been the promised Messiah, why didn't he save himself is what the people have been heard saying." Vespian shook George's hand. "I have to go. I have to organise a guard for his burial site."

"Really?"

"Micah requested it from Pilate. He, and the council, also know about the claims of rebirth. They are concerned the followers will steal his body, to give truth to the claim."

"Their pettiness holds no bounds," George said. "I will let you go then." They shook hands again, and parted company.

Returning to the hotel, George spotted his son sat at the bar with Derek. Taking a deep breath, he went over to join them.

James was clearly in shock.

This, George thought, is going to be another late night.

Part Three
Saturday

Chapter Six
A Life Reclaimed

George was pleasantly surprised at how good he felt when he woke the next morning. Virtually no hangover. Which considering the quantity of alcohol the three of them had consumed the previous evening, definitely qualified as a miracle.

The conversation had been a rambling one, bouncing from one subject to another. A lot of the talk had, naturally, been about the week's events. He had got into a minor argument with his son, who still held to the philosophy of Bartholomew. James had persuaded him to meet with some of the others, and with some who had not been followers.

George got out of the bed and headed into the shower. Despite his cynicism, or maybe because of it, he found he was still intrigued. The old journalist was waking up, just as Charlie had said, and it was telling him there was more to this than first appears. He also felt somewhat useless, he didn't want to know more, he found he needed too.

As he dried himself, he looked over the list of names they had put together. There were only five names;

Mary Da'Magdalena.

Peter?

Judas Iscariot

Joseph Arimathea

Nicodemus

The question mark against Peter was due to the fact that James had realised he had no idea what his second name was.

George, with the exception of Joseph Arimathea, did not know any of them. James had told him a little about each of them, except Mary. He said he had not wanted to prejudice him.

Peter was one of the most prominent of the disciples, had been with him since the early days in Galilee. His most trusted out of them all, James had said.

Judas, that was an interesting addition. The suggestion had been James's. The traitor, as he called him. James just wanted to ask him why.

Finally, James had suggested he meet with the Rabbi, Nicodemus. A member of the council, a respected scholar of the scriptures who had been open to what Joseph had to say.

Dressed, George put the list in his pocket and headed down for breakfast. He spotted his son sat at a table. Helping himself from the buffet, he ordered a pot of coffee and joined James.

"You look rough," he told him.

"Thanks, I feel it," James responded.

"Well, the three of us did attempt to drink the bar dry between us."

"Feels like we succeeded."

"Not quite, but it was a close fought battle." James smiled at the joke. "And otherwise, how do you feel?"

"I'm not sure, numb. Still can't believe what's happened."

"Well, it all happened, and he is dead, sadly."

"Is that all you can say?" James stated impatiently.

"What else is there to say? What's done is done. I'm sorry your friend had to die, and in such a barbaric manner."

"Barbaric just about describes what I saw."

"Why on earth did you go? Surly you understood what was going to be done?"

"I wasn't the only one."

"Who else was misguided enough to attend?"

"Peter was there, and Andrew. Some of his family. It was the least we thought we owed him."

"That's not much of a reason."

"Well, we thought... I don't know...that maybe..."

"He would prove to the world that he was who he claimed? Fly off the cross and reveal himself in all his glory?"

"Perhaps, I suppose we just wanted something more."

"He didn't. He was just a man, like any other. Now he is gone, and nothing can bring him back, despite his claims to the contrary. His death has left a trail of disappointment, left those who followed him in danger of their lives." George looked at his son, he appreciated that he could not begin to fathom what he felt. He continued speaking, "As far as I am aware the authorities are no longer interested in pursuing this any further. However, should they change their minds, at least you can tell them you were sent by the paper to cover the story."

"Why would I do that?"

"To keep yourself alive."

"Abandon the others? Abandon him?"

"If necessary, yes. He is dead, you don't owe him anything."

"Deny it ever happened? I couldn't do that. The things he did. The words he spoke. I don't know if he was their Messiah, but I am sure he was sent by their God."

"Even after everything that was done to him?"

"His death does not change what he had to say. His teaching, the criticism of the authorities. Those things are still true."

George stared at his son, stunned by his stubbornness. "So, you intend to carry on his work, this mission of his?"

"In any way I can. The corruption within the council has not gone away just because he has." George looked at his son. There it was again, that fire he had seen last night whenever he spoke of Joseph.

"You still believe in him, you think he was their promised Messiah."

"I never said that, I don't know what to think at the moment; But you can't expect me to just forget everything I've seen and heard."

"O.K. Tell me, what was so special about what he had to say?"

"What do you want to know?"

"Everything, from the beginning."

James began, and George poured himself a coffee and settled back to listen.

"He was born thirty-three years ago, in a small town called Nazareth. The story begins even before then. His mother was promised in marriage to Joseph, a carpenter. He wasn't born into wealth, his family were hard working people. His father was respected, his skills were well known.

"His mother, Mary was from a good family, a devout and respectable girl. Not long after they were betrothed, she fell pregnant. It was a scandal, an outrage in their small town. Joseph swore he had not touched her, until they threatened to take her to the town square to be stoned to death for her infidelities. They were married soon after. They still maintain that Joseph never touched her before they married. She maintains that she was a virgin when they married, that the child she carried had been conceived through God's spirit. That the child was his.

"The Roman census takes place every ten years. The Roman's still insist that everyone returns to their birthplace to be counted. Joseph was born in Bethlehem, so they travelled there. It was a difficult journey, Mary was heavily pregnant by this time. When they reached the town, every pub, lodge and hotel was full. The one they should have stayed in had cocked up the booking, so they had nowhere to stay.

"Fortunately, a woman took pity on them. She owned a farm, allowed them to bed down in one of her stables. That's where he was born.

"Joseph tells how he was visited in a dream, warning him of impending danger, that they must leave as soon as possible. That morning, once they had registered for the census counter's, they fled across the border into Egypt. I have no idea what this perceived danger was, and I have not been able to find anything out."

"If the dates are right, I think I do."

"The dates are right. What do you know?"

"I had not been out here long, it was only my third placement. I'd been here about six months, this was around twenty-nine years ago. One night a couple of us decided to go for a beer after work. While there, this woman grabs me, 'Your new' she stated. I just thought she was another prostitute plying her trade. I shook her off, but she wouldn't leave me alone. She asked if I would write her story, as no one else would. I asked her what story? She told me that the temple guards had murdered her baby boy, that she wasn't the only one. According to her, Herod, the current one's uncle, had ordered the murder of all children below the age of two; provided they had been born in a specific location."

"Bethlehem."

"Yes, Bethlehem."

"Was it true?"

"I think so, but there was no real evidence, only gossip and rumour. Without any proof, we couldn't say anything."

"Did you believe it?"

"Yes, I did. The other women I spoke to were very convincing."

"You think this is why they fled?"

"No idea, how would they know?" George said. "Anyway, born in a stable, fled to Egypt. Carry on."

"Of course. So, it wasn't long before the stories started. Shortly after he was born three men arrived. They claimed to have been told a new king was born, that it had been foretold in the stars, and that a new star in the sky confirmed the prophecy. They had travelled from the east in order to pay their respects, to bring this new king three gifts." James stopped, thinking. "If that story about Herod's uncle is true, it could have been them that told him."

"Why?"

"As visiting dignitaries, protocol would require them to call on King Herod. He may have asked what had brought them here."

"It's possible, but there's no use in speculating what may or may not have occurred. Stick to the story."

James continued his narrative. "Other stories sprang up during his childhood. That he cured a lame girl when he was six. Revived the crops after a blight. Healed his uncle of a debilitating disease, it was reported to have been leprosy. Little else is known about his childhood other than these rumours.

"There is one story of his going missing when he was about twelve. His parents where frantic, searching everywhere they had been. When they finally tracked him down, they found him in the temple, talking with some of the rabbi's. I tried to find out more, but I couldn't track any of the people he spoke with.

"After that, nothing for years. No stories, as though he had just disappeared. Then, he suddenly appears, a fully grown man. Turns up to be baptised by another preacher at Jordan. All I know about that is again rumour. Those that bore witness maintain that after he was baptised, a dove appeared out of nowhere. The heavens opened up, one said, that the dove was sent by God. As if it was a sign of approval.

"Then, again he vanishes. Walked off into the desert, so I was told, only to return about six weeks later. It is from that moment he began his preaching. It is also from that moment that the stories really start to gain momentum. How he turned water into wine at a wedding celebration, casting out demons, a miraculous catch of fish. How he fed thousands with nothing more than a few loaves and some fish.

"Then he arrives in Jerusalem. The same stories follow him here, he sets himself at odds with the council. The rest you know."

James had been talking for over an hour. George had listened closely to everything he had said. He had some questions, he started at the beginning.

"A virgin birth?"

"That's what the family maintains."

"Not a tale to hide an illicit affair?"

"I told you what was said to me."

"How do you know Joseph isn't the father? Afterall, he said he was."

"To protect her, after the elders of the village threatened to deal with it according to their laws."

"Why would he do that?"

"People do strange things when in love."

"Even accepting someone else's child as their own?"

"Not my problem. I believe them, I can tell you that after meeting them, they are totally devoted to each other. We should all be so lucky to find such love."

"This Baptist, John, who was he?"

"Another preacher, he believed redemption for past sins was possible through baptism; and an acceptance of God's will."

"But he wasn't the Messiah?"

"No, he claimed to be a messenger sent to prepare the way."

"For what?"

"The coming of the Messiah. 'Someone is coming who is greater than I am – so much greater that I am not worthy to stoop down like a slave and untie his sandals. I baptise you with water, but he will baptise you with the Holy Spirit.' His words."

"You think he was talking about Joseph," this was said as a statement, not a question.

"Yes, I do. Unfortunately, I never got an opportunity to ask him. He was very vocal in regard to the state of Herod's marriage. Accused them both of being in an adulterous relationship, called her a whore."

"According to their laws, they are."

"Well, it was that truth that got him arrested and killed." James paused. "That is a story in itself."

"Why?"

"Salome, his stepdaughter. If you think the council are conniving, she leaves them in the lower leagues."

"What happened?"

"The short version, Herod held a celebration. No idea what it was for, may have been his birthday. Anyway, there were important guests from the city, and around the world in attendance. Salome is an accomplished dancer, it is said she can make you forget everything as you watch. Her abilities are famous around the world. Herod wanted her to dance for his guests, she refused. He persisted, offered her anything she wanted for one dance. She performed, then asked for the head of the Baptist served on a silver platter."

"She always was a charmer," George said.

"I told you, she's a rattlesnake."

George was well aware of what a poisonous creature Salome was. Even her name was a contradiction, a derivation of the Hebrew word shalom, meaning peace. He continued his questioning.

"He turns up, gets baptised by John. Then he disappears, by all accounts, into the wilderness for days on end. Why? You must have thought about it?"

"Some. Frankly I have no idea. Maybe to gather his thoughts, before beginning his mission. To commune with God, who knows?"

"Well, that does make sense. Even so, how did he survive? There's nothing out there, just miles of desert. You don't think it odd?"

"Odd? Everything about this is odd."

"I can't disagree with that. The idea he was communing with God, that is what he would want people to believe. It would give the impression that he was given a mission directly from him."

"That is a particularly duplicitous way of looking at it."

"I'm a journalist. I'm supposed to be objective, consider all the possibilities. Something you have lost in the middle of all this."

"I've been with him, walked with him, eaten with him. I got to know him."

"And in the process you have lost that objectivity. You all wanted to believe he was who he claimed." George stopped, he wasn't here to chastise. "How do you know he didn't have a breakdown out there in the wilderness? Maybe he heard what happened to John, decided to take some sort of revenge in a misguided attempt to get him justice?"

"If that was his plan, it resulted in both their deaths. Besides, I told you. I got to know him. He didn't do revenge. It would be impossible for him to even consider it. He spoke only of love for your fellow man, compassion and understanding. As to a breakdown? No. He couldn't have spoken with such clarity if that had been the case."

"But no sane man, knowing the possible consequences would have claimed to be the Messiah."

"I been thinking about that. I can't recall him ever making that claim. Not once."

"He claimed exactly that at his trial. In fact, he told Caiaphas that's who he was. It was those words that sealed his fate."

"Well, I never heard him claim that. I know some of the others believed he was."

"Do you?" George immediately reconsidered that question, waving James's response away. "Never mind. What about all these so-called miracles, for want of a better word. Do you believe he fed a few thousand people with virtually nothing?"

"Yes, I do," James responded. "I wasn't there, but I have spoken to those who were. They are very compelling, convincing when they speak. Or at least they were, I'm not sure what they would say now."

"It makes no difference how compelling. It just isn't possible."

"That's why they call them miracles."

George changed the subject, "What about his preaching. Do you remember any of it?"

"Yes. When he spoke, you listened. I remember his words."

"Tell me some of it."

"Have faith in God. I tell you the truth, you can say to this mountain, 'may you be lifted up and thrown into the sea' and it will happen; but you must believe it, and have no doubt of it within your heart. Faith can give you anything, if you pray to the father. Before you pray, make sure you have forgiven anyone you are holding a grudge against. Then the father in heaven will be able to forgive your sins also.

"I am the true grapevine, and my father is the gardener. He cuts off every branch of mine that does not produce fruit; and prunes the branches that do bear fruit, so they can produce even more. You have already been pruned and purified by the message I have given you. Remain faithful in me, and I will remain faithful in you. For a branch cannot bear fruit if it has been cut from the vine, and you cannot be fruitful unless you are faithful to me.

"If you love me, obey my commandments, and I will ask the father who will give you another councillor who will never leave you. He is the Holy Spirit, who leads into all truth. The world cannot receive him, because it is not looking and does not recognise him. But you know him, because I live with now and later will be in you. Soon the world will no longer see me, but you will see me. Since

I live, you will also live. When I am raised to life again, you will know I am in my father, and you are in me and I am in you. Those who accept my commandments, and obey them, are the ones who love me."

George looked into his son's eyes. Again, that fire. "That sounds like he is giving you all a job. Getting you to continue his work." James merely nodded his agreement, George did not press the point. "You mentioned, 'when I am raised to life', do you believe it? That he will come back from the dead?"

"Of course not. It was not meant to be taken literally, it has some other deeper, spiritual meaning that none of us have understood."

"Convenient, what do the rest of them think?"

"I don't know, other than Peter, I haven't been able to get hold of them. They are in hiding, frightened the council will come after them next."

"Understandable. As I said, from what I have been told they have no plans to do anything. The Roman authorities don't care about you one way or another. The council don't want to do anything, as all it will do is keep it in the people's minds. They just want it to be forgotten." George lit a cigarette, then continued. "So, if they are all in hiding, how do I get to speak to them?"

"I spoke to Peter, he is expecting us for a late supper. Joseph, Judas and Nicodemus have no reason to be concerned. Mary will be in work, she has agreed to meet us on her break at two."

"What do you know about Judas?"

"He lives in the Potters Field apartments."

"Expensive."

"Very. His father still supports him to some extent."

"Privileged?"

"Not particularly. His father owns a dozen grocery shops, they are moderately successful. Daddy made sure his son received the best education he could afford. He had ambitions for his son, wanted him to gain a place on the council, to ensure the family's future. Make sure their name was spoken with respect. Judas, however, had other ideas. While attending university, he became…radicalised I suppose you would call it. His family hoped it was just a phase, youthful high spirits. I am looking forward to seeing him."

"What order are we seeing them?"

"Mary first, at two. She works in the Eucalyptus Restaurant, just a ten-minute walk. Then, Joseph has said he can see us at four, Judas lives round the corner from his offices, so we will see him after. Then, Nicodemus is the Rabbi at a small synagogue in a village on the outskirts. I have arranged a car for the drive, then we will head to Peter."

"Why do you think he did it?"

"Who, Judas?" George nodded. "I don't know. That is the one and only question I've got for him."

"Maybe he was a true believer. That Joseph would reveal himself. Did it to force his hand." James made no comment, George asked one more question. "Do you believe he was the Messiah, the chosen one?"

"I thought I did. Think I still do at times, then I don't know what to think. One minute I'm sure if it, the next I have no idea what to think. I am confused, after everything he said and did, I still find it difficult to believe what has happened. Anyway, we need to make a move, Mary will be expecting us soon."

Both of them left the hotel, James had been true to his words. The restaurant was only a short walk away. As they made their way, James confirmed he had left the car in the hotel car park.

George had always hoped his son would have taken up a different profession. However, it had been clear from early on that his son loved the business. He had used to come to the paper with him when younger. From those first visits had grown a love affair with the world of news. Then, George had been offered the posting to Judea when James was seven, he had accepted the posting. That decision had sealed the fate of a marriage that was already struggling.

When James had enrolled in the college run by the paper, he had been proud as well as a little disappointed. He had hoped that James would change his mind after bearing witness to what the job had cost George. His mother had been furious, but she had to eventually admit that he was too much like his father. One of the tutors had even passed the odd piece of James's work. They had been good, very. The boy had a rare talent. Not just in his style of writing, but also in his ability to see through the lies that had been embedded within the assignments. He graduated top of his class, and Charles had immediately invited him to join the paper. The facts around his graduation meant nothing to Charles, James started in the same team all new comers do. The obituaries team. He thrived in the atmosphere of a real paper, within two years he was offered the Junior post here in Judea.

Now, here they were, father and son working the same story.

James tapped George on the shoulder and pointed across the street towards the eucalyptus restaurant. When they entered, George realised it was more of a bistro place. James left his side to speak to one of the waitresses. When he came back, he stated, "Mary has arranged a private booth for us, where we can't be overheard. Number thirty-two, it's near the back."

George followed him, taking seats opposite each other. The waitress appeared, carrying a tray of coffee. She placed them on the table, then greeted James with real warmth, kissing him on both cheeks. While they talked, George noted the name on her badge. This was Mary. He took the opportunity to look her over. There was evidence of a former beauty, she was a strikingly good-looking woman. She had incredible green eyes, George noticed. The bone structure of her face also spoke of a former beauty now lost. Her hair was losing its colour, he could see the beginnings of some grey flecks in the red. He estimated her age at mid-forties, it was obvious that life had not been easy from the lines formed there.

She had finished talking to James, and now turned her gaze on George. It was a cool look he received. While quietly assessing each other, another waitress brought a mixture of pastries. Chocolate raisin babka, rugelach, surganiyet, Bourikas and hamantaschen.

James made the introductions. "Mary, this is my father, George. He works for the paper in London. He wants to help us, he wants to know more about Joseph. The effect he had on the people around him."

"So he, and his paper can make fun of us, show the world what a bunch of idiots we all are?"

James was about to answer, when George spoke, "No, I don't do that, and I haven't decided what I am going to write, or if I will write anything. Most of what I've been told wouldn't be believed anyway. Miraculous healings, driving out demons, raising the dead. If anyone is going to look like a fool, it will be me for writing such fanciful stories. However, should I write anything, no names will be used. At this point I am just trying to discover the man behind the hype."

"Please Mary, you can trust him."

"Can I? Can we?"

"I promise, you can."

Mary continued to look a James, then turned her attention on George. "I'm not happy about this." George was about to respond when she held her hand up. "I'm only going to do this for two reasons, One, because it is what Joseph would want, and secondly because he," with this she nodded at James, "says I can trust you. Despite what the council are saying publicly, I do not believe for one minute that they are finished with us. That they will just forget us." She settled back in the booth, gathering her thoughts. When she started, it was hesitantly at first. As she continued her nerves began to settle, and by the end there was that same fire in her that George saw in his son.

"I was born in a small village, far from here. With no real Roman presence or council to deal with, we were able to live relatively free. It was mostly a farming community, everyone worked in the fields side by side as soon as you could walk almost. We had a Rabbi that came once every four weeks to lead us in worship. Everyone attended. It seemed, from the outside, an idyllic life. Especially if you were born male. The elders of the village took the scriptures very seriously. Particularly the phrase, the woman will be subject to the man. They wrap it all up in religious jargon, but it essentially meant women of the village had no rights.

"I would have been about twelve, I suppose, when I started to notice the looks I got off some of the older boys, and the elders of the village. I wasn't much older, when I was ordered to attend to one of them. I was to spend the night, to do whatever I was told. He raped me, there is no other way to describe what he did that night. I was told this was God's punishment on the woman, for what they had done in the garden of Eden. I knew no better. It was a closed community. I assumed this was what went on everywhere.

"When his son came of age, after his bar mitzvah, I was given to him as a present. He, and two of his friends, took their turns with me. It went on all night.

"I tried to get some support, somehow. Both my mother and father told me this was God's will, not to defy the elders. When I was fourteen, I ran away. I decided enough was enough, I didn't see why I should stay. They soon found me. I received a public flogging for my disobedience.

"The next time, I planned better. By the time they had realised I was missing, I was miles away. They didn't find me, not this time. I found a job in the market, gutting fish. An old couple rented me a room. It wasn't much, but it was better than what I'd had.

"I was happy there. For three years.

"Then one afternoon, I saw one of them, one of the elder's sons in the market. I found out he had moved there, I have no idea why. It was only a matter of time before we would cross paths. I packed everything I owned into my bag and left.

"I came here, to Jerusalem. I thought I would be safer in a big city. Where it was less likely to be discovered, even by accident. Safety in the numbers. I could get lost.

"Again, I was lucky and managed to secure work. I was employed in one of the clubs, as a floor walker, hostess if you like in one of the better bars. I was good at my job, the customers liked me and I made a good living. I thought, if this carried on, I would be able to open my own place in ten or twelve years.

"Then I met him, David. I fell for him. Totally. I was still, really, just that naïve little village girl. I was head over heels in love. He was the man of my dreams, or at least that is what I thought. I shared my dreams of opening my own place, how it was hard to save the money. He said he could help. He had some friends who would pay a lot of money to spend the night with me.

"I was horrified at the suggestion, told him no. Think about our future, he said. Once he had the idea, he wouldn't let it go. He continued to bring it up at every opportunity. Saying, if you really loved me, you would do this for our future."

"You gave in," George stated simply.

"I did. It was hard, at first. But I just thought about the future, that it was just an ends to a means. I never handled the money, he took care of that. For my own protection. I drank more, started taking pills. I suppose I was terrified of losing him.

"David assured me, whenever I asked, that the money was safely put away. So it went on. I felt empty, filled that void with drugs and alcohol.

"One night, another girl in the club saw me talking with him. Afterwards, she warned me to keep away from him, he's nothing but trouble. I told her, she must be mistaken. He was my fiancée I told her. She laughed, you and five others she said. Besides, he was already married, had two kids. I persisted in telling her she was wrong, she had the wrong the person. If I didn't believe her, I could see for myself. Every Sunday, he took his family out to the local park, then for lunch at a nearby restaurant.

"I just ignored her, but the thought wouldn't go away. It played on my mind. After a couple of weeks, I went there. Of course, everything she had told me was true. There he was, kicking a ball around with his kids. I followed him, saw him meet another woman for a nice family meal.

"The next time I saw him, I confronted him. He laughed, didn't even deny it. As if he would marry a cheap slut like me. I told him I was finished, demanded my money. Which is when I realised the full extent of my stupidity. He punched me, told me there was no money. Told me he owned me, no one leaves him. He pulled out knife, told me if I ever tried he would make sure no one would ever want me again.

"I had no choice, I carried on. Only now I did the odd one for me, kept the money. Naturally, he found out. He came to my flat, brought two of his friends. Demanded the money, I told him to get lost. He hit me, reminded me I worked for him, none of his girls went freelance. That I needed to be taught a lesson. That's when he dragged me into the bedroom, left me with his friends. While they did what they wanted, he tore the flat apart. He found all the money.

"Then they took me downstairs, threw me in the back of his van and beat me. When they had finished, he threw me out of the back, telling me he had no further use for me, I was past my prime, then drove off.

"When I got back to the flat, it was locked up. All my stuff was in bags, the landlord told me to get out. I was trouble, he ran a respectable place. I picked up what I could and left.

"It becomes a bit of a blank after that. I assume I must have passed out, fainted. The next thing I know, I wake up in a hospital bed.

"After I was released, I had nothing left. No job, nowhere to stay. So, I did what I did best, I became another one of the numerous whores on the streets of Jerusalem.

"It was one of my regulars who told me about Joseph. I had been shouting at some local lads, the usual thing. When I calmed down, he told me not to worry. According to this new preacher in town, I am forgiven for all my past deeds. I told him I was long passed redemption. Not according to this new preacher doing the rounds, he said. If we ask, we will be forgiven."

Mary paused in her story to allow the noise of a speeding ambulance, sirens blaring, to recede into the distance.

"I was curious. What did I have to lose? I heard he was preaching nearby, so I went to listen. It was outside the city, an hour's walk, there were thousands heading the same way.

"I remember that day as if it was yesterday. He even fed us, everyone. I had never tasted bread so good. The words he spoke, the way he spoke filled my heart.

"I told you, after I left the hospital, I was at my lowest point. I had nothing to live for, suicide was something I considered often. That night, I sat at home drinking. As I did, my whole life came crashing in around me. I could see no escape. I was desperate.

"I went back out.

"I just wanted to believe. That maybe there was a chance for me. A chance of redemption. I wandered aimlessly, when I overheard a conversation. A new preacher was staying at a house nearby.

"I had to push my way through the other people, they shouted abuse, called me names. Said I had no right to be here. I was going to leave, when I saw him. He was sat there, staring straight at me. I can't explain, it was as if he could see right through me, into my heart and soul. I couldn't help myself, I went to him. Fell at his feet, sobbing.

"He looked at the others, spoke to them. 'I came here as your guest, yet you did not offer to wash my feet. Yet this woman, she has washed them with her own tears, and dried them with her hair.'

"I felt him place his hands on my head. There was real power there, I felt it surge through my body. I know, you are going to think I am talking nonsense. I don't care, I know what I felt that night. A warmth spreading throughout my body, taking all my despair with it.

"He lifted my face, to see me clearer." Then said, "Your sins, and I know they are multitude, are forgiven you." Then he handed me a small pot, saying, "Take this, use it to anoint my body when I am gone. Now go, and sin no more."

"I don't pretend to understand, but from that day I have not been with another man, taken another drink or pill. For the first time in my life, since that day, I have hope. I believe I have a future."

"That's quite a story," George said with sympathy.

"It's all true, every word," she said definitely.

"I Don't doubt it. I know bullshit when I hear it, know a liar when I see one. You're neither."

"Well, thank you for that at least."

"Did you believe him to be the Messiah?"

"I did. Whether he was or not has no consequence, all I know is that he saved my life."

"Did you see him again after that night?"

"Only when he preached."

"What did you think?"

"His words, they speak to you. To your heart. He made the old scriptures accessible. He breathed new life into the words."

"What about tomorrow, will you visit the grave, anoint the body as he requested?"

"Of course. There are three of us, we will all go, anoint and clean the body and wrap it with fresh linen."

"Do you expect him to still be there?"

"Where else would he be?"

"Well, according to talk been heard, he has promised to rise from the dead three days after his death."

Mary looked at James. "Did he really say that?"

"Yes," James began, "but as I have already said, there is a spiritual message. It isn't supposed to be taken literally."

"You didn't know?" George asked.

"No, as I said I was not with him all the time."

"And what do you think?"

"I suppose I will find out in the morning, won't I?" George stared at her, there was no mistaking the hope, the conviction with which she had spoken. "Now, I must return to work." She hugged James, told him to be careful, and left them.

James watched her walk away, then turned to his father, saying, "Did you believe her?"

"Strangely, yes, I did. I've no reason not to. If, with one touch, he changed her life, then he must have been a remarkable man."

"I told you."

They got up to leave, heading back to the hotel to pick up the car. As James opened the doors, George asked him, "Tell me about Joseph Arimathea."

"I will fill you in on the way."

Chapter Seven
Millionaire, Traitor and Holy Man

James talked as he drove. "He was born in Ramula, into extreme poverty. His parents managed to scrape enough together to provide him with a basic education. When he was eleven, he went to work, like everyone else, into one of the numerous sweatshops.

"He realised that if he didn't get out of there, he would be lucky to make it to thirty. So at age fourteen, he walked out and started his own small delivery service. Nothing much to begin with, newspapers, groceries. He was a likable lad, people instinctively trusted him. Businesses as well as customers.

"By the time he was eighteen, he was employing four other lads, pulling in profits of couple of thousand a year. Not much, but where he lived it was considered a small fortune; and he used it to invest in other small business. The stories claim he was pretty ruthless in those early days. If a business wasn't turning a decent return he pulled out. If that business then went on to fail, he bought them out. However, he always ensured the employees were looked after.

"Now, nearly forty years later, he is one of the richest men in the region, the country. Owns a couple of department stores, here and in other cities. Three newspapers, with interests in four others. He also owns the biggest of the TV studios, a film company and an airline company. His estimated worth is seventy-two million.

"He is known as a bit of a philanthropist, something he tries to keep private. Rumour says he, almost, single handily financed the refurbishment and upgrade of Jerusalem hospital.

"He is divorced, three boys. The eldest is reported to have struggled with drugs and alcohol, from what I know he has been clean for the last year or so." James finished talking.

"What about the other two sons?"

"The youngest is still in school, the middle one is studying law in Oxford, Briton."

"What does the eldest do now?"

"He works for his father. I think he is one of his personal assistants."

James was turning the car into the basement parking of an office block. Settling the car into an available space, they followed the signs to the stairs. Walking up the three flights, they emerged into the main concourse. Reporting to the receptionist, they were told to take a seat and someone would come and collect them.

It was only a couple of minutes before a young man came over and introduced himself, "Good afternoon, I am Elias, would you please follow me?"

They stood up, shook Elias's proffered hand, then followed him to the lifts. There were four, but the one on the far right was the express taking them all straight to the twenty sixth floor. Elias escorted them down the corridor and through a set of double doors into an office.

"This is our conference room. Mr Arimathea is just finishing a call. He hopes you will join him for afternoon tea?" The conference table was already set for three people, and an assortment of sandwiches and cakes had been laid out.

"Thank you, that's very kind," George answered.

"Good, I will let the kitchens know. Please take a seat." Elias left them as they sat at the table.

When Joseph Arimathea joined them ten minutes or so later, it was obvious that Elias was his son. The likeness was undeniable. He dropped a bag on the floor next to the chair.

"Good afternoon. My apologies for keeping you waiting. I trust my assistant has looked after you?" He did not wait for a response, as he reached for a jug. "Coffee?"

Both men nodded, and as he poured three cups, Joseph told them to help themselves to food. Each of them selected a couple of sandwiches, and a cake. Joseph Arimathea continued to serve them, providing napkins, forks and passing the sugar over with their coffee.

"You must try one of the lamb, I have no idea what they do with it, but it is superb. I've tried to get the recipe out of the cook, but he refuses to give it up."

"I can see why you have been successful, Mr Arimathea."

"Why is that? and please call me Joseph."

"You have an affinity with people. Most men in your position would never serve his guests himself. You don't mind doing the menial stuff."

"Well, I believe in making people feel welcome. If you look after your people, they will want to work for you. At least, that's what I have found, Mr Ambrose."

"If I'm going to be calling you by your first name, I think you can call me by mine," George said. "Your assistant, Elias. Your son?"

"Yes, we thought he might benefit from a more structured life."

"How is he coping?"

"Like any other in his position. He has good and bad days. We take it one day at a time, but he is doing well, and he attends meetings which help."

"I'm glad. I wish him well."

"That is kind, thank you. However, you did not come all this way to discuss my son's health."

"No, I didn't, and thank you for making the time."

"I assure you, that was not a problem. I would not have missed the opportunity to meet the famed George Ambrose. I have a copy of your book, I hoped you might sign it for me?" Joseph said all this as he pulled a thick, hardbacked volume from his bag.

"So, that's who bought it. Of course, with pleasure." George took the book from him, opened it to the title page and signed it with a small flourish.

Joseph was asking another question, "What was that African warlord you met like in person?"

"Scary, and as charming as they come."

"It must have been fascinating."

"He was an interesting character, I grant you; and one of only three truly evil men I have ever met."

"Who were the other two?"

"The serial killer, Jonathan Barnett, and the South American head of the drugs cartel, Mendoza."

"Well, perhaps we can talk about it another time," Joseph had sensed the reluctance in George's voice, and the need to move on. "What can I do for you?"

"You paid for a burial site for Joseph Bartholomew, I was curious as to why."

"Because I could. Because I wanted to."

"Why?"

"I liked him. I only met him a couple of times. I admired him, and agreed with a lot of what he had to say. The council is a disgrace, instead of taking care of the people's welfare they line their own pockets. As a result, it falls to people like myself, and the other businessmen I know, to try and do what we can. I did not want to see a good man go into the pits with the rest of the city's garbage. He deserved better than that. I also happen to believe he was a real believer, that he spoke from the heart without malice."

"Sent from God?"

"I have no idea. You would have to ask God."

"Based on that, you footed the bill for his burial?"

"Yes, his family had nothing. And they would never have been able to convince Pilate to release the body back to them. Besides, it was the right thing to do."

"How did you get the council to agree?"

"I didn't, I went straight to Pilate. It was his decision."

"I bet the council loved you for that."

"Yes, well I am fortunate enough to be in a position that what the council thinks does not concern me. If they want to make a fuss, I will simply pull my financial support from their ambitions to refurbish the Temple of Jerusalem."

"Have they? Made a fuss, I mean?"

"Only for show. I have insulted them, disregarded their authority. I hear Micah was particularly annoyed," Joseph said this last with some sense of happiness in his tone of voice.

"You don't like him?"

"I despise anyone who treats the law as his own personal weapon, to be bent to suit their needs. I fully expect him to arrange for my arrest on some trumped-up charge."

"Why?" James spoke for the first time.

"Because, as for as he is concerned someone of my prominence paying for his funeral gives credence to what he had to say. An approval, if you like."

James continued, "That's ridiculous."

"Of course it is. As is his preoccupation with finding a reason to come after you, and the rest of his disciples. He really does hate you all."

"How?" James asked.

"Obviously, as one of his followers you are aware of his claims that he will rise from the dead? Return in glory."

"Yes, but…"

Joseph held is hand to stop James, then continued, "It does not matter what he meant when he said that. Micah does not care. All he wants is an end to you all, by any means. The point of it is this, Micah has arranged for the body to disappear. He intends to blame you all, that you stole it in order to back up his words, so you can claim he was the Messiah. That will give him the excuse he needs. He intends to make you all pay for the humiliation the council has suffered."

George spoke this time, "Is that how you saw him – as the Messiah?"

"I have an open mind about that. I don't know, is the real answer. I only understood half of the things he said to me, but then I am no theologian. The interpretation of the scriptures, who knows whether his was right, and the councils have got it wrong. What it comes down to is simply this. I paid for his burial, because his family couldn't and because I liked the man. I enjoyed his rants against the council, he really made them squirm." Joseph looked back at James. "What the council did was cruel, spiteful. Caiaphas, Micah and about ninety per-cent of the rest of them can be extremely vindictive. Especially when they think their position is being threatened.

"They are also very adept at playing the people. As you would have seen during the release of Barabbas. It won't take much to convince them that you all took the body."

"How do you know?" James asked.

"I have my sources. They can't do anything until tomorrow, after that Micah will start making noises. I'd say you have about forty-eight hours before they begin the hunt for you all. I have it on good authority that arrest warrants are ready to be issued. I would strongly recommend that all of you make plans to get out as soon as possible."

"I don't understand," James said. "Isn't what they have done enough?"

"For a normal person, it would be. Unfortunately, Micah is psychotic when it comes to the protection of the council's reputation. His hatred for everything that does not conform is all consuming, that includes you. As far as he is concerned, the council has been granted authority over the people, and that authority is given to them by God. Therefore, in his mind, anyone that questions that authority is questioning God's purpose. A strict obedience to the will of God is all that is expected from the people."

James turned to question his father, "Didn't you say they had appointed guards around the burial site?"

It was Joseph who answered, "Roman guards."

"Yes," George said. "That's really quite clever." Seeing the blank look on his son's face, George continued, "Roman guards don't answer to the council, so what reason would they have to back up anything Micah says?"

"So why would they?" James asked.

Joseph continued the explanation, "A Roman private earns about ten thousand a year, a pittance. Micah is a very wealthy man." The inference was obvious to all of them.

George spoke, "He won't convince Vespian though. He will see right through it, and he will advise Pilate accordingly. I suspect they will offer to help search for the body, but little else."

James again, "And if they don't find it?"

"They won't, Micah will ensure that," Joseph said. "Pilate will be left with no choice. Micah will push them into a corner, accuse them of incompetence. Threaten to inform the emperor of their failings, insist the only option left is to find Bartholomew's follows, to question them. Micah will hand any caught straight over to their inquisitors."

"He really is a fanatic." George stated simply.

"Of the highest order," Joseph said. "Now, if there is nothing else, I have a family celebration to attend."

"You have already been more then generous with your time," George said as he stood.

"You know, Micah really dislikes you," Joseph told him.

"The feeling is mutual. Thank you again for your time."

As he was showing them out, Joseph handed one of his business cards to George. "Micah puts you in with the others, he believes you are a danger to the council. Should you find yourself in need of help, no matter what, call me."

George thanked him and was surprised at the offer, He found he liked this Joseph, he was a good man.

They left his conference room and returned to the car park. As they drove out of the entrance, George noticed another car pull away.

"Judas lives around the corner," James said.

"Take the scenic route," George replied.

James did not question the reason, just took a right instead of left. It was a full fifteen minutes of twists and turns before they arrived back where they started. As he took the left turn, they found the road blocked. An ambulance, together with council security vehicles had formed a cordon across the road. A small crowd had gathered.

"Stay here," George told James, then got out of the car. He walked around, mingling with the people gathered. He could not learn much from the snatches of conversation, heard nothing specific. Continuing to make his way through the crowd, he saw a sergeant of the Roman forces stood to one side, leaning on a jeep. He recognised him as the driver that had taken him from the airport to his hotel.

Taking a cigarette out, he wandered over. "Excuse me, officer. Do you have a light?"

The soldier reached into his pocket, offering his lighter. "Thank you," George then acted surprised. "Oh, hello again."

The man slowly recognised him. "Mr Ambrose, isn't it?"

"Yes, that's right."

"How have you been sir?"

"Busy couple of days. What's going on here?" George looked at the sergeant. "Sorry, shouldn't I ask?"

"No, nothing like that. Just a local man killed himself. We're really just here to assist with crowd control."

"Suicide? Nasty."

"Yeah, the cleaner found him hanging from one of the roof beams."

"That must have been a shock."

"She screamed the whole apartment block awake. Understandable, not what you expect to find when you arrive for work."

"Anyone we know?"

"I wouldn't think so, sir. I said, local chap, name of Judas Iscariot." George muttered under his breath, the soldier spoke again, "I'm sorry, sir. Did you know him?"

"Only by name, I was hoping to talk to him. He was one of those that followed that Bartholomew."

"Didn't know he was one of them."

"It is definitely suicide?"

"Oh yes, they found thirty pieces of silver scattered on the floor. Doubt they would have left that behind if it wasn't suicide."

"No, I suppose not," George stamped his cigarette out. "Nothing for me here now, I will leave you to it sergeant." He walked away, back to the car.

Climbing back in to the passenger seat. "Judas is dead. Suicide, apparently. The cleaner found him hanging from the ceiling, thirty silver coins on the floor."

"He wasn't even well paid his treachery."

"Possibly."

"Why did he do it, I wonder?"

"Which, the betrayal or the suicide."

"Either, I suppose."

"I would assume the suicide was out of some sense of guilt. Drive us to Nicodemus, it's getting late."

James put the car in gear, and they set off.

"You knew him, do you have any idea why he would kill himself?"

"I knew him slightly. I never spoke with him as much as I did with the others. He always seemed…I don't know…remote? He was never really that talkative. I only met him six days ago." The reality of that suddenly sunk in. "Hell, six days. How did it all end up here? How did it become so complicated in just six days?"

"I tend to find that when things start to fall apart they can become very complicated very quickly. Judas, was he a true believed like the others?"

"You mean like me? I always thought so, until the betrayal. Why do you think he did that, betrayed him I mean.?"

"How should I know, I never met him."

"It makes no sense."

"Most things seldom do." George looked over at his son. "Did you know that when you talk about Bartholomew there is a light in your face, a demeanour and intensity about you." As he said these things, George realised that he was jealous. Of the thing he had found. George had never had anything like that in his life.

"That's his temple, just up the hill," James said. He looked where indicated. A small building sat on the hill at the top of the dirt track James was negotiating with the car. It was plain in design, neglected in places. They passed through the village to reach it. A scattering of about fifty dwelling. George glanced in the side mirror as James parked up. There, at the bottom of the hill sat the car he had seen back in the city. Someone was having them followed.

As they walk the short distance to the entrance, James gave a brief history. "Nicodemus is a revered scholar, he is also a member of the council in a religious, advisory capacity only. He holds no power, but he is highly respected by the others. He studied under the great teacher, Rosen. He was always open to what Bartholomew had to say."

They opened the door, and went in. A boy of about twelve was struggling along, weighed down by a pile of books. George and James moved forward and relieved him of some of the burden. The boy muttered his thanks.

"Where do you want them?" George asked. The boy nodded at the shelves in the corner. All three of them stacked the books back on the shelves.

"Do you know where we can find the Rabbi?" James asked.

"I will take you to him," the boy answered. He led them behind the alter, down a short flight of steps and knocked on the door to an office. A gentle, kindly voice said, "Come." The boy opened the door and went in.

"Rabbi, these men are here to see you."

"Thank you, Isaac. Please take a seat, gentlemen." He turned to address the boy. "Have you finished clearing the books away?"

"Yes, Rabbi."

"And I suppose you now want to go and join your friends outside?"

"Yes please."

"And I am guessing they will have a football?"

The boy just smiled.

"Then you had better go and join them, yes?"

"Thank you, Rabbi," the boy said as he left, running up the stairs, whooping as he went.

"He is a good boy," Nicodemus said. "The second son. His older brother will work for their father, but his family insist that he is to be a Rabbi, a gift to God. It is still something of a tradition here. Isaac, however only dreams of playing football for Beiter FC."

"What do you think?" George asked.

"I think God has other plans for our young friend. He is a much better footballer than student. I have explained this to his family, but they are determined. Perhaps his next report card will convince them, at least I hope so because that is what it will show."

"You will falsify it?"

"A little. Sometimes it is necessary to give God's plan a little nudge here and there." He smiled, turned to James saying, "It is good to see you again. How have you been?"

"Keeping busy, sir."

"Keeping busy is good, but it will only delay the grief you feel. You must allow yourself time to face it, and the longer you leave it the worse it will be."

"Yes, sir."

"Nico, I have told you. Call me Nico. No formalities, speaking of which, you have not introduced your friend."

"This is my father, George Ambrose, he works for the paper in London."

"You kept that secret, young man. In all the years I have known you, you never once told me you had a famous father."

"Not that famous." George retorted.

"Notorious then?"

"That is probably closer at the moment."

"I know. I had the misfortune to overhear our illustrious council member, Micah talking about you. Not, I might add, in the most flattering way. He seems to hold you in very low regard, something I suspect does not greatly concern you."

"It doesn't concern me at all,"

Nicodemus turned back to James. "I have been informed that Judas is dead. Is that correct?"

"Yes, he killed himself," James answered.

"That is regrettable. He must have been deeply troubled, I will say El Maleh Rachamin for him. Have the family made arrangements?"

"I don't know."

"They may have some difficulty in finding someone to perform the service. Suicide, you know? If they do, please tell them I am available."

"I will, if I see them."

"I assume you have brought your father here to talk about Joseph?"

"If you don't mind, Nico."

"I am happy to."

George spoke. He had listened to the conversation, having no idea that his son and the Rabbi had become such obvious, close friends. He had also sensed an awkwardness in Nicodemus, as though this behaviour was new to him.

"I am told you are the finest scholar of your age."

"People are very kind, they do overestimate my abilities however."

"Still, you are one of the foremost scholars."

"That's kind of you to say so."

"You spoke with Bartholomew, what did you make of him?"

"I only met him on two occasions. I found him intelligent, erstwhile. He believed in what he had to say, that I don't doubt. Many of the things he spoke of, I agreed with. There were also those times when I did not understand."

"Yet, in those two meetings he has changed you."

"Why do you say that?"

"It is the same with everyone I have spoken with, and, with all respect, you don't strike me as a typical Rabbi or scholar."

"I begin to appreciate why you are so respected, you have a natural instinct. You are right, of course. He made me see the world different, or even for the first time. I lived inside my books, he made me realise that I needed to take my eyes off them, to look at the needs of those I have responsibility for. He had a genuine connection with the people, A humility about him. He understood the people in a way I never had. He made me realise that, and I have tried to do better. When he spoke to them, he did not confuse them by wrapping it up in jargon, he spoke plainly."

"And when he spoke with the council?"

"He spoke the same way. Used terms that made it quite plain, left us in no doubt of his meaning. We all knew he was criticising our actions, our status. It was these things that brought the council to take the actions they did. I was unable to speak on his behalf, I was not aware of the gathering. It would not have changed anything, I have no voting rights on the council."

"You said there were things he said that you did not grasp the understanding of?"

"One conversation had me running back to consult my books. 'Unless you are born again you cannot see the kingdom, the God,'" he said. Nicodemus saw the look of confusion of George's face. "I had the same look when he said those words. I asked him, how can a man go back into his mother's womb and be born again? He responded, saying, 'you are wise in the scriptures, yet you do not see. Humans can only produce human life. In order to enter the kingdom of God you must be reborn of the spirit' I consulted the books, without any success."

"Do you understand now?"

"I think so. You must devote all of yourself to God. By relying constantly on my books, I was only giving a part of myself to him. I was neglecting the heart, the soul."

"When did you next see him?"

"In the synagogue, when he was speaking to the people. It was what he said here that really made me look closer at my life, changed me. I remember those words. 'Come to me all you who are weary and carry a heavy burden, I will give you rest. Take my yoke upon you, let me teach you for I am humble and gentle at heart and you will find rest for your soul. For my yoke is easy to bare, and the burden I give you is light. All nations will be gathered in His presence, and he will separate them as a shepherd separated the sheep from the goats, He will place the sheep at his right hand and the goats to his left. Then the King will say to those on his right, 'come you who are blessed by my father, inherit the kingdom prepared for you from the creation of the world. For I was hungry, and you fed me. I was thirsty and you gave me drink. I was a stranger, and you invited me into your home. I was naked, and you gave me clothing. I was sick, and you cared for me. I was in prison and you visited me' it was powerful.

"So, from that day I spent less time in my books, and more time with the people under my care. They live in relative poverty, they are hungry so we feed them, as best we can. Some of them have fallen foul of the authorities, we ensure they receive a visit from someone. To let them know we have not forgotten them, that there is still a place for them here."

"That is quite something."

"Love thy neighbour, as he said, you know I tried to get some of the council to listen to what he had to say. They refused any such suggestion. I tried to explain this was an opportunity to learn more. It is a sad truth that the majority of the council are more interested in their own self-importance. They would not entertain the idea. That someone with little education could teach, enlighten them, provide a greater insight into God's word."

"I assume, as a member of the council, even a non-executive member, you were required to attend the execution?"

"I was there. My last official duty."

"Why?"

"I resigned my position the next day. I have no desire to witness such malignant behaviour again. I will work here, look after my people. You know, even there, on the cross, he quoted the scriptures. Eloi, Eloi; lema sabachthani."

"What does that mean?"

"My God, my God, why have you abandoned me. He was quoting from the Psalms of David. Some of the council thought he was calling on Elijah." George was about to say something, changed his mind as Nicodemus continued, "They said, 'let's see if Elijah comes to take him down' Still others called out, 'he saved others, let him save himself' and 'If you are the Messiah, save yourself' at one point, as he hung there in agony, he actually asked God to forgive them for their actions."

"What?" George asked, astonished.

"He said it, 'Father, forgive them, for they do not know what they are doing.' Even then dying in the most horrific manner imaginable, he asked God to forgive us."

"Do you believe he was the Messiah?"

"Is he the Christ?" Nicodemus seemed to ask himself. "I don't know. He does fulfil a number of the Messianic Prophecies."

"What are they?"

"A series of promises, clues if you like, scattered throughout our scripture."

"Like?"

"The prophet Micah wrote, but you, oh Bethlehem, are only a small village among all the people of Judea. Yet a ruler of all Israel will come from you on my behalf."

"Hardly conclusive evidence."

"Isaiah. He stated that the Messiah will be born of a virgin. His mother constantly affirms that she was a virgin, conceived through the spirit of God.

"Zechariah. Rejoice oh people of Zion! Shout in triumph, oh people of Jerusalem! Look your king is coming to you, He is righteous and victorious, yet he is humble riding on a donkey.

"Isiah again. He stated that the Messiah would be rejected by his own people, would be tried and condemned. That he would be silent before his accusers, spat upon and abused by his enemies. Two of David's Psalms predict that he would be betrayed by one of his own."

"Which infers that Judas had no control, that his actions were pre-ordained."

"Exactly."

"This could still be just circumstantial."

"For one or two, perhaps. But I have studied these things, He meets sixteen of the eighteen prophecies."

"And those other two are?"

"Problematic. They state that he will return, rise from the dead to take his rightful place at God's right hand."

"Ah, the whole rising from the dead thing."

"Yes, I know. Madness."

"Totally," George said, although neither of them had spoken with much conviction.

Nicodemus spoke again, "Now, I must leave you. I have a meeting with the council."

"Why, if you have resigned?"

"They are not pleased that I went with Joseph Arimathea to claim the body on behalf of the family."

"You risked your reputation by doing so."

"I did, but it was the right thing to do. I will play the old fool, pretend not to have understood the implications."

"Will they believe you?"

"Oh yes. They all think of me in that way to be honest. I am their scholar, I do not understand how the real-world works. I will apologise, and they may fine me; but that will be an end to the matter."

"Then I wish you luck," George said as they parted company.

Walking back to the car, James asked, "So, what do you think now?"

"I don't know, the more I learn the more confused I become."

"Well, maybe Peter can help clear up that confusion. He was with him from the very beginning."

"Are you going to introduce me to anyone who wasn't an admirer?"

"What for? You can find them anywhere on the street."

Chapter Eight
A Most Devoted Man

The drive through the village, into the city then back out the other side to Peter's hideaway took just under an hour. They arrived a little after eight. The drive, for the most, was completed in silence. The only conversation coming from James as he provided some background into the man they were meeting.

"He can be stubborn, infuriatingly so some times. He appears brash, speaks before he thinks. He is one of Joseph's most devoted followers, having been with him from the beginning. Since those early days in Galilee."

George had only been half listening, consumed with his own thoughts. It was vexing, the more he learnt about the man, the less he understood. The people he had spoken to, they all seemed convinced of his holiness, that his mission had been given to him by God. Not one of them could say that he hadn't changed them for the better. The most striking change was, perhaps, in Mary.

The other thing he noticed, that he no longer dismissed out of hand those things he was being told. He, himself was changing. He could feel it. Nothing he could point at and say, this is what is new about me. He also realised that he had stopped jumping, the twitchiness that had plagued him for so long was in abeyance.

All the people he spoke to, some of them had talked about the changes they had made in their life. Mary. Nicodemus. Was the same thing happening to him by some strange osmosis?

George could no longer deny that Joseph Bartholomew must have been a remarkable man. The words he spoke had power. The power to make people want to be better than they were. At least, in those who had been willing to listen. Mary was living proof of the power of those words.

George Ambrose, the cynical journalist had arrived only forty-eight hours earlier. Convinced this Bartholomew was just another in a long history of cranks and conmen. Another religious fanatic.

And now?

Now, he wasn't sure about anything. He was beginning to have a grudging admiration for Joseph Bartholomew. There was a part of him that regretted he had not been able to meet him in person. He was even a little envious that his son had, he found himself wanting whatever it was that they had found.

The car was slowing, they had arrived at their destination. Just to confirm his suspicions, James announced, "We're here," as he pulled up behind a ramshackle building. They both got out, walked back round to the front and knocked on the door. As they waited, George looked around, seeing the same little blue car from earlier in the day.

The door was opened and they were quickly ushered inside. Peter took them through to the kitchen area, were the table was laid with a selection of breads, cold meats and cheese. He told them to sit, and poured them each a glass of wine. George spoke, "I apologise, but I am fairly certain we have been followed."

Peter responded, "I would have expected nothing less. It was inevitable, but it is of no concern. It was only a matter of time before they found us. I won't be here much longer. We are all leaving tonight, Simon still has some contacts. He has secured us a place of safety." He turned to James. "You will need to come with us, your name is on Micah's list."

George responded to this information, "I agree. You can go with them, they will keep you safe until arrangements to get you away can be made. I doubt the excuse of working the story for the paper will hold much sway with Micah. He is determined to have his revenge." James had been about to object, but he knew they were both right. It was no longer safe for him, he would have to go into hiding. "Do you know where you will be going?" George asked.

"Of course. I will let you have the information." Peter had forestalled George's next question. "Please, sit and eat something. James has told me a little, so how can I help you?"

"I just wanted to know more about the time you spent with him, before you all came to Jerusalem."

"That may take more time than I have, But I will do my best." Peter helped himself to some food, while he gathered his thoughts. "I was with him for almost three years. My brother introduced us. Thinking back, I was not in the best of moods…"

Peter stepped off his fishing boat and stood on the shore. It had been another disastrous day. Their catch was paltry, it would barely cover their expenses; and now, here was his brother, Andrew with yet another preacher.

"What use is another holy man?" He bellowed at him down the shoreline. "What use are holy words when my crew cannot earn enough? When there isn't enough of a catch to go around?"

"Peter, please. Just meet him," Andrew pleaded.

"What happened to the last one, that Baptist fellow? You change your holy men with every change in the wind. Why do you keep falling for their nonsense?"

"John told us to follow him."

"And like the good little sheep you all are, you went. I've no time for this, Andrew." Peter turned, dismissing his brother to attend to work. He found his way blocked, he was about to yell at the man to get out of the way, but something stopped him. Andrew had eagerly come over.

"Peter, this is Joseph," Andrew said before turning to Joseph. "My brother, Peter."

Joseph spoke, "You seem ill at ease, Peter."

Peter looked at this man, scornfully saying, "Another bad day of fishing, like it has been all week. What can you do, holy man? Offer a prayer? Provide us with some words of wisdom? Meanwhile I won't make enough to pay my men, so again we will go hungry."

"Go out one more time, I will come with you," Joseph suggested.

"It's late, and my men are tired."

Andrew jumped in, "Please Peter, what's one more trip?"

Peter looked between them both. Looking at Joseph, he felt uncomfortable. It was as if this man could see right through him. He shrugged his shoulders, laughing he turned to his crew. "Make ready, we are going back out. The holy man wants a fishing lesson."

Andrew was delighted. Joseph stepped aboard, taking a seat in the corner. Once they were underway, it was a short time before they reached the fishing ground. Peter turned to Joseph. "What now?"

"Cast your nets on the right of the boat."

"Very well," impatiently he relayed the order to the men, who quickly carried out his demands.

"Leave them in the water for ten minutes," Joseph said.

Peter nodded to the men, muttering under his breath about how much he knew about fishing. Waiting with mounting impatience, Peter felt the boat lurch to the right. Then it happened again.

He waited out the time, looking over a Joseph he said, "Let's see what you have holy man." Then ordered his crew to bring the nets in.

As one of them moved to do so, he shouted, "We can't pull them up!"

"That's all I need, my nets tangled up on the rock bed."

More men moved to help pull in the nets, each was straining with the effort. Peter came over to join them, when he heard one of them say, "That's impossible."

"What is?" Peter asked as he came over.

"Look, the nets are full."

Peter reached them, looking down he saw the nets were full to bursting point. Thousands of fish flopped about as the nets were finally pulled in. The catch spilling from the nets. It was crazy, they covered every inch of the deck.

Back on shore, the news of their catch had spread. Crowds gathered to buy, they needed to feed their families. The men were gutting and preparing the fish as fast as they were selling.

Peter sat by his boat, confused and amazed in equal parts. How was this possible? For the last four days they had been lucky to break even. He thought that, maybe, the area had been overfished, needed time to recover. He had even reached the point where he needed to consider laying some of the crew off. Now, this haul that would see him and his crew financially secure for a couple of months.

Andrew had told him they would be staying the night, they would stay with Peter. Which would place more pressure on their mother. She had been quite unwell of late…

The four of them walked through the town to his home. His mother was nowhere to be seen, she was resting his wife said as she cooked the evening meal. His two young sons were preparing the table to eat.

Joseph made a request. "May I pay my respects to your mother? I promise if she is resting, I won't disturb her."

Peter pointed, "Down there, last room on the left." He watched Joseph go where he had indicated, then hugged his sons, kissed his wife. Turning, he saw his mother stood there, smiling.

Joseph spoke, "It seems your mother was awake, and not as ill as we thought,"

Peter went to her, saying, "You should be in bed, you're not well."

"Hush, Peter, I'm fine. Much better. Andrew, do you not have a kiss for your mother?" Andrew did ss he was bid, hugging her fervently. "Now, please sit, I will help Rosa with the meal." Peter watched her go to the kitchen.

They passed the night pleasantly, enjoying the food and each other's company. It was good to see the brothers together again, it had been a while since Andrew had last visited. Although, Peter assumed he would be leaving the next day to follow this new preacher.

There was a loud, determined knock at the door.

"Who is that at this time?" His mother complained. Peter rose from the table to answer the door. When he saw who was stood there, anger welled to the surface.

"What do you want?" he spat out.

"I heard you had some good luck today, I have just come to collect the tax you owe. Save you a journey, and I was curious to see this new preacher everyone is talking about."

"You are not welcome hear, bloodsucker. Leave us alone."

The visitor looked past Peter, saw Joseph sat at the table. He shouted to be heard, "It seems we must meet some other time." As he turned to leave, he heard something being said, but did not catch it clearly. He turned, asked, "What did you say?"

Joseph replied, saying, "Is your own house far?"

"But a short walk," he told him.

"Good," Joseph replied, rising from the table he walked over saying, "Show me."

"This way. My name is Matthew."

"I know who you are, and what you do."

Peter and Andrew grabbed Joseph, both speaking at the same time.

Andrew; "You can't go there, he is a pariah, the people will assume you are one of them."

Peter; "His house is full of the worst of society, the scum of the area. You can't associate with these people."

Joseph replied, "Healthy people have no need for a doctor, sick people do. My message is not for those who think they are righteous, but for those who know they are sinners." Then he left them and followed Matthew.

Peter looked over at the rest of them, his whole-body questioning what he should do. Should he stay, or should he follow? His mother provided the answer. "Go. All of you, stay with him. Protect him from those people." Peter, together with Andrew and his two friends left, walking quickly.

Matthew had been true to his statement, his house was not more than a five-minute walk away. Peter's description of the people who would be there had also been accurate. The room was full of the outcasts from society. Matthew announced their arrival, telling everyone that the preacher had come to visit them. Some mocked Matthew, jeering. A woman approached Joseph, her intent clear. Matthew told her to leave him be. As all those present looked at this stranger in their midst, slowly a silence came over the gathering. Another woman stood up, offering her seat to Joseph.

Joseph thanked her and sat down. Then they all began to speak at once, asking him questions. Joseph looked over at the doorway, which had remained open. He could see Peter and the others stood there. He turned to the others, saying, "How about I tell you a story, instead?" They all cheered at this, shouting their agreement. Make it a good one, a voice called out.

"There was once a king," he began, his audience cheered appreciatively. "This king decided it was that time of the year to bring his accounts up to date. As he did this, he noticed there where a number of outstanding debts owed to him. Some were only small, and settled easily, In the process, a man was brought before him. His debt was huge. He could not pay such a large amount. So, the king ordered that all his property be seized and be sold to pay the debt. This would not cover the whole amount. Therefore, he ordered that his wife and children be sent to debtors' prison, until such time as the man worked off the remainder that was owed.

"The man broke down, falling to his knees in front of his king and master. 'Please, please be patient with me. It has been a difficult time, give me time and I will pay it.'

"The king was filled with pity for him. Releasing him, he forgave the debt, writing it off.

"The man left the king. Upon leaving he went to one of his own servants, a man who owed him a debt. He grabbed him, violently about the throat and demanded instant payment. His servant fell to his knees, begging for more time to repay him. But his creditor would not wait. He had the man arrested and thrown in prison, then seized his property to pay the debt.

"When the king heard what had happened, he became angry, calling for the man to be brought before him. 'You evil man' he shouted 'I forgave your tremendous debt because you pleaded with me. Should you not have done the same, had mercy on this man who owed you?' The king then had him arrested and thrown in prison until his debt was paid."

Joseph looked at those around him, then settled his eyes on Matthew and Peter. "This is what God will do to you. If you refuse to forgive your brothers and sisters from your heart."

Peter and Matthew were looking at each other, sadness on their faces. "What happened to us?" Matthew asked. "We have been friends since childhood."

"I don't know," Peter responded. "I have missed that friendship we had."

"So have I," they then fell into each other's arms, happy. The room cheered at this renewed friendship.

The next day, Peter took them all across the lake. Andrew, James, John and Joseph. Matthew came with them, as they reached the opposite shore, they all jumped from the boat.

Matthew hesitated, then gave up and followed Joseph. Peter stood watching them all walking away. Looked back across the water to his home, his wife and sons. He knew it was useless to resist. Turning to his first mate, who stood in the boat he said, "The business is yours now – look after my family." With that said, he pushed the boat out, then turned and followed.

Over the next weeks, months and years Peter followed wherever Joseph led. He heard his words, felt them in his heart.

He watched as Joseph healed the sick.

Made the deaf hear.

Made the blind see.

The crippled walk again.

Cast out demons.

Watched as those first of them grew to twelve.

Watched as the people brought the sick to him to be healed from miles around.

Across the land his fame was spreading. Yet he remained a humble man. Never gave the impression that he was better than any of them. They ate whatever they were given. Slept in the open air, or as invited guests in someone's home.

People came from all over to hear him speak. Peter had never seen anything like it, it was astonishing.

The biggest gathering occurred a couple of months before they went to Jerusalem. He spoke that day about the gifts God had for them, the blessing he would bestow on those who were true to his word. Thousands were gathered as he spoke.

"God blesses those who are poor and realise their need in him, for the kingdom of heaven is theirs.

"God blesses those who mourn, for they will be comforted.

"God blesses those who are humble, for they will inherit the whole earth.

"God blesses those who hunger and thirst for justice, for they will be satisfied.

"God blesses those who are merciful, for they will receive mercy.

"God blesses those whose hearts are pure, for they will see God.

"God blesses those who work for peace, for they will be called the children of God.

"God blesses those who are persecuted for doing right, for the kingdom of heaven is theirs.

"God blesses you when people mock and persecute you, and lie about you, and say all manner of evil against you because you are my followers. Be glad about it for great rewards await you in my father's kingdom."

Afterwards, the people remained. Peter and some of the others went to him, saying, "Master send these people home. It is late and they will become hungry."

"You feed them."

"We have nothing to give them, we only have five loaves and two fish."

"Go into the crowds. Divide them into small groups." They did as they were asked, returning to him upon completion. Joseph took the small amount of fish, split it between the baskets then said, "Take this and go among them. There will be enough."

They were all doubtful, but did what was asked. Apologising to the people as they went, saying there wasn't much.

The people began to shout, telling them there was plenty. Peter looked down at the basket he held to see it was full. He looked around, it was plain the others were experiencing the same thing.

When they had finished, they collected twelve full baskets of leftover food. "This," Peter said to himself, "is a miracle." When he re-joined the others, they were saying the same.

From then on, Peter never had any doubts. That night, as they were sat together, one of them asked Joseph, "Who are you?"

Joseph answered with another question, "Who do you think I am?"

It was Peter who answered him, "You are the Christ, the son of the living God."

Joseph had looked at him intently, saying, "You are blessed, Peter, because my father in heaven has revealed this to you. You did not learn this from any human being."

A few weeks later, Joseph had gathered them all together. "I am sending you ahead to Jerusalem. Spread the word of my coming. Do not go to the Gentiles, only to the people of Israel. God's chosen ones, his lost sheep. I give you authority. Heal the sick, make the crippled walk again, cast out demons. Tell all, the kingdom of heaven is at hand."

So, that's what they did. They visited the towns and villages on the way. People were amazed by what they did, the words they spoke. When they returned to Joseph they spoke of these things. He told them, "All that you have done comes from God, and it is to his glory."

That same day, he taught them a new prayer, teaching them to pray to God on high with these words.

"Our father, in heaven, may your name be kept holy. May your kingdom be on earth, as it is in heaven. Give us this day the food we need. Forgive us our sins, so we may forgive those who sin against us. Do not let us yield to temptation, and rescue us from the evil one. For yours is the power and glory, forever."

Finally, the day came for them to enter Jerusalem. The crowds lined the streets, cheering. It was a glorious arrival, that seemed to fulfil the promises.

It was during this final week, before his arrest, that he spoke for the last time about his death. "Listen to me. We are in Jerusalem, where the son of man will be betrayed to the leaders. They will sentence him to death. Then they will hand him over to the Romans to be mocked, flogged and crucified. But, on the third day he will be raised from the dead."

None of them understood. Who amongst them would betray him?

At the end of the week, they had gathered for that last meal. He had told them it would be their last together, as the time of reckoning was near. He took the bread, blessing it he shared it with them saying, "Eat, for this is my body." Then he blessed the wine, "Drink, for this is my blood, which confirms the covenant between us…"

At this point Peter stopped his narrative. "The rest you know. He was arrested that night," Peter looked embarrassed, finally confessing, "Do you know what I did that night, the night they took him?"

"No," George answered.

"I denied ever knowing him. A man recognised me, accused me of being one of his followers. I told him he was mistaken, that I was new in town. Three times I did that." Peter paused. "And he told me that would happen. I remember telling him, never."

George did not know what to say at this point, instead he asked a different question, "Do you still believe his is the Christ, as you put it?"

"I do," Peter said. "I know it makes no sense to you, but I know the truth of it."

"So he will rise from the dead?"

"I hope so. The things he said would happen, happened. I have no reason to change my mind about him."

George had nothing to say to this. One thing was certain, Peter had spoken the truth. George had known liars, this man sat opposite was not one. Which left him in a predicament. Was Joseph truly the promised saviour?

James was speaking, "He arrived here to great acclaim, now here we are less than a week later, his mission in tatters. We, his followers soon to become hunted men."

"What was that mission?" George asked, for something to say.

It was Peter who answered. "To bring the kingdom of God to within reach for everyone, He said, 'do you think I have come to bring peace on earth? No, I have come to divide people against each other! Father will turn against son, and son against father. Mother against daughter, daughter against mother!' He was saying, if you choose to follow me there will be a cost to pay."

"What will you do now?"

"Go into hiding. Wait for them to forget about us. Maybe return to my family, to fishing for a living."

George stood up. "I will let you get away then. The sooner you are on your way the better." He turned to his son, asking for the car keys.

"What for?"

"So I can head back to the hotel, and take our little blue friend with me."

"I can drop you off. I need to go back to my flat, grab a few things."

"Give me a list, I will get them for you. Peter has told me where you will be, I will come tomorrow night. Late."

James felt like he should object, but also knew it would be a waste of time, Besides, his father was better at this sort of subterfuge that he was. He handed over the keys.

George shook hands with Peter, then walked to the door with his son. Peter had stayed where he was, allowing them some time to talk privately.

"You belong here, with them, I know it, and deep down so do you. I will find you, and don't worry about me. Just get yourself to safety."

"What are you going to do?"

"Drive around a bit, I know a twenty-four-hour café. I may waste a couple of hours there, keep our friend busy." He turned to Peter. "I will leave through the back, if that's possible?"

"Of course."

Father and son hugged, then George walked out the back door. James stood watching him get in the car, start the engine and drive off.

"I wonder if I will see him again." He muttered.

"I think you will. I don't think your friend's involvement in this in over just yet."

James turned to Peter. "He isn't just my friend. He's also my father."

Chapter Nine
Reflections

Peter and James had packed a few essentials. Now they travelled on foot to the safe house, located further outside the city. All the others had been contacted, each of them would arrive at their allotted time. It had been arranged in this way in the hopes they could all arrive with the smallest amount of fuss, arriving unnoticed.

Both men travelled in silence, partly for practical reasons, partly because Peter was immersed in his own thoughts.

Joseph was dead. Peter had suffered a momentary lack of faith. A weakness that had led him to deny his friendship. That would not happen again. He had been deeply ashamed of his actions, after all he had seen and heard, how could he have behaved in such a way?

Fear, pure and simple. Privately he had been in despair in those first hours leading up to his death. All of them where frightened. On that day, Peter had realised Joseph wasn't the man they had all thought he was. It seemed, on the surface, that this man they had all, that he, had given up everything for was a liar. Now, if Micah had his way, they would all meet the same fate.

For three years, Peter had followed him. Dedicated himself to Joseph's teachings, to be like him. He had fully committed himself to Joseph, to service to God.

When Joseph had told them he was going to die that first time, Peter had reprimanded him. Well, now he was dead. This man that Peter had believed, that they had all believed, was their promised saviour. He hadn't just been their leader, Peter had come to love him as a brother. The grief he felt was as if he had lost a member of his family.

Peter, along with all of them, had believed Joseph was who he said he was. He wasn't supposed to die. He was meant to be their leader, to evolve into a powerful political force, freeing them all. Vanquishing their enemies, releasing them from the grip of Roman occupation. He had done none of these things. Joseph had turned out to be just like the other's that had been before them. Another false prophet; and he had been treated with the same ruthless efficiency the council always employed. Now, the whole city knew him for what he was. A liar and a heretic. He was not the son of God, and now the council had placed him under the curse of God.

Peter had believed in him, believed he would fulfil the prophecies. Now he was dead. The council had been right about him, and now everything Peter had come to believe for the last 3 years was a lie.

Peter still grieved at his loss. He was also angry. At Joseph, at himself. How had he fallen for this man? Peter had done everything he could in order to be more like Joseph. When he had shown courage, Peter had tried to do the same. When he told them all he would be willing to die for his beliefs, Peter had believed he would have done the same. To die with him, at his side. Now, here he was running for his life.

Peter had to assume the others would be feeling the same mixture of emotions. The same anger, despair and disappointment. There would be a lot of talk tonight, and into the early hours. Arguments may spark up as each of them tried to understand what had happened. How they had been sucked in by this false prophet.

Had it all been an act? The things they had seen, the miraculous healings, had all seemed so real. How could they have not been? Joseph was dead, killed in the most horrendous fashion. Therefore, he can't have been the saviour. So it must follow, that all the things he did and said where false. A trick of some sort.

On the other hand, if he had been the Messiah, and everything they had seen was real, why had he not saved himself? How could he save the people now he was dead?

Which brought Peter round to that promise. On the third day after his death, he would rise from the dead, another impossible thing. Once you were dead that was it, there was no coming back. This then raised the question, what had he really meant? Peter could not grasp the significance.

That was yesterday. Those feeling had slowly subsided to be replaced by a stronger faith. A belief that he had been the one. That he had saved him, Peter. Changed his life, given it a greater meaning, a closer relationship with people and with God.

One other thing continued to puzzle him. Why did they all still refer to him as Joseph, refer to him by his middle name? They all knew his true name, Jesus.

However, he suspected that was the one question no one would be asking tonight; And they would all be looking to him. Expecting him to provide the answers to their numerous questions.

Answers he just didn't have.

Across the city, in his office another man was deep in thought. Pontius Pilate stared out of his window, watching these people he had sway over. These troublesome Jews, a people defeated by the might of Rome. Defeated, but a people who would never be dominated.

Naturally, his mind mulled over the events of the previous twenty-four hours. Joseph Bartholomew, in his opinion, had been an innocent man. He had committed no crime that he could see. Pilate knew he had been expertly manipulated by the council, Caiaphas and Micah in particular. But the whole council had been involved. Once he had realised he was been driven into a corner, Pilate had tried to find a way out. A way to save this Joseph.

It had been a stroke of genius when one of his assistants had mentioned the ancient ritual. The mercy of Rome on the night before the Passover celebrations. It was all for show, the granting of clemency for one condemned man. If Pilate had just decided and announced the release of Bartholomew, there would have been problems. Both Caiaphas and Micah would exact some form of revenge. So, in a twist to the usual ritual he had passed the decision onto the people.

It had been a gamble, one he had lost. If there was one thing in life that was guaranteed, it was the stupidity of people. They made their decision, and now Pilate had to live with it. He had told the crowd, about the ancient custom, the release of one prisoner at Passover. He had not thought for one moment they would make the choice they did.

Pilate could still here the screams of the people vividly. Especially their demands concerning the manner of Bartholomew's execution.

It remained a mystery to him why the people, and the council were so determined to kill him. Because that's what it was, state sanctioned murder.

Pilate was beginning to wonder which of the two men offered up that morning had really been the more dangerous. He also knew he should have stuck two fingers up to the council and done the right thing. That self-preservation gene had kicked in. His survival instinct that had kept him alive all these years in the service of Rome.

Pilate had always had a stormy relationship with the Jews, and their council. Over the years his Roman toughness, his sense of fairness had been eroded away. To be replaced by cynicism. Compromises had been made, and he had made mistakes.

Some of his actions had led to arguments with the council. They had maintained that he had acted inappropriately. That he had offended their God, their religious laws. There had been riots, civil disorder. Within six months of taking up this appointment, he had wondered what he had got himself into.

Nevertheless, here he was. Governor of Judea. Trying to control people he had little affection for. A populace that treated the Roman occupation with a total lack of respect. Militarily defeated, but never, ever dominated.

The matter of Joseph Bartholomew was just another in a long line of problems. The day-to-day continuous struggle to rule over the Jews.

The trial, which was in itself a contradiction in terms. The decision had already been made, the verdict assured. Even so, it had been a bizarre event. Joseph Bartholomew had just stood there, silent. Offering no explanation, no defence. As though he welcomed his fate, embraced it.

Pilate had hoped that after ordering a flogging, he may have been more inclined to talk. Not so. He just stood there, bleeding from the earlier punishment. Dressed in the robe Herod Antipas had draped over him. One of the guards had made him a crown out thorns, pushing it onto his head. Blood ran down his face from where thorns had pierced his skin.

One thing had come out of this whole sordid affair that did please Pilate. He had ordered that a wooden, engraved sign be placed on the head of the cross. Written in Latin it proclaimed Joseph of Nazareth, king of the Jews. It had incensed both Caiaphas and Micah. There affronted sensibilities had amused him. He had thought that would be an end to the matter.

However, later that night commander Vespian had turned up with Micah. The council were demanding a huge guard be placed around the burial site. Pilate had been inclined to refuse the request, until Vespian had explained why the guard was wanted. The problems that might have been caused by refusal were ones he did not need in his life. He had agreed, in part. He allowed two men to stand guard at the burial site.

Pilate suspected this affair was not over. Micah was plotting, he wanted more.

The owner of the name that preoccupied Pilate's thoughts was also sat in his office. Unlike Pilate, however, Micah was in a much happier mood. So far, everything was falling into place.

Micah had a real hatred for all of these so-called prophets. The latest had been a little more troublesome admittedly. He had proven to be quite intelligent, with an exceptional knowledge of the scriptures. Which was why Micah knew something had to be done. If he had allowed Joseph to continue, he would have undermined them all. The power of the council would have been subverted, weakened in the eyes of the people.

Micah considered them all to be nothing more than ignorant peasants. They needed a strong council to be able to lead them. To ensure they followed the right path. They had to be controlled, order must be maintained. The status Quo had to be preserved, therefore, Joseph Bartholomew had to be destroyed.

It had been easy to poison the minds of the council. Made so by Bartholomew's constant complaints about them. His disregard for their authority, his complete lack of respect for their position. At first, Micah had sent out his spies to find something he could use to discredit this new prophet. They had questioned people, sought out his old acquaintances. Nothing had been discovered, it appeared that Bartholomew had led an exemplary life.

After that, he had sent some of the councils' brightest scholars to question him in public. Set traps in their words to trip him up. It seemed he had an answer for everything. The man saw through all the traps Micah set. Nicodemus, the old fool had even returned at one point arguing in Bartholomew's defence. Micah had needed to take steps to strip him of those few privileges he had held on the council.

It was becoming clear that a mere discrediting would not be enough. The man had to be destroyed completely, and in a very public manner. That's when he started the whispers. The smear campaigns. Little things to begin with, building up to the claim that he was the promised Messiah, the fabled son of God.

During all of this, the biggest surprise had been the approach of Judas Iscariot. That, Micah had admitted, he had not seen coming. He had been suspicious of his intentions at first. What possible motive could he have? What advantage was in it for Judas?

Micah soon realised that Judas was delusional. He actually believed that handing him over would work in his favour, force him to reveal his true calling.

That Bartholomew would convince the council of his authority. Learning that had been important, it meant Judas had no understanding of what would happen once they had him. Micah had negotiated, had not even quibbled over Judas's price.

From that moment, everything had gone according to plan. It had been a close thing, especially when Pilate had insisted that Herod Antipas should decide on his fate. The king was unpredictable, no one knew what he would do on any given day. Fortunately, the king had concluded that he was being mocked by Bartholomew's refusal to speak. That paranoia had saved the day.

Even then, everything could have been undone if it hadn't been for Micah's quick thinking. The announcement of the Passover ritual by Pilate had caught him off guard. He had forgotten about that long tradition. He had needed to act quickly to ensure he flooded the crowd with people who would shout the right name. The inclusion of a large number of Barabbas's followers in the crowd had also helped.

It had all worked out in the end.

Now, he just needed to ensure the second half of the plan went as smoothly. He had managed to get a guard placed at the burial site. They had both been paid handsomely to turn the other way. In the early hours of the morning his men would take the body away. Micah would then take steps to ensure the right people were held responsible. That would make it easier to convince the Romans of the danger these disciples represented.

Micah intended to ensure every one of them was erased permanently from memory. He even had a preference for the officer he wanted to carry out the hunt.

Once she had finished in work, Mary had fully intended to go home. Grief stricken, in the depths of despair she had been surprised to find herself entering a bar. One of her old haunts from her previous life. Now she was sat at the bar, staring at the glass of whisky in front of her. She had been at the execution, convinced he would save himself. Become the saviour she believed him to be. It had not happened, he had just died there on the cross.

Died, just like any other man.

Mary reached for the drink, lifting it to her mouth. Its journey was interrupted by a man's hand. She had looked up into the face of Thaddaeus. "I don't think you want to do that," he stated simply.

"Why not?" she asked.

"You know why?"

"I don't care."

"I think you do. You like this new version of you, more than you care to admit at the moment."

"What difference does it make?" she said angerly. "He's dead, he can't do anything now."

"He already has. Remember who you were before."

"Leave me alone."

"No, I don't think I will." Thaddaeus took the drink out of her hand, she gave a token resistance. Taking her by the arm, he manoeuvred her towards the exit. After the last couple of days, she had very little fight left in her.

As they walked away, the grief finally took over and she broke down in tears. Thaddaeus held her close, comforting her as best he could. Once the tears subsided, he dried her face, as she declared, "It's not fair."

"I know, we all thought he was something he wasn't."

"But the things he did, the way he made me feel."

"That doesn't change. You still felt those things. Just because he wasn't who we hoped, doesn't change that. What he did for you, the change he effected in you."

"So, why?"

"I don't have those answers."

They had arrived at Mary's house. Thaddaeus kissed her goodnight, then headed back the way they had come.

Sitting in her room, Mary stared at the small pot on the table. The pot he had given her. At first, Mary had been unsure whether she would join the others on the morning. To visit the burial site, to wash and anoint the body. It had been his wish that she does this, and even after everything she had decided to keep her promise. Strictly speaking, the cleaning and anointment should have been carried out today, but this was the Sabbath, the day of rest. Mary had not recognised the Sabbath rules since she was a young girl. The other women did though, so it would be tomorrow when the rituals would be observed.

They had all agreed to meet first thing, as soon as the sun rose signifying the end of the Sabbath. 6:30 in the morning. Mary was not looking forward to it, religious ceremonies always made her feel uncomfortable. Unworthy, unclean she supposed in her own mind. Because of who, what she had been.

Thaddaeus had been right about one thing, she did like this new version of her. She was privately pleased he had been there to stop her making a catastrophic mistake.

George Ambrose was sat outside on the balcony of his hotel room. He stared across the city, deep in his own thoughts. He no longer knew what he believed.

He had spoken to believers and non-believers alike. Each in turn had spoken about Joseph Bartholomew in glowing terms, or with complete condemnation. There had been no middle ground. It was either one or the other. Except, George thought, there was Joseph Arimathea. George was still unsure which side he came down on. He had donated the burial site to the family, why do that if he didn't believe? It was true he was fabulously wealthy and well known for his philanthropic actions. Was that what this was about, just an act of charity?

Then there was the Magdalena woman. George had found her story interesting, and a familiar one sadly. He had heard it many times, in various forms before when he was working on a story about the sex trade. The escape from an abusive member of the family, or relationship only to end up falling into the sex trade. It was, unfortunately a common theme that ran through a lot of these cases. The only part he had doubts about was the sudden and miraculous recovery from her addiction. He had met many people who were addicted to drugs, or alcohol or both. It was a long and painful process to come off. Unless, of course Joseph Bartholomew had cured her as she claimed. That he was, in fact the man they all had claimed him to be.

Which brought a whole new set of questions. If this Joseph was the son of God, the Messiah, why hadn't he saved himself?

Peter, another puzzlement. Obviously, a true believer. Unless he had just been saying what he wanted George to hear.

But why would he do that?

To avoid looking like an idiot? It that was the reason he had said the things he had, he could end up paying a serious and painful price. All to avoid the stigma of being made to look a fool? George thought that was unlikely. There was no denying the fervour in his voice when he spoke of Bartholomew, nor could he hide the fear he had detected in Peter.

George sat considering all these things. Like other stories he had worked on, he had three independent sources all saying the same thing. In journalistic terms, that was enough to go to print.

Still, something was holding him back.

If only he could have met him in person. Had the opportunity to have spoken with him.

George had also considered trying to find some of the people who had been cured through meeting Joseph. However, that seemed like an impossible task. Plus, through the climate of fear the council had created it was unlikely anyone would be willing to speak to him.

Thinking about those people naturally made George think about his own health. Since arriving, he realised, he had slept better than he had for nearly a year. No sudden awakenings in a cold sweat because of the nightmares. George had expected his fears to have been heightened, but they hadn't been. If anything, those fears had been placed on a backburner. Considering he was surrounded by memory triggers on every corner, he had not had a single panic attack. Other than his attendance at the trial, he had not had any serious attacks.

Nothing.

Did this mean that he too had been healed?

If so, was this due to him facing his fears by returning to their origin? Or was there another, more unusual explanation?

George stood up, abandoning these thoughts and heading in for sleep. It was fruitless to carry on, he had more questions than answers.

And the only person who could provide the answers was dead.

Part Four
Sunday

Chapter Ten

The Hunt – Part One

There was a persistent knocking in George Ambrose's dream. At least he thought that's where it was coming from. The realisation that someone was actually knocking on the door arrived as he slowly came out of his sleep. Shaking his head in an attempt to clear his mind, he threw the bed covers off and answered the door.

Two men in the uniform of the Roman Army stood outside. One of them spoke.

"Colonel Vespian sends his apologies for the early call, but he would appreciate your co-operation."

"What time is it?"

"Just a little past five, sir."

"Come back in a couple of hours, when I will be more than happy to co-operate." George replied and made to shut the door. One of the soldiers put his hand out to prevent the completion of this movement.

"He did say it was most urgent, sir. He was quite insistent that we did not come back without you. If you don't mind, Sir?"

George realised they were not going to leave without him. Letting out a sigh he told them, "Well, one of you can make the coffee while I shower and dress."

"Thank you, sir." The two men entered his room as he made his way into the bathroom. Twenty minutes later he was sat in the back of the jeep heading out of Jerusalem. Both of the soldiers had taken the front seats, so at least it didn't look like he was under arrest. He asked them where they were heading.

"Golgotha," the soldier in the passenger seat told him.

The drive took them through the back streets of Jerusalem. The city was starting to awaken. The market stalls were being erected in readiness for the first day of the Passover celebration. It would be a busy day, hopefully for the stall holders a profitable one. This was the biggest festival of the year, they could make enough to survive the rest of the year if they were lucky.

Apart from a couple of delivery vans, the roads were quiet making their progress swift. It took a little under ten minutes to leave the city, yet again through the Damascus Gates. Once outside the city limits, the usual bleak view was interrupted by a sea of tents. The encampment had appeared over night as the people arrived to celebrate Passover in the famed city of Jerusalem.

The jeep lurched as they turned sharply to the right, off the main highway. Here the roads were not of the same quality. It seemed as if the driver was aiming for every one of the potholes and imperfections in the road as George was tossed around in the back.

A little ahead he could make out the figures of two men. George assumed one of them must be the Colonel, as he came closer to them, he recognised the other as Micah. The soldier parked the Jeep, jumped out and opened the rear door for George. Leaving the vehicle, he made is way over to the two men. He was beginning to suspect the reason for his being brought to the middle of nowhere, but he asked the question anyway.

"Why am I here?"

Before Vespian could respond, Micah spoke, "A question I have been asking. Well, Colonel?"

"Because I wish it. I would appreciate a second pair of eyes, and I thought it would interest you."

Micah spoke again, "And I do not think this required the involvement of the press."

"Mr Ambrose is here on holiday. He attended the trail at my behest, of his bosses here and in London. He is currently off duty. That is correct, yes?" The Colonel turned to George to direct this question.

"Yes, it is." George confirmed, instinctively backing up lie.

"It has been my experience," Micah continued, "that the worlds press is never off duty."

George was starting to dislike Micah more with each encounter. Turning to Colonel Vespian he asked again, "Why am I here?"

Vespian answered him, "This is the burial site of Joseph Bartholomew. Who, it appears, has indeed risen from the dead."

Micah interrupted before George could say anything, "Do not say that. Even as a joke."

George continued, "Can one of you please tell me what you are talking about."

"The body," Vespian said, "has gone."

"That is a surprise," George said, not even bothering to hide the sarcasm in his voice.

"Seriously, take a look for yourself." Vespian pointed off to the right, up a slight incline.

George headed off in the direction indicated. Instinctively he moved slowly, looking at the ground closely. He moved deliberately, trying not to disturb the site any more than it already had been. There were numerous footprints. At first glance, it looked like they had all been made by the imprint of army boots. As George moved on, he noticed there was one set of prints that may have been made by someone not in army boots. He considered that these would be the prints made by Micah's sandals. Unfortunately, the ground had been so disturbed by the coming and going of everyone, it was difficult to be sure, but he thought the assumption a fair one.

As he progressed up the pathway, it veered off to the right. Following the route, George stopped in order to take stock of what he saw. The stone burial chamber was directly ahead. The large, round plug stone was rolled away to the left of the tomb, the ropes used to secure it broken, some of it was still hanging in place around the stone. Portions of the wax seals were still intact, others had been damaged. George mentally calculated that this plug stone must weigh a couple of tons at least. It would not have been a simple job to, it would have required a couple, three at least he guessed, in order to role it to one side. Possibly even more, depending on the size and strength of the men.

He moved closer, inspecting the ground as he went. There was no chance of distinguishing who had been here. The ground again was too disturbed by the traffic of human feet. He made a closer examination of the plug stone. Looking at the ropes, it was clear they had not been cut. From what he saw, the ropes had been pulled apart. Their broken edges did not have that smooth look about them, which they would have shown had a knife been used. The same was evident with the wax seals, they showed the seal had been stretched before breaking.

Finally, George entered the chamber. It still had that damp feeling from the early morning chill. He could see some moisture on the stone walls, created as the day warmed. He was surprised at the amount of space there was, he guessed at two hundred square feet. The centre of the chamber was dominated by the raised, rectangular stone block. On the top of which lay a discarded, linen sheet. George looked closer at this, he noticed the dried blood stains. This wasn't a sheet, it was the shroud that had wrapped the body. He spent some time looking around the tomb, but there wasn't anything else to see. Leaving the tomb, he made his way back. Again, all he had were more questions and no answers.

He met Vespian on his way up. He immediately asked him, "What do you think?"

"What do your guards have to say for themselves?"

"That they were overpowered by Bartholomew's followers, who must have stolen the body."

"Do you believe them?"

"Not in the least. There are a number of empty wine flasks. They got drunk and passed out."

"Why lie?"

"I didn't get here first, when I arrived Micah was already here. I rather suspect money has changed hands."

They had reached the bottom of the small walk, Vespian left him to speak to the soldiers. Micah saw them and made his way over, Vespian ignored him. Micah spoke directly to them all, determined to ensure his version of events was the one they took away. "It seems obvious that his followers have stolen the body. You already have the statements of the guards. I see no reason to doubt them. His followers intend to hide the body, then claim he has risen from the dead."

"Why?" George asked.

"To perpetuate their claims that he was the promised messiah of our scriptures."

"Why? To what end, who is going to believe a story so ridiculous?"

"You have no knowledge of these things. The people have lived for thousands of years in the belief that he will come to save them. These claims, Colonel, will divide the people. They will cause factions within the city. Civil unrest would follow. His body must be recovered, his followers claim quashed."

"What for?" George persisted. "Why would they make these claims?"

"For the reasons I have already stated," Micah responded impatiently.

"You executed him, his followers are in hiding. Terrified of what you are going to do next, so why would they bring attention to themselves?"

"They are zealots, they are not rational. All they are concerned with is proving their lies as truth."

"I imagine that the only thing that concerns them is their own safety, what action the council intends to take against them. Or was that what your intention was all along? Find an excuse to persecute them? After all, this would be the perfect motive to ensure they are finished off once and for all."

"What are you insinuating?"

"Exactly what I said."

"I see, you have already made your own conclusion. The council has arranged all this, conspired with the Roman's. As usual, the press will write the most sensational version of the event, regardless. Never let the truth get in the way of a good story."

George was becoming impatient with this man. "Tell me, exactly how did they achieve this? Most of the ground disturbance looks as though it was been made by army boots, there is one other set, which cannot be made out clearly, but which I assumed was made by your own inspection of the tomb."

"Impossible, I have not been near the tomb. Those prints must belong to the follower who stole the body."

"Just the one? You really believe that one man could achieve all this? One man turned up, overpowered two trained, Roman soldiers, then single handed pushed that stone to one side. Did so with enough pressure to crack the seals and snap the ropes?"

George was pleased to see Micah was losing some of his composure. "Obviously there was more than one of them."

"Where are the signs of the others? There are none."

"As you have already said, the ground is badly disturbed. Obviously, the evidence of their involvement has been destroyed. I assure you, Mr Ambrose, I understand the truth of this better than you."

"And what is that truth?"

"As I have stated, his followers came in the night and stole the body away." Micah turns to address the returning Vespian. "I must inform Caiaphas of what's happened here. The council does not have the resources in order to search the whole city to recover the body, I am sure he will be speaking to the governor this morning." Smiling, he turned to George and continued, "I will also be making the strongest recommendation that the governor invokes a complete press blackout." Having said his piece, he turned on his heels and walked away.

George watched him go in disbelief. As he passed by the guards, he could have sworn he saw a sly grin on his face. Looking at the two soldiers, he noticed they would not return his look.

Vespian was speaking, "I told you what he was like."

"I don't get it."

"It's simple really. He is determined to destroy any reference to Joseph Bartholomew." He surveyed the area around him, thoughtful. "I was supposed to be having a day off. I was going to take a trip, relax. Now it looks like I am going to be searching for a missing body all day. Micah really is living up to the little shit he is today."

"You think it's a mistake to look?"

"I do. It just brings more attention to the man. If he would just leave it, forget about his personal ambitions, this would all just fade away. What do you think happened here?"

"I have no idea. The ground has been overrun with footprints, I couldn't tell you with certainty how many people have been up there. I do know one thing, if what I was told is correct. This was all done at the connivance of the council, whoever has the body, it won't be any of his disciples. Everything I have seen, everything I have heard, none of it makes any sense, other than the certainty that they would never defile his body."

"Welcome to my world. This place is full of contradictions that I have to deal with on a daily basis. Still, thank you for coming. My men will take you back to your hotel." George knew he was being dismissed, that he would not be privy to any further actions. He thanked Vespian, then made his way back to the jeep.

Vespian turned his attention to the two soldiers who had been guarding the tomb. "How much did Micah pay you?"

"Nothing sir, I swear." The both answered.

"Of course not. Get back to the barracks, do not under any circumstances go anywhere until I have decided what to do with you."

Both of the soldiers scurried off, Vespian knew they had been bribed. Micah would want to ensure it was his story that got out. With a resigned acceptance of the day ahead he made his way back to his vehicle and the office of the governor.

When he arrived, Caiaphas was already there. Upon entering Pilate's office, the governor turned to him, annoyed. "Is this true? The body is missing?"

"Yes, sir."

"How? I thought you had guards to prevent this?"

Before he could respond, Caiaphas spoke, "How is no longer important, with all respect governor. What is important is that we find it."

Vespian spoke directly to the high priest, "I assume Micah has already provided you with his version?"

"What of it? Micah did his duty by the council, and by me. He is a good servant to the city, and the people."

"Well, that's one view point."

"I know that from what he has said, that you, Colonel, have no wish to address our concerns. Hence his urging that I impress the urgency of this personally with the governor."

"Oh, I'm sure he made his feelings quite plain."

"He has; for example, I am confused as to why you allowed the press access." He turned to Pilate, continuing, "I'm sure you agree, governor, that the last thing we need is their involvement. It would be an embarrassment to both of us, and to the emperor. Not to mention the Roman Army will be the laughing stock of the rest of the world. The elite forces of the empire, overpowered by a couple of locals, unable to even protect a dead man."

"I disagree," Vespian responded. "It was one journalist."

"And he will just muddy the waters, dreaming up another conspiracy theory to embarrass us all."

"Enough," Pilate said. "What do we do next?"

"We must recover the body, before his followers start spreading their nonsense that he has risen from the dead," Caiaphas said vehemently.

"You think the people will believe such rubbish?" Pilate asked.

"That is not the point. The people will believe, or not. The real danger is the faction that will use this to stir up the people. Use this story of his resurrection to claim it is time to drive Rome back into the sea." Caiaphas paused, gaining some calm he spoke again, "The people are like sheep. They will follow where they are lead, as evidenced by these events of the last week. Regardless as to how ludicrous it may sound."

Turning to Vespian, Pilate said, "Opinion?"

"There is a proportion that would use this to their own means. To use the opportunity to further their own aims, but we know who these people are. We can ensure they do not give us much trouble."

"I can't afford any disturbances. I have just been informed that Tiberius has come down from his mountain. He intends to visit us, he arrives in one week." Pilate sits at his desk. "We will do all we can to help, High Priest."

"Good. Find the body, and his followers are to be handed over to the council. We will deal with them."

"No, I will order the search for the body. His followers have not been proven to have committed any offence. They are your problem." He turns to Vespian. "You have your orders, see to it."

"As you wish, Governor." Vespian left the office, heading across the corridor to his own domain. As soon as he entered, from the other door his sergeant came in.

"Morning, sir."

"I need Lieutenant Aurelias, now."

"Sir." The sergeant left to out carry out his request.

Within twenty minutes, the young Lieutenant was stood before him. Vespian addressed him, "You're my newest officer, arrived, what – two months ago?" The young man nodded. "All the reports I have received tell me you are an exceptionally able officer. Now, you have your chance to prove it to me."

"Thank you for the opportunity, sir, I won't fail you."

"I hope not. It's not going to be an easy task. You know of the man they called Joseph Bartholomew?"

"Yes sir, I was ordered to oversee his execution."

"Then you know who he was, what he claimed to be. Well, his body is missing and we have been tasked with finding it. The council believe his followers stole it overnight to give some credence to their claims he would rise from the dead."

"Do you have suggestions?"

"I will make some enquiries, any information I get, I will pass on. However, it is imperative that the body is found as quickly as possible. I don't care what methods you use to achieve an outcome, just find him." Vespian moves closer to the officer, lowering his voice. "We both know men do not come back from the dead, so his body is somewhere in the city. Find it, or at least find one we can easily pass off as his." Vespian moved back to his desk, dismissing the soldier.

His assistant returned as the soon as the Lieutenant had left. He explained what they had been asked to do, "Any ideas?"

The sergeant was no fool, he knew what his boss wasn't asking him, "I will see what I can discover, sir."

"Thankyou. You can mention, if it leads to something I am willing to be generous in my appreciation."

"Yes, sir." The sergeant left.

Vespian heard his assistant telling the corporal he shared his office with that he had somewhere to go. Vespian had no illusions about the sergeant. He was the one who had caught him trading in the black markets when he had been a mere lieutenant. After making further investigations, he had been astonished by the network of contacts the sergeant had. Instead of charging him, he had suggested a different type of relationship. It was largely through those contacts, and the ones he had made for himself, that he had risen through the ranks so quickly.

As he left, the sergeant made his way to the market place. He had no problems with the relationship he had with the Colonel. He knew he had been lucky, and the agreement had been mutually beneficial. In return for the use of his contacts, he was allowed to continue his off-book business deals. The sergeant had slowly become reasonably wealthy. Not fantastically so, but certainly enough to ensure a comfortable retirement. Once in the market, he spoke to as many of his people as he could, making sure they all understood the offer of a reward. After the market, he headed over to speak to a number of the temple guards. He spent most of the morning talking to people. Within the hour the word was spreading.

Back in his office, Vespian was making calls to his own contacts. His spies. The request was simple. Find me the body of one Joseph Bartholomew. The whispers spread throughout the city. People spoke to people, who spoke to other people. The Romans wanted something, and they were willing to pay handsomely. So the word spread.

All of the morning, into the afternoon.

Nothing definitive was heard, but there were some moments of hope.

In the early afternoon, his sergeant had returned with news that the body may have been found. "The manager of the body pits has come forward, he has three bodies that cannot be accounted for. No documentation, no official paperwork. He thinks one of them may be the one we are looking for. He is outside, the bodies on the back of his truck." Vespian went with the sergeant to check.

He looked at each of the bodies in turn, it didn't take him long to realise the one he wanted was not among them. He shook his head at the man.

"Your honour, are you sure? You barely looked at them. Please, take a closer look. I am sure what you want is here."

Vespian turned on the man, grabbing him by the back of his neck he dragged him, protesting to each body in turn. "This one is a woman, this one has been dead for at least six months, it has been eaten by so many creatures I can't even tell what sex it might have been. Finally, I can see the sex of this, but he is too old. Most importantly, none of them where crucified." He released the man from his grip, throwing him to one side. "Try to con me again, and you will join them in the pits."

He walked away from the bodies, back to his office.

Later that afternoon, another man turned up at the office. His sergeant came in and told him he might want to hear what this person had to say.

"Bring him in," Vespian ordered, his impatience beginning to show.

The man who appeared before him was dressed poorly. Vespian assumed this was another looking to get a hand out. "Who are you?"

"They call me Ridzik, sir."

"What do you have to tell me, Ridzik?"

"That the man you are looking for his alive." Exasperated, He was about to have the man kicked out of his office. "At least, that's what I was told."

"He is dead, I watched him die. Who told you this ridiculous nonsense?"

"A woman I used to know."

"Does this woman have a name?"

"Mary Magdalena."

"Magdalena? I know that name." Vespian muttered the name under his breath over and over, trying to remember. "Magdalena, the whore?" he asked, looking up as the Lieutenant came into the office.

"Former. She claims that Bartholomew cured her."

"Cured her? Since when has being a prostitute a disease?"

"Well, made her change her life, then. And she says she has seen him. This morning."

"That's not possible, the man is dead. How many times do I have to say this? I watched as they nailed him to the cross, watched as they hung him up for all to see. I witnessed the guard thrust a spear into his heart." Vespian turned to his sergeant. "Get this fool out of my sight." Ridzik was dragged away by the sergeant.

Vespian turned to the Lieutenant. "Do you have anything?"

"Nothing."

"Someone must know something."

"What about the woman just mentioned? I think it may be worth speaking to her."

"I don't, but we have nothing else to do, find her."

"I am new here, were do I look?"

"Well, she is a whore. I suggest you start by asking our own men if they know her."

"Yes, sir." The officer left the office and headed across the square to the men's barracks. Opening the door he shouted, "I need the whereabouts of one Magdalena, the whore." Several of the men raised their voices to say they knew where she could be. Lieutenant Aurelias told them to grab their kit and come with him.

From his office, Vespian could see the councillor Micah leaving the governor's residence. Seeing him, he was struck by a thought. Calling his sergeant, "Is there anything new in regard to Ambrose?"

"I'll check now, sir." The sergeant returned to his own area, Vespian heard him speaking to someone over the radio transmitter in his office. "Returned to his hotel and is still there, hasn't moved."

"Damn. I was sure he would have been eager to act. Shame, maybe he has decided that this lunacy is a waste of his time." He turned to look out the window again, deep in thought. "Micah has a real hatred for him. See if he had him watched, I'd be surprised if hadn't. Try talking to Lucas Spellman first."

"Do you really think Micah would have had him watched."

"Yes, I do. He is well aware who Ambrose is." Vespian turned to look at his assistant. "I have known, sergeant, five really brilliant investigative journalists over the years. George Ambrose is in a league of his own, his instinct is exceptional. You should have seen him this morning, he had the feel of what happened instantly. Don't judge him by appearances. He is the best I have ever seen. Micah will know this as well, I am sure he will have had him watched. Speak to Spellman, I can't imagine Micah trusting anyone else with this. Persuade him to tell us what he knows."

"Yes, sir." The sergeant left.

In another part of the city, Lieutenant Aurelias was busy searching the residence of Mary Magdalena. The woman wasn't home. This was the third address the soldiers had provided. They had searched the house, one of the soldiers had informed him of her absence.

The Lieutenant was stood in the kitchen area. "We missed her by twenty minutes at the most."

"How can you know that?"

"The kitchen, the stove is still warm. Leave someone behind, in case she returns. Let's move to the next location."

Unknown to the officer, they were being watched from across the street. The man looking out of his window said, "You're no longer safe. You can't go home." He turned to look at the woman.

"I have already made arrangements. I am leaving the city, I have a cousin in Spanish Gaul. I will be safe there."

"You can wait here until its dark. It should be safer for you then."

"Thank you, Tobias."

Tobias turned back to watch through the window. There was a sadness about him. He had known Mary only a short time, maybe three months. He knew what she had been, but he didn't care. Now, he would probably never see her again, and his heart was pained by the prospect.

Back in his office, the Colonel was becoming impatient. He found it difficult to believe that no one knew anything. It was during these contemplations that his sergeant arrived, pushing a man into his presence. "Who's this?"

"His name is Cleopas. He was one of Bartholomew's followers."

"You admit this?" Vespian asked the man.

"Gladly." He replied happily.

"Where is the body?"

"There isn't one, he lives, I have seen him."

"This nonsense again. Tell me, where did you see him? Having a drink in a tavern? Maybe you all had dinner together, a nice reunion?" The Colonels voice rose as he spoke.

"I tell the truth, he lives."

"When, when did you see him?"

"Little more than an hour ago." Vespian laughs. "You don't believe me? Why would you, I wouldn't. But it is the truth, and I'm not the only one."

"This is ridiculous. I saw him die in front of my own eyes."

"He is back. Two of us met him. Walking to the village of Emmaus. We were discussing everything that had happened. As we walked, we met and were joined by another traveller. He asked what we were talking about. I asked him surely, he must have heard of the recent events. He asked us, what things. So we told him all that we had seen and heard, how we were sad that he had died. That was when he scorned us, told us we did not understand the scriptures. It was late when we arrived, so we invited him to stay and dine with us. That's when he revealed himself to us."

"So, the two of you walked over five miles together, with this man you had followed for years and neither of you realised who he was?"

"Not until he broke bread with us."

"You didn't recognise a man your lived, slept and ate with for three years until you all sat down to eat?" Vespian said scornfully.

"We did not travel with him, we were not part of his inner circle, we just followed to hear him speak. It is the truth. We aren't the only the ones, they have all seen him."

"Really? Do you have any idea what the Jewish Council want to do to you all?"

"I don't care. Nothing they could do to me can change what I know to be true."

"Which is?"

"He is the Messiah, the son of god."

Vespian gave up. There was no dealing with these lunatics. He told his sergeant to throw him back on to the streets. As his orders were observed, the Lieutenant and his soldiers could be heard returning. Vespian left his office and went down to the square to meet them. He called to them, "What progress?"

"None, sir. The woman Magdalena has disappeared. We have not heard anything from anyone."

"Well, apparently that's because there is no body to find. Because, according to the man you just saw been escorted by my sergeant, Joseph Bartholomew is alive and well. He's just been having a long conversation with him all afternoon, they even had dinner together." Vespian grew angry, shouting at all those present. "Find him, dead or alive. I want his body, it is somewhere in this city. Find it!" He turned and walked back to his office.

He could feel his career disappearing in disgrace. This was one of those assignments that can kill a man's future. If that happened, he knew who was responsible. All eleven of them. If they were instrumental in the halting of his promising career, he would personally hunt them into extinction.

Chapter Eleven
A Version of Truth

The soldiers dropped George back at his hotel. He thanked them, making sure they could see him as he had collected his key from the receptionist and headed up to his room. He realised there wasn't much he could do until later, so after three late nights and an early morning, he went back to bed. He fell asleep almost immediately, waking five hours later. He checked his watch, it was almost mid-day. Rising, he headed into the shower, dressed and made his way to the hotel's restaurant.

While he ate, he planned. Top of his list was his need to have a conversation with the one, or both of the guards. That look Micah had given them, and their reluctance to meet his gaze had convinced him. There was more to be discovered about the events of that morning. The best chance of meeting either of them would be in one of the bars favoured by the soldiers.

He remembered some of the ones they frequented, he knew of six or seven from the time he had spent in the area. He just hoped their preferences hadn't changed in the time he had been away. He took his time over lunch, there was no point in rushing around. The soldiers normally left the barracks for the local taverns after four in the afternoon.

Once he finished, George made his way to the entrance of the hotel. Standing outside he lit a cigarette and looked around. As suspected, sat in the coffee bar opposite was the man who had been tailing him since Friday. Obviously, Micah had not forgotten, or given up on him. Continuing to look around, he was unable to notice anything out of the ordinary. He found that strange, he was sure Vespian would have put at least one man on him. It was as he lit a second cigarette that he noticed him. He had not given the man much thought at first, but he had been stood staring in at the shop window for five minutes or more. George watched him, the man stayed where he was. He decided this must me Vespian's man, there was a military feel to the way he stood. Unless he had an incredible penchant for handbags and women's shoes. George stubbed his cigarette out and returned to his room.

He would not be returning after today. After the events of that morning, his only concern now was to ensure his son's safety. He grabbed the essentials. Passport, wallet, keys, throwing them into his knapsack. It was time, find the guards and then get his son out of the country and safe. He left the hotel, turned left and headed towards the main shopping district. George wandered around, nipping into this shop or that with no particular route in mind. He was pleased to see both of his companions continued to keep him in their sights. Seeing one of the men's clothing stores was busy enough for what he needed, he entered. Passing the serving area, he picked up one of the stores bags and carried on. Passing the jackets, he quickly slid one of its hangers and into the, bag, a peaked baseball cap followed and then a pair of cheap sunglasses. Looking around, he saw the sign he looked for. Staff only.

Moving quicker, he stepped through this door, slamming it behind him. Steps led up to the other floors, and down to the staff area below. He took the steps down briskly, putting on the hat and glasses as he went. Discarding the bag, he put the jacket on over his t-shirt. He reached the bottom, banged against the release bar and stepped swiftly onto the pavement of the staff car park. Now running, he headed across the parking lot, through the barrier ignoring the guards protest and straight across the road and down into the subway. At the bottom of these steps he made a quick turn left, then took the next right and then another left. Down another flight of stairs. At the bottom he stopped, took a moment to look around, his two companions where nowhere to be seen. This did not mean they weren't far behind. He walked off towards another flight of stairs and followed the signs for the subway, and a randomly picked track. He jumped on the first train that turned up, purchasing a ticket to take him a further three stops.

Ten minutes later, he was emerging from the underground into the sunlight, alone. George took a moment to get his baring's. Realising which area of the city he was in, he walked down the road and took the first right. He continued along this road for another seven minutes, then turning left he walked to the entrance of The Lamb and Lion tavern.

The bar was only small, with enough room for about a dozen people to stand comfortably. However, to day being the first day of the holidays, it was tightly packed, customers had taken to standing on the pavement outside. George entered and headed over to the bar, situated on the left as you came in. He ordered a glass of ale, then made his way back. Neither of the two men he was looking for was inside, nor where they stood outside. He drank his beer as quickly as he could without bringing any undue attention to himself. Leaving his empty glass on the window sill outside, he walked away.

The next nearest place was a good twenty-minute walk. George did it in fifteen. The Star of David was a well-known haunt for both soldiers and sailors alike. More often frequented by the sailors, there was still a chance they would be there. The entrance was at the top of a short flight of stairs, past a door on the left that led to the hotel reception. The bar area was on the right, stools stood next to the bar. On the left tables and chairs occupied the space along the wall. As you walked further into the bar, a raised seating area was to the right, with another area further down on the left. Just like the Lamb, this bar was also busy. George ordered another ale, then wandered around searching. It took a little longer this time, but they were not here. George left his half-finished drink on a passing table and left.

Crossing the road, he walked down a narrow back street. The Angel was five hundred yards down, on the right. This place had four rooms with seating areas for the customers. The service area was in the far-left hand corner as you enter, and consisted of a small hatch way. You gave your order, and the server disappeared into a back room, and returned with your order. Above the hatch there was a price list, which included the cost of hiring one of the seven rooms available above the pub. This was a popular place for the whores of Jerusalem to bring their client's. They liked using this place because the owner never insisted in taking a cut of their earnings. As long as the cost of the room was paid, she was happy. George joined the queue, then took his drink and went to have a look around the various rooms. Again, he was disappointed. Finishing his drink, he left, declining the offer of company from one of the women outside.

The next place was the White Horse. An establishment favoured by the black marketeers as well as the army. Run out of cigarettes and everywhere is closed? Speak to David, sat by the fruit machines. Looking for a little extra to make the night fun? Simon's your man, sat under the painting of Moses. When he entered, George was surprised to see it was three quarters empty, it took him all of two minutes to realise the people he wanted where not present.

George turned left at the bottom of the street, walked down the road for five minutes then turned left. Up ahead he could see the lights of the Lion of Judah.

George entered and headed straight over to the bar. The place was laid out with booths lining the wall opposite the service area. Other seating was scattered about. The Lion of Judah was different from most others, in that they had their own brewing facilities on site. George ordered a glass of their house brew. He was about to turn around to survey the areas, when he caught sight of one of the men he was looking for reflected in the mirror.

Looking at the reflection, George realised he was much younger than anticipated. He couldn't have been more than twenty. The table in the booth he occupied was littered with half a dozen empty glasses. It was obvious this young lad was already half drunk. He hoped this might work in his favour.

When the barman returned with his order, George apologised and asked for another. Picking up both drinks, he made his way over, sliding into the seat opposite he placed the beer in front of the lad, saying, "You look like you could use this."

The boy looked up, squinting through the fog of alcohol he said, "What do you want?"

"Nothing, just thought I would buy one of our brave soldiers a drink."

"I'm not a puff, if that's what you think."

"I don't. You just looked like you needed some company, but if you want to be left alone. No problem." George got up to leave, the boy waved him back into his seat apologising.

"Sorry, sorry. Companies good." He was already slurring some of his words. "Sure?"

"Yeah, sit down old man."

"Cheers, my names Tom." The boy picked up the full glass, clinked glasses and swallowed a third of his drink.

"Am Marcus."

"Rough day?"

"Just come off a twenty-seven-hour duty."

"Bloody hell, that's a long shift."

"Well, I'm in the lower ranks, aren't I? We just get the shit duties no other fucker wants. The officers don't give a rat's arse about us. Should been sent a relief, never turned up. What we supposed to do? Couldn't just leave, be shot for disobeying orders."

"Puts you in a hard place though, they should have sent the relief."

"Told you, officers. Don't give a fuck about us. We're just fodder for them to use for the crap jobs."

"It's the same outside the service. I do all the work, bosses take all the credit. Rich gets richer. And if you do manage to crawl your way up, they still keep you out of their club. You have to be from the right family, wear the right school tie."

"That's it, exactly. It's all a massive shit pile." Marcus paused to belch. "Take that poor bastard they nailed up the other day? What did he do? I'll tell you, pissed off the wrong people."

"You talking about that Bartholomew nutter?"

"That's the fellah." Marcus leaned forward. "I could tell you a thing or two about that," he said, shushing and putting his finger against his lips drunkenly.

"Really, like what?"

"Can't say, it's a secret."

"Shame," George replied, reluctant to push too hard. "Hey, your glass is empty. Let me get you a refill." George went to the bar, returning a moment later with the drink.

"I was one of the guards at his tomb," the soldier suddenly admitted to George.

"Yeah? So you know what happened? I heard his followers had stolen the body."

"Nah, that's bollocks."

"So who took it?"

The boy tapped his nose with his finger, saying, "It was all arranged."

"Arranged? What do you mean?"

"That bastard Micah. Paid us both to turn a blind eye. Told us he was sending some people. Was going to take care of everything."

"What did he mean by that?"

The boy shrugged his shoulders. "Who knows? I'm just a humble soldier, I don't understand these things. All I know is he gave me a month's wages to shut up."

"So Micah stole the body?"

The young man looked down at this question. The atmosphere had subtly changed between them. "No. They never turned up. We never told him though. Just in case he wanted the money back," he said, giggling. "We got one over him."

"So what happened."

Now there was real fear in the boy's young face. "It just went."

"That makes no sense."

"I'm telling you, it just vanished. We were both sat there. The ground started to shake, there was a blinding light. When it cleared, it was gone and the tomb stone was moved."

"Just like that?"

"Just like that. Poof!"

"I don't understand."

"It's simple. Shaking ground, blinding light, crack and Poof! Gone." He laughed, snorting down his nose as he did.

"You must have been scared."

The young man sat opposite him seemed to sober up at that, as though he was suddenly taken back to that morning. "Terrified, both of us. Never known anything like it. This blinding light, seemed to be coming from inside the chamber. It felt like all the power of the world was in it." He shuddered at the memory, then reached for his drink. He sat back in the seat. George looked at him. There was no denying it, the boy was speaking the truth as he understood it. George was dumbfounded. He had not known what he might learn, but it certainly wasn't this.

The young soldier sat opposite had drifted off into a drunken slumber. George left him in peace and moved outside to smoke and think. What had happened to Micah's people, he wandered? He assumed that, as the guards hadn't come forward, Micah still believed everything had gone as planned. George really wanted to be there when he found out the truth, that his people had not turned up. What would he think, more importantly, what actions would he take? George had a horrible feeling that things were about to get extremely nasty. Micah would assume that the followers had actually stolen the body. Whilst it had just an imaginary accusation, he would be the one to write the narrative. Now, it was real. Which meant he was not in control of the events. He would take every step he could in order to wrestle back that control. George felt a chill on his soul. He needed to warn them all, and get his son away.

As he reached this conclusion, he was distracted by a disturbance up the road. A group of teenage lads were shouting, name calling and throwing stones at someone walking down the road towards him. He moved towards the lads, telling them to clear off. He realised it was a woman they had been attacking. He went over, asking, "Are you alright?"

"I'm fine, please do not concern yourself." The woman was covering her face, trying to get away from him. George had recognised that voice.

"Mary?"

The woman stopped in her tracks, looking up. "Your James's friend."

"Yes, well his father actually." George paused. "Are you sure you're OK?"

"Yes, maybe a little shaken. But, I'll survive." She made to move off, then stumbled.

George rushed forward to support her. "Come with me, there is a late-night diner round the corner. You can rest there for a bit." She didn't resist as he guided her away.

Settling at one of the tables, he ordered a couple of coffees from the passing waitress. The smell of the food being cooked made him realise he was hungry, so he ordered a plate of sandwiches. He sat down opposite Mary.

"What was that all about?"

"Having a past. I'm used to it, though it has been a while since anyone bothered me."

"You get that a lot?"

"Not that much these days."

The drinks and food arrived. They both remained quiet while the waiter fussed around them. Cups. The pot of coffee and the milk and sugar were placed precisely. The waiter then left, returning with a plate of mixed sandwiches.

"Help yourself." George invited as he selected a lamb filling. Mary hesitated, then reached for an egg filled sandwich.

"What have you been doing?" he asked her.

"Making my preparations to leave this place for good."

"Where will you go?"

"I have a cousin in Southern Gaul, in Spain. I will go there, I have spoken to her, she is expecting me. Tells me there is plenty of work available too." She finished eating, then continued, "What have you been up to?"

"Having a beer and listening to more implausible stories."

"Who with this time?"

"One of the young men ordered to stand over the tomb last night."

Mary suddenly became agitated. "What did he say?"

"Nothing that made any sense."

"But what exactly. Please." George could see the desperate need to know the details written all over her face and demeanour.

"He told me he was paid off. Both of them. To look the other way."

"There's more though, isn't there?"

"Yes. He also said that during the night the ground shook, throwing them both to the floor. Then, he claims there was a blinding light that seemed to be coming from inside the chamber. When everything cleared, and they could see clearly again the stone had rolled back and the body was missing. He described the light as containing the power of the world."

"No, not the power of the world. The power of God." Mary face was alight with the certain knowledge that they all had when talking about him. "He is returned to us."

"Ah, of course. Because only the power of God could raise your Joseph from the dead."

"Yes, he is risen. I know, I saw him."

"Really? Where?"

"This morning, at the burial site. I had made a promise to him, that I would attend to his body. Wash, anoint and wrap it. When the three of us arrived, we saw the empty tomb. I was distraught. A man tending the grounds asked me, 'woman, why do you weep?' I told him and asked if he knew what had happened to the body. He replied, saying, 'Why do you look for the living among the dead?' that's when he revealed himself to me. My master, my lord. The true Messiah." Mary paused, looking intently at George. "You don't believe me? The others didn't when I told them. Can I ask you a question? Well two actually."

"Of course."

"Firstly, why do you refer to him as Joseph?"

"Because that's what everyone called him. Why, is he known differently?"

"Joseph is one of his other names, the full name is Jesus Joseph Joshua Bartholomew."

"And the other thing?"

"You have not believed any of the things you have heard. You consider them to be far-fetched. Exaggerated. But your still here, still asking about him. Why?"

"I have no idea. Other than trying to prevent my son from making a rash decision, one that could possibly cost him his life. I honestly don't know why I am still pursuing this story. It's certainly not why I came out here."

"I know you don't believe me, when I say he is risen. I don't blame you, I wouldn't if I had not seen it with my own eyes. The rest of them certainly had severe doubts. Thomas even told me I was a crazy woman."

"You've spoken with the others?"

"Yes, He commanded me to tell them what I had witnessed." Mary stood up. "I need to go, or I will be late."

George looked up at her. "Good luck, Mary. Be safe."

To his surprise, she bent down and kissed his forehead saying, "God bless you, George Ambrose. I will pray for your eyes and your heart to be opened to what you have seen here." Then she was gone.

George no longer had the inclination to argue the point anymore. He knew he was passed the point where it would make any difference. Again, he had that nagging disappointment of not being able to speak to Joseph. Or Jesus as he was called. At least he had only ever preached about love for your fellow man. Experience told him it could have been a lot different.

George finished the food, drained his coffee cup and paid his bill. All he wanted to do now was see his son, and try to convince him to come back home with him.

Leaving the coffee house, he hailed a passing taxi and had him take him to the bus station. After being dropped there, he walked across the station's concourse to the other taxi rank. This time he gave the destination of the Damascus Gates. After his arrival here, he stood around, walked aimlessly smoking. After twenty minutes he was happy that he had not reacquired his friends from earlier that afternoon. Looking at his watch, he saw that it was just past mid-night. The safe house was a brisk twenty-minute walk. He would arrive there in good time, at least half an hour before the time he had agreed.

Part Five
Seventy-Two Hours

Chapter Twelve
The Road to Galilee

George stood in the small clump of trees, in sight of the safe house. He was confident he had not been followed. His philosophy in these situations was better safe than sorry; so he stood, watching the approach. He had observed two men arrive, separately from different directions. He stood as Peter had come out, looked up and down the road, saw his son do the same thing.

They seemed concerned; someone was late.

It wasn't just the concern for the latecomer, there was an urgency, an excitement about the way they stood, how they moved. When the other two had arrived, he had heard shouts of what he could only describe as joy. It was understandable, the pleasure of seeing their friends safe. The happiness at the reunion.

It was time for him to join them, he had waited long enough. As he moved into the open, he heard someone else coming and shied back into the trees. He listened for the knock on the door, watched as Peter greeted the newcomer warmly. Once he had entered, George moved forward and gave a short double knock on the door.

Again, it was Peter who opened the door. George knew instantly that something had happened. Something momentous judging by the sheer joy written all over Peter's face. George did not have long to wait to find out what.

Everyone was gathering around a central figure, the last arrival was on his knees, saying something. It was then that George saw who he was talking to, making him stop in his tracks. Actually, fall into a nearby chair in astonishment.

This was not possible.

It simply couldn't be.

His mind was playing tricks.

Any minute now he would wake up in his hotel bed.

He pinched himself, no he was definitely awake.

Sat there, looking straight at him. Jesus Joseph Joshua Bartholomew.

A dead man. A talking, breathing dead man.

"How…What…" he stammered. He sat, staring across the room.

Staring at this impossible man.

Peter was coming back over to him. George suddenly remembered what he had come to tell them. Still staring, he said, "You need to get away from here. Micah is coming for you."

"We know, we are leaving for Galilee soon."

"What happens after that?"

"We will each receive our mission, to spread the word across the world."

"What?"

"The truth of this. The Messiah has come."

"About that…"

"I know," Peter said, there really wasn't much else he could say. He left to return to the others.

George watched him go, opened mouthed in astonishment. Closing his mouth, he once again looked at the man, this time he could make out the scars in his wrists where the metal spike would have been driven in.

After the initial shock, the cynical journalist was beginning to return. This was not possible. It had to be another person. They must have hired a doppelganger. Except George had seen him close up. He had got to know that face, observed it in front of Annas, then Caiaphas and finally in front of Pilate. Twice.

Still, common sense, the laws of reality told him it just was not possible. It had to be a double, an exceptional lookalike, even a twin perhaps.

Which meant what?

That this had all been elaborately planned years in advance?

To what purpose, though? And why would twelve perfectly normal men agree to such a thing? When they knew from the outset, that such a hoax would present a very real threat to their lives. They had all given up many things to follow, friends, families, jobs, reputations and status.

And, if they were twins, how did they decide which of them would die? Whichever one it was, he had to be an extraordinarily single minded individual. To be willing to go through with it. George realised this was ridiculous, no one would go to such extreme lengths. Again, what would be the purpose, the reason?

In his time, George had investigated many a complex confidence trick; and they all had one thing in common. Financial gain, to make money by fleecing the gullible.

There was none here.

Or, at least none that he could see.

There was no reason to it.

George became aware of someone standing over him. Looking up he saw his son, he was holding out a bowl of food. He took the proffered meal, and his son sat next to him.

James looked at his father's confusion, smiling he said, "You still don't get it, do you?"

"Who is he?" George asked.

"You know who he is."

"That's not possible."

"Yet, there he sits, twenty feet away. Still you refuse to grasp the reality of it all. It is simple. He came to preach his message, they rejected it, they killed him. Now, as he promised, three days later he has risen. Come back to us. He is the son of man, the Messiah, the Christ." George looked at his son. "You can't accept what has happened, because it contradicts all that you know, all that you understand about life and death. Even Thomas doubted it. He insisted on inspecting the wounds, pushed his fingers into the scars. Thomas, who travelled with him for three years."

"So, you have your Messiah, what next?"

"We all leave, to meet up again in Galilee. To re-group, to receive our final instructions."

"How will you get there?"

"Some will travel on public transport, others will drive. Myself, Peter and Simon our walking. Simon still has contacts from his revolutionary past. He has arranged a number of safe places for us to stay on the way. Come with us?"

"Maybe."

"Please?"

"I will think about it." George looked at his son squarely. "Am I allowed to talk to your Messiah?"

"He is yours as well. And yes, once we reach Galilee."

"Why not now?"

"Because he has gone on ahead. He left a couple of minutes ago." George looked over to where he had seen Him. The space was no longer occupied.

"Then, if I want to talk to him, I suppose I will have to come with you." He paused. "They will find you, you must know that?"

"Eventually, but not before we finish the tasks given to us."

"I wouldn't be so sure."

"I'm not. But he is." George had no need to ask who 'he' was. "So, you will come with us?"

"Yes, you may need someone sneaky, if you are going to arrive safely." George smiled. "And, as you know, there aren't many as sneaky as me." James, his face aglow, took their dirty dishes into the kitchen.

While he was gone, Peter came over. "James is pleased that you are coming with us," he commented. "Simon says he can get us to Galilee safely, without much trouble. He has contacts from his resistance days."

"James said."

"For my part, I am also pleased that you have decided to travel with us. At least as far as Galilee, anyway."

"Thank you."

"Simon insists that day travel is best, rather than overnight."

"That makes sense. At least in the day you can see where you are walking, making accidents less likely. I assume you will be going across country were possible?"

"Yes, Simon wants us to avoid the main roads."

"In that case, day travel is less conspicuous. No one will think twice about a group of friends hiking through the countryside in daylight. Doing the same at night could draw attention. It also has the added bonus of being able to see if you are being followed, watched."

Peter nodded.

George continued, "Micah has already started to spread his poison about you all. He will not rest, night or day, until he has each of you."

"He is known as a stubborn man."

"You have no idea," George said. "Which route will you take?"

"Simon has it all mapped out. Tomorrow, at first light we will leave for Jericho, where we will spend the night. After that, I am completely in his hands." As they spoke, Simon had walked over, took up the thread of their conversation.

"From Jericho, we will move to Hemdat, then onto the village of Beit Yoser. Arriving in Galilee on the fourth day."

"So, an average of what? …thirty miles a day?"

"Yes, easily manageable for all of us. I have secured travel for all of us to Mo Ale Adumim. I think we should move tonight, to another safe area. Just to be cautious, we leave in twenty minutes. Pack light."

Both of them nodded, making moves to get ready. George had little to do, having already packed before leaving the hotel. He was passed a couple of items, which he stowed away. George walked over to Simon, shaking his hand, looking down at the maps open on the table.

"You have planned a good route, one that does not take you to close to the highways."

"And it is adaptable if required. We can veer off the route without taking ourselves to far in order to come back on track."

"Good," The sound of a vehicle could be heard coming to a halt outside.

Simon went over to the door, opening it slightly to peek out. He then turned to everyone. "That is our transport. It's time to go."

George pulled his bag onto his shoulder, then joined the others as they headed out. Outside an old school bus awaited them. One by one they climbed aboard, taking a seat. Simon spoke with the driver, who nodded at what he was told, pushed the vehicle into gear and, with a jerk, they moved off.

It was slow going at first, but one they reached the main road they soon picked up speed. The drive was uneventful, apart from the odd pothole. In less than an hour the driver took a sharp left turn down a dirt road, eventually pulling up outside an old, disused building. Everyone quickly moved from the bus inside. Simon spoke again with the driver, then watched as he drove off.

Inside, they had all found a space to settle down for the night. Simon came in telling everyone to try and get some sleep, it was only a couple of hours before first light.

Nobody needed telling twice. Getting as comfortable as was possible, George closed his eyes. It seemed only a moment later that he was being shook awake. He stretched and stood up. James told him there was bread and cheese to eat, and the coffee was on the go.

George thanked him, grabbed some food and a coffee then headed out the back of the building. He placed his coffee cup on the wall outside, finished off his food then lit a cigarette, looking out across the landscape.

The little village of Mo Ale Adumim was beginning to waken. He could see some of the inhabitants making their way into the fields. Primarily a farming community, the village and the surrounding valley could date its history back to the days of Moses. The valley boundaries rise up from Achor to Debir, then turn north to Gilpal. Facing the ascent of Adumim, the village name actually means Ascent of the Red, taking its name from the reach that rises from the dead sea. It was a perfect place of isolation, surrounded on all four sides by the Judean desert. Jericho lay twenty-five miles way to the west.

"Beautiful, isn't it?" George heard Simon say.

"Stunning," George agreed.

"I was born right over there," Simon told him, pointing. "I love this country. I fought for its freedom, believed that real freedom lay in kicking the Romans out. I was wrong."

"What is real freedom then?"

"Living with a purpose, being able to live with myself, the decisions I have made. I did some terrible things in the name of freedom. Real freedom comes from within, He taught me that."

"Joseph?"

"Yes." He turned and headed back inside. George continued to finish his cigarette and coffee, enjoying the scenery. He watched as he recognised four of the disciples leave, heading off to the left and the local bus shelter. As he turned to return inside, his son's face appeared.

"We will be leaving shortly, are you ready?"

"I am," he said, entering the building and colleting his bag. Judging by the weight he suspected other things had been added. James confirmed his suspicions.

"We needed to share out the supplies. I hope you don't mind."

"Of course not," he confirmed as Simon and Peter joined them.

"We leave through the rear entrance," Simon stated.

Heading out the back door, they walked down into the valley. The sights and sound reminded George why he had originally accepted a posting here all those years ago. Taking a little used path, they began to rise up to a view over the whole of the valley. The town of Bethany lay off to their right as they dropped back down the other side of the valley. Walking for another ten minutes, they emerged on route one which they followed for half an hour before bearing left to head back uphill again. It was a slow, arduous climb. The sun beat down on their backs, their necks. Once at the top, Simon pointed off into the distance, telling them all, "We can rest there."

"What is it?" Peter asked.

"It is a holy retreat. We will be made welcome," he replied as he moved off downhill.

George looked into the distance as indicated by his travelling companion. Even this far out, the structure looked spectacular. As they descended to the Wadi Qelt Valley the building became clearer to the eye. What came into focus first was the vivid blue of the cupolas. The retreat itself had been carved out of the rockface, appearing as though it is clinging to that rockface.

As they continued to walk, George estimated they had covered over half the distance to Jericho. As Simon had said, the member of the holy retreat welcomed them warmly. The head of the order invited them in, showing them to the room whilst encouraging them to take a seat. As they did as they were bid, other members appeared carrying trays of food and refreshment.

They rested for an hour; Refreshed and fed they headed back onto the road, walking up the steep steps out of the retreat. At the top they walked away from the cliff face towards the settlement of Mitzpe Yerino. The village lay at the end of the cliffs that mark the trail of the Judean headlands. It overlooks the rift valley of Jordan, the dead sea and, in the distance the oldest recognised city on earth, Jericho.

It took another hour of walking to arrive at their chosen destination. They were accommodated on the outskirts, by one of Simon's old friends. The building lay at the end of what remains of the famed walls.

George sat in a vacant seat, the others doing the same, while their hosts prepared a simple meal of roasted meats and rice.

After a good night's sleep, they were on their way again. They left the sanctuary of the building, heading down into the rift valley, towards the Jordan. They crossed the river via the famed Allenby Bridge. Originally built in eighteen eighty-five by the Ottoman government. After throwing them out, the Roman authorities built a stronger, more permanent structure. Not strong enough, as it turned out, as it was destroyed by the earthquake of nineteen twenty-seven. It fell apart and then collapsed into the river.

A wooden structure was built to replace the bridge, which was again destroyed in the June uprising of nineteen sixty-seven. Again, a wooden structure was built, the wooden way eventually being given a modern paved crossing in nineteen ninety-four. The terminal is operated by the Jewish council, providing income for the upkeep of the bridge. Unrecognised the four of them crossed without incident.

Heading north they followed the flow of the river. Apart from the impressive Karamen Dam, their walk crossed desert land only, interspaced with the occasional small village. They ate as they walked, in almost complete silence as the struggle to walk across the desert terrain took most of their energy and concentration.

After walking between four and five hours, they turned to head in a north westerly direction, beginning a slow, gentle descent. This was the Jordon river valley, and their destination lay some distance ahead. They would climb again to the altitude of six hundred and thirty-four feet. Climbing uphill through desert sand is hard going, and when they reached the summit, they were all drenched in the sweat and heat of the walk.

Where they intended to stay was a relatively new settlement, formed a mere forty years earlier. Formally a military outpost, it had been demilitarised and handed over to a group of young pioneers in nineteen seventy-nine. Due to the heat, remoteness and other obstacles it had laid abandoned for the last twenty-five years.

As they approached, Simon saw movement around one of the outbuildings. He stopped everyone, and with George moved cautiously forward to observe. Pulling off his back pack, Simon brought out a set of binoculars and scanned the settlement. "It's Andrew and Matthew," Simon said, concerned. "I wonder what brings them here."

Rising, he indicated that it was safe for them to continue into the settlement. As they descended down into the valley, Matthew spotted them and came running over.

"We have news," was the first thing he said.

"It's good to see you, too," Peter responded.

"And you," Matthew answered, taking him into a bear hug. "We are in the main building. Andrew has already lit a fire and is making coffee. You know what he's like, he must have his caffeine."

As they entered the building, Andrew greeted his brother warmly. There was little of use that remained inside, but they had managed to construct a temporary table from the wooden pallets that covered the floors. They stood around, and Matthew brought them up to date.

"We started as planned. Taking the train from the station in the village, across country to Ofra. There were some temple guards there, but we managed to keep out of their way taking cover in the waiting room. We had to wait two hours for our connecting train, we were both sure they never saw us, or if they did, they didn't realise. We caught the train as planned, it was when we arrived that we ran into trouble. Terminal was busy, there were temple and Roman guards. It was obvious they were looking for us, they had photographs they showed to other passengers. We were spotted, but we managed to get away.

"Since we considered it unwise to continue, we decided to take a more circuitous route on foot. When we came here, Andrew remembered Simon talking about it as a safe place. So, we decided to wait and see if you turned up."

Everyone was quiet as Matthew finished talking. "They can't know where we are heading," Simon told them, seeing their worried expressions.

"What about the others?" James asked. "They may not be aware of the search for us."

It was George who spoke, "They will have to take their chances, just like us. You can't take the risk of trying to get in touch to warn them. We all need to stick to our plans. We will need to be more cautious, more watchful that's all we can do."

Simon agreed, reemphasising the need to stick to their plan.

George asked Simon for the map, which he spread out on the makeshift table. Simon pointed to a spot. "This is where we are. In the morning we will head up to Shadmot Mehola, onto Tirat Zvi, passing Ma'oz Haim through the valley of springs to Beit Yosef. We will spend the night there at the Augustus memorial, there is a reasonably habitable disused old barracks behind the monument.

"The final walk will take us into Galilee. Through the national park of Yayne'el. Through the town of Tiberius, and then down to the shores of the sea near Ginosar." Simon had used his forefinger to trace the route. "What are you looking for?"

"A false trail. Something to throw them off the scent if we need to. The problem is making sure they fall for it, which we can't do without the foxes contacting the dogs."

Simon grasped the problem. Both men studied the map more closely. George pointed at a location on the map, saying, "If we could convince them you were making for here, that would be ideal."

Simon looked at where he pointed, "The airstrip? It's no longer in use, been abandoned for a couple of years now."

"Even better. If you are trying to make an escape, where better to head?"

"But how do we make them think that?"

"Absolutely no idea, perhaps fortune will give us the opportunity."

Peter had joined them, listening to their talk. "God will provide it," he announced. "That is why he brought you to us."

"Let us hope so," George told him. "Meanwhile, I need to give this more thought," he said, then headed out the door for a cigarette. Mulling the problem over, he could see no way of achieving what he needed without giving themselves away. He paced around, smoking, thinking. It was an hour later that the solution hit him, he had his hands in his pocket, playing with a small piece of card he had put there a couple of days earlier. It was so simple, he realised.

Two phone calls, that was all that was needed. And the agreement of the men at the other end of the call, which should not be difficult to achieve. Afterall, one of them had already offered his help, George thought as he continued to turn the business card over in his hand.

He had one last cigarette, then returned inside. Everyone was bedding down for the night, apart from Simon. He was bent over his maps, George grabbed a coffee and joined him.

"What is the terrain like in the area? Would it be possible to land there?"

"Land what?"

"I have a friend who may be able to help with your final escape. To take you wherever you need to go. He has access to aircraft."

"Impressive. We never had access to that sort of thing when I was a revolutionary. It would have been useful."

"I bet."

Both of them switched their concentration back to the maps. Simon continued, "As you can see, it is all sand. It would be difficult, but not impossible. It would depend largely on the size of the craft."

"Well, it would need to be able to carry you all, so it would have to be a fair size."

"You could land a helicopter, I have seen it done before by the Romans. It stirs up a lot of sand, and it is tight, but it is possible."

"I don't know if he has one. I know he has an airline he part owns."

"Which one?"

"I don't know, just that he has an interest in one." George turned and called his son over. "James, which airline is it that Arimathea owns?"

"Ellet," he answered.

"Do you know if they have access to a helicopter? In particular, one big enough to carry you all?"

"Several. They use them for tourists transfers."

"Good." He turned to Simon. "I will make the call in the morning, I just hope his offer of help was genuine. If so, that's your escape sorted. Then we just need to convince the authorities that you are actually heading somewhere else. I think I know how to achieve that. Right now, it can wait till the morning. I need some sleep." Having said this, George bedded himself down and was asleep minutes later.

The morning arrived, bright and fresh. The building was warmed by the sun, the light shining through the cracks in the roof. As he grabbed a bite to eat, he asked where Simon was. Andrew told him he had headed outside.

George found him, lying down on his front with the binoculars pressed against his eyes. George joined him.

"We have company," Simon told him, passing the binoculars over. George put them to his eyes, looking in the direction he was shown. A single army vehicle came into focus, two soldiers standing next to it. Simon directed him over to the right of this to another view. One man, dressed in desert garb, knelt down on one knee examining the ground. Simon continued speaking, "I don't know the soldiers, but the little man knelt I do know."

George heard the tension in his voice, saying, "Sounds like you have history."

"We do, his name is Izsak Abraham Sheenah, a tracker of some reputation. He is a repulsive individual, with an ego the size of the empire. He particularly takes great enjoyment in the tracking of humans, he considers it great fun. A sport," Simon told him, further saying, "he is responsible for the capture of a dozen or so of my former revolutionary friends, including my brother. It was him the Roman's used to track Barabbas, one of his rare failures."

Both men continued to look in the distance. "This makes things difficult," Simon stated. "We will need to move with more speed, travel over land that will make it harder for him. It won't stop him, but it may slow him down enough." He paused in his conversation. "I am sorry about what happened to you, what you went through last year."

"You know about that?"

"Yes, I was with Joseph by then. I wanted nothing to do with them by that point."

"Then you have nothing to be sorry about." George told him. "We need to move." Both of them stood up, heading back into the building to find everyone ready to get going. They did not tell them about the tracker, instead they grabbed their own bags and led the others out through a hole in the building at the rear.

George remained behind, telling them he would catch them up. Once they had all left. George removed his mobile from his bag. Turning it on, he was relieved to see he had a decent signal strength. Taking the business card out of his pocket, he dialled the number printed.

It rang four times before it was answered and he heard the voice of Joseph Arimathea. By the end of the conversation, everything had been agreed. George got the impression that he enjoyed the idea, and was looking forward to ruining Micha's plans. He came away from the call with even more respect for the man.

The second call was to the editor in chief at the Judean office for the times newspaper. Derek listened to what he was told, promising to do what was requested at the time George wanted.

Calls finished, George removed the battery and sim from the device, throwing it all back into his bag. He threw the bag on his shoulders, then left the same way as everyone else. Rather than heading in the same direction as the others, who would be taking a more roundabout journey, George headed in a more direct route. It was heavy going, but six hours later he stood on the top of the Valley of Springs. Below him, about another half hours walk away lay the settlement of Beit Yousef. George could just make out the monument to Augustus, and the building behind it as he approached.

He was surprised to find that he had made better time than he thought, the others had not yet arrived. He made some preparations for their arrival. He was astonished to discover that the power was still attached, throwing the light switch as a matter of habit. The room was in better condition than expected, even reasonably clean. He looked around, found a kitchen through a door at the far end. Turning the oven on, he was disappointed to find it no longer worked. Still, you couldn't have everything.

He settled down to wait for the others. It was about twenty minutes later that the door opened, only for the tracker Izsak to enter. George just stared at him.

The man looked at George with surprise. Ignoring him, he began to look around, then addressed George in an arrogant manner.

"Who are you?"

"I might ask you the same," George responded calmly.

"I am asking the questions. So, your name?"

"I'm not inclined to tell you."

"I am a representative of the Jewish Council, and I am here with the authority of Rome. Refusing to answer my questions is an obstruction of my duties, punishable through law. Now, perhaps you will change your attitude?"

"Why didn't you say that to begin with?"

"I am the one in charge here, not you. Now, answer the question. Who are you?"

"Just a hiker who got lost, needed somewhere to spend the night."

"That was not the question I asked."

"It all the information you will get, my name is of no consequence."

"I am the authority here. Either answer my questions, or I will place you under arrest."

"I have told you why I am here, I have not caused any problems, what do you think you can charge me with?"

"I will think of something. I don't believe the reasons you have stated for being here."

"What exactly do you think I am doing here, in the middle of nowhere?"

"I do not have to explain myself to you," as he said this, he produced a short-barrelled pistol. "Get up. You are coming with me for further questioning. Move!" he shouted the last word. As George got to his feet, the man continued, "You won't be so confident when the inquisitors have finished with you."

"That's the problem with all you little people, a little power goes straight to your head. You think you have all the power, when you have nothing, and you use that to bully others."

"I have the gun, so I think I do have the power."

"Yes, but I know something you don't."

"Really," the man said scornfully, "what that might be?"

George never got the chance to respond, as the man was plunged into darkness when James knocked him unconscious.

"Nice timing.," he told him as they hugged each other.

Peter came into the room, saying, "Violence does not answer anything, James. However, on this occasion I think we can make the exception." They all laughed appreciatively.

George spoke to Simon, "If he is here, the soldiers won't be far." Simon nodded, grabbing the binoculars out of his bag they both went outside. George looked down at the unconscious tracker. "Find something to tie him up with, and someone get the lights.," he stated. They all began looking around, James hit the light switch.

George noticed some of the wiring in the kitchen had come loose. Checking it would not cause any further problems for them, he pulled it free. He returned to the main hall, turned the body over and tied Isaak's hands behind his back. Andrew removed is neckerchief, which he then used to gag their unwelcome guest.

Simon returned after they had finished, stating, "They are about a mile away, travelling fast. We need to hide, there is a crest behind the building, we can all take up a position behind there."

"Good, let's move everyone, take him with us," he told the room, pointing at the tracker. Two of them grabbed him, dragging his body out of the rear, up the hill and over the top.

George and Simon lay on their front, watching as they saw the jeep, trailing a dust storm pull up at the building. One of the soldiers went into the building, the other staying with the vehicle. The one inside soon reappeared, going over to speak with the other. They split up, and began an unenthusiastic search of the area, eventually joining back up at the Jeep. One of the soldiers spoke into the radio. George and Simon could not hear clearly what was said. Whatever it was they were told they, it caused them to climb into the Jeep and drive off.

They waited, watching them disappear into the distance. They remained hiding on the crest, waiting to see if they would return. After half an hour, they deemed it safe to return. Simon spoke to them all once they were back inside. "We stay to eat only, then we move into the mountains to the south to spend the night."

"What about him?" Andrew asked, pointing at Izsak.

"He comes with us," George told them. "If he is as good as I have been told, we can't afford to leave him behind."

Matthew spoke, "He will just slow us down."

Peter spoke, "What do you suggest, that we kill him?" Matthew dropped his head, "We take him with us."

"Besides," George said, "he might prove useful." No one thought that, looking at him, he would be any use. James was looking at his father, when he spoke.

"You have a plan to use him, don't you?" George said nothing.

They all set about organising their evening meal. Simon told them no fires, it was to be a cold supper. Fires attracted attention he told them. He then came over to talk quietly to George.

"Was James right, do you have a plan?"

"The beginnings of one, yes. Unfortunately, whichever way I look at it, I don't like the way it ends. It needs more thought."

Simon nodded, leaving him to his deliberations.

George knew how he could use this prisoner of theirs. Plant a false trail into his head, the same that would be backed up later the next day by Derek Watling. It would mean that someone would have to stay with the prisoner, allowing the others to continue on. There was only one person they could leave, and that was himself. He spoke to Simon, outlining what he intended. Simon was reluctant at first, but soon realised it was the best option. He left George to speak to the rest of them, giving them precise instructions.

An hour later they had reached the small outcrop, taking it in turns to watch their guest, they all tried to sleep.

Dawn arrived all too quickly, they were all tired as they set off.

Within the hour they had reached the national park, passing the Belvoir Fortress. It was only a ruin now, but you could still make out the two circuits of the defensive walls, one within the other. It was one of the earliest examples of what became called a concentric castle plan. It would be adopted and used widely in later buildings.

They walked past the ruins, heading northwards over another crest and down into the town of Yavn'el. This was a much larger town, covering twelve and a half square miles. The area, according archaeological claims, has been occupied for over four thousand years, some say since the bronze age. They moved quickly through, picking up some supplies as they went, anxious not to draw to much attention, especially with their unwanted companion.

They next passed through Poria Illit, a small community around four miles outside of the city of Tiberius. They headed west, avoiding the city by skirting its borders, eventually turning to the east and into the Ginosar farms. They were expected, Simon had arranged to stay with his uncle.

They entered his little house gladly, to be greeted with the smells of cooking. His uncle and his wife bid them take a seat, and served them a stew of spiced beef and lamb.

George sat with their prisoner, removing his gag and untying his hands so he was able to eat. George told him there was no need to talk, just eat. The prisoner did just that, wolfing down his food hungrily. Once he was finished, the gag was replaced, and then the ties around his hands. As he did this, George told him, "It won't be for much longer. Just another day." Then he left him sat in the corner.

The meal over, the dishes cleared they all sat around the table. Simon's family excused themselves, leaving them alone to talk. It was George who spoke first.

"Tomorrow you will be reunited with your Messiah, then transport has been arranged for your escape. I don't think it is a good idea to take our friend with you, so I will take him with me."

"Where are you going?" Peter asked.

"I will go directly to the airstrip, to ensure everything is ready for you. Remember, you must be there by no later than two thirty. Once the plane enters their airspace, once it touches down, we will only have a short time to get aboard and back in the air. Every minute you are late, brings the danger of capture ever closer."

Simon replied, "We will be there, as soon as possible. It is only a short walk."

Andrew asked him a question, "What will you do with him?" pointing at Izsak.

"Once I am sure it is safe, I will release him. Far enough away that he can't say anything in enough time to make a difference. So, that's it. Let's get some sleep." They all made themselves comfortable, settling in for the night.

The next morning, George went over the details again. His son came over to talk to him. George spoke to him first, "I have never said this, and I should have. I am, and have always been, immensely proud of you."

James sensed something amiss, "What's going on?"

"Nothing. Just, in the last few days I have learned so much more about you. No matter what anyone else said, you stuck to your beliefs. I'm jealous, a little of the conviction, this faith you have found. A faith I have only just started to understand. I wish I could have had that conversation with your preacher."

"You can, anytime you want. It's called prayer."

"Well, maybe when all this is over you can teach me about it all in more detail."

"It would be my pleasure, and honour."

"Now, I need to get going." They hugged, embracing each other firmly. George went over to their prisoner, helping him stand. He picked up his bag, shook hands with them all, wished them luck and said he looked forward to meeting them later that afternoon.

Pushing Izsak towards the door, they left.

Chapter Thirteen
The Hunt – Part Two

It had been just over twenty-four hours since the discovery of the empty tomb. Still, with all their contacts, with all their power, that was the only thing they were sure about. That the tomb remained empty.

Micah was growing worried, and angry at the lack of progress Having discovered that his people had not carried out the deed, he was no longer in full control of the situation. At least he now knew for certain these so-called disciples were responsible, despite the protestations of the reporter. Who else could it have been? No one else gained anything from it. No, it had to have been his followers.

Pilate was frustrated, the situation was getting out of control. He needed this settled, before Tiberius' arrival in a weeks' time. He could just imagine the malicious enjoyment Micah and Caiaphas would get out of telling the emperor all the details, suitably embellished. Promising careers had been destroyed by a lot less.

Which were the same thoughts that passed through Colonel Vespian's mind. After another unpleasant meeting with Micah, he was beginning to see his own promising career disappearing over the horizon. Unknown to Pilate, Vespian knew one of the purposes for the emperors visit. The offer of a new posting back in Rome and a promotion to head of the praetorian guard, a promotion that would seal his fortune, and a future appointment to the senate upon retirement.

The Colonel was at a loss. He had used his contacts, used the sergeants contacts, offered a reward for any information. Yet, nothing of any use had been learned.

Just the fanciful tales from the informant, Ridzik, and the preposterous ramblings of Cleopas. He was unsure of the wisdom of letting that one go, the rumours were already spreading through the city like a pandemic. He could not place the origins firmly at Cleopas' door, but he had his suspicions.

What was really worrying was the number of people who seemed perfectly happy to believe it.

Micah was also aware of these rumours, the chatter coming from the streets. That had been the one fun thing in all this, to see the panic Micah was experiencing. That had not stopped the weasel from ranting at him, calling his competence into question, threatening to inform the emperor of his failings when he arrived.

The young lieutenant was scouring the area for the whore, Mary. With no success.

Vespian had even ordered out a couple of battalions. They had left, travelling the length of the city, kicking down doors, making threats, offering rewards with no success.

Vespian was beginning to really dislike these so-called Christians. Intensely.

It made no sense. Eleven people, with zero experience of any clandestine operations, no military experience was making fools of the Roman army, a mockery of him and the governor.

The council, meanwhile, remained untouched by it all. Micah had made it clear to all that the Roman authorities had insisted in handling the matter, no mention of the council begging for their help. He had no illusions, any failures would be laid at his feet by the council. Rome would be humiliated, and he would pay the price.

The sergeant knocked and entered, calling out, "We may have them, sir."

"May?"

"We have received information that they are holed up in a building on the far side of the city."

"Get a dozen men, now. We leave in twenty minutes. Get my driver ready, I am coming with you." He barked these orders out, and his sergeant hurried to fulfil them. As he pulled his cap on, he glanced at his watch. It was eight thirty in the morning, twenty-seven and a half hours since the discovery of the empty tomb. As he left his office, Vespian considered informing the governor, then changed his mind. Better to come with good news rather than a suspicion.

His jeep and driver were just pulling up as he emerged onto the barrack square. A flurry of activity continued around him. Soldiers running, pulling on their tunics as they went. Orders being shouted, one soldier was fastening up his pants as he went, another through a rifle to his friend.

As the military truck turned into the square, there was no hesitation as the dozen soldiers jumped aboard. Vespian told the sergeant to have them follow his vehicle, then ordered him into his jeep.

His driver gunned the engine, and in a cloud of dust they accelerated out of the barracks, the truck following closely behind.

With the sergeant giving directions, they sped through the streets towards their destination. It was a credit to the drivers' capabilities that they arrived in half the time it would normally take.

The soldiers were jumping off the back of the truck as it skidded to a halt. Vespian told them to spread out, covering all exits, forming a parameter around the building. Picking two of the soldiers out, he approached the main entrance, nodded at them and they kicked the doors down and rushed in, rifles raised. The same action was taken at the rear. A couple of minutes later and Vespian heard one of them shout, "All clear Colonel."

Vespian entered the building, looking around, seeing the evidence of occupation. His sergeant joined him, "There are indications of a large vehicle being here out back."

"How recent?"

"Can't tell, could be hours, could be days. We can follow the tracks, but once we reach the main highway, we have no way of knowing which way they went."

"I know a man who does, though," Vespian said. "Search this place from top to bottom. They're amateurs, they may have left something behind."

"Yes sir."

Vespian took one last look around, then left taking his driver with him. They drove back to the barracks at a more leisurely pace, the Colonel grabbing some sleep in the back. Upon his return, he headed over to the governor's office. When he entered, he was annoyed to find Micah stood there.

As he walked across to the governor's desk, Pilate asked him, "Do you have any news, Colonel?"

"Nothing much," Vespian began, he was about to continue when he was interrupted by Micah.

"Then what is the point of you being here? And, why have you no new information?"

"I never said I didn't have any information, just that I didn't have much."

"You really have nothing to tell me? I shouldn't be surprised, you have dealt with this incompetently from the start. I will be…"

Vespian had had enough, and spoke straight across Micah.

"I am sure you will be making a full report to Caiaphas, and to the emperor next week. In meantime, why don't you do us all a favour and crawl back into the hole you came out of. What I have to say is none of your fucking business until I decide it is, because I don't report to you. So, if you want to continue enjoying the cooperation of this office, I suggest to keep your shitty comments to yourself, because I really couldn't give a fuck what you think. If you are unhappy with the way I have handled this business, your fucking cock-up incidentally, please feel free to take over," Micah remained silent. "That's what I thought."

Pilate spoke, "So what information do you have?"

"We received a tip off that they were hiding out in a building on the outskirts."

"Why was the council not informed?" Micah demanded.

Vespian ignored the question. "When we got there, they had already left. We missed them by a couple of hours would be my guess."

"This is not acceptable, another example of…"

Pilate interrupted him, his anger rising at the constant stream of criticism from that quarter. "Micah, you are here at our agreement, so either make a useful contribution to this conversation or stay silent." He refocused his attention back to Vespian. "What do you propose to do now?"

"We aren't going to find the body, not without reliable information, which we can't get. The council have found out even less than we have. I think it is time to change the focus onto the followers, they are the ones who know what we want."

"How do we find them? As you said, it appears they have flown."

"There is a man, a thoroughly repulsive human, but he is unsurpassed as a tracker of others. He is currently finding Barabbas for us, but that can wait."

"Really?"

"Yes, he will pop his head up eventually, he won't be able to help himself. When he does, I will be there to shoot it off. Meanwhile, the city is buzzing with stories of the risen one, as they call him. The emperor is due in five days, this needs to be sorted before then."

"I agree," Micha said. "His followers hold the key, hunt them all down. Find them, then pass them to the council. We will deal with it from there."

"I don't think so," Vespian said. "The council no longer has any authority in this matter."

"We have all authority in this."

"But you told me that these people represent a threat to Rome, only thirty hours ago at the tomb. Are you now saying they aren't? If that is the case, then we are more than happy to hand this whole matter back to you to deal with."

"They are our responsibility, not yours."

"No, they are Rome's problem now. As a threat to our empire, as you happily told me yesterday."

Pilate looked at his Colonel, he could overrule him; but after the amount of crap he had put up with from the council over the last couple of days, he was not inclined to. He looked up at Micah, who stared back at Pilate with expectation. "What?" he asked. "He is correct. I have lost count of the number of times you have told us about the type of threat these followers are to Rome." Turning back to Vespian, he continued, "Do it, use this tracker." Back to Micah, "Once we have them, we will inform you of their capture, we will then decide what is to be done, and I may include your council in those decisions if I feel so inclined."

Vespian saluted his governor, then left to carry out the agreed plan. Entering his office, he called out to his sergeant, "Get hold of the tracker, Izsak Abraham Sheenah."

"Yes, sir. Any idea where he is?"

"With the unit currently hunting Barabbas. In fact, bring them all back in, we have another job for them."

The sergeant left to carry out his orders. He returned shortly after, speaking as he walked, "They are on the way back, should be with us in a couple of hours."

"Good, now I want you to inform the commanders that I want a watch put on all local train and bus terminals. Make sure they all have the photographs, tell them these men are to be arrested on sight and brought back here."

"Yes, sir."

While he waited, Vespian decided to take the opportunity to clear up some overdue paperwork. Nothing important, just the daily reports from the commanders of the individual regiments. Minor infractions, punishments given. More important acts would be brought directly to his attention, accompanied by the commander's recommendations. He trusted the men appointed to command the individual units. He had ten units, each with a contingent of one hundred men in each. Ten thousand soldiers, all answering to him. Each of these units had a captain in overall charge, supplemented with two lieutenants with responsibility for fifty men each, and under them the sergeants with ten men each to command. It was an efficient hierarchy, it worked well.

Reading through his reports he found most of the troublesome behaviour was due to drunkenness. These had been dealt with as usual by the commanders. There was one man's name that he recognised, checking back he confirmed this was the fifth time he had appeared in the daily reports. He would have to look more closely at this man, get a better picture of what was going on. He reached for the phone to make the call, when he heard vehicles arriving outside.

Within a couple of minutes, the two soldiers, and the tracker were shown into his office. One of the soldiers did not look happy, speaking immediately on being ushered into the room.

"May I ask, sir, why we have been taken off this assignment?"

"Because there is something more important I need him for." Pointing at the Izsak. "I will overlook your lack of respect, soldier and put it down to your eagerness to put Barabbas back where he belongs."

"I apologise, sir. I have good reasons for wanting that bastard caught."

"As have us all. However, something else has come up which requires Izsak's particular skills. Something that can't wait."

The soldier nodded his understanding, realising he had been granted a reprieve for his insubordination. He listened intently as the Colonel continued.

Speaking directly to Izsak, "You will, I am sure, have heard of this so-called prophet, Joseph Bartholomew?"

"I know of him, yes," the little man replied. His voice sounding bored, as if being there was an inconvenience. Despite the huge fees he charged for his services, he still treated each assignment as if he was the one in charge. Vespian had dealt with him on a number of occasions, he found this tracker to be arrogant to the point of rudeness. He had an over inflated opinion of himself, believing the skills he possessed to be indispensable, so making him untouchable in his eyes. Vespian would have reminded him that the graveyards were full of equally indispensable people. The Colonel did not trust him, every time he shook hands with the man he was tempted to check he still had four fingers and a thumb.

Vespian continued, "As you will also know, he was executed on Friday afternoon. Then, on Sunday his body disappeared from the tomb."

"Ah, the rising from the dead rumour," Izsak said. "I heard about these tales, these claims. However, I can't help you. I can't track dead people."

"I'm sure you underestimate your abilities, but that is not what you are here for. As I said, the body has disappeared. We have searched without any success, and now the stories of his having risen are beginning to spread through the city. Nothing serious at the moment." To his annoyance, he was interrupted again by Izsak.

"And you need to put an end to them, or at least the council want you too."

Vespian spoke again, with a trace of impatience, "Yes, precisely. Before this whole business gets completely out of control. Therefore," he held his hand up to prevent the man interrupting again, "we need to question these followers of his. That is where you come in, I want you to find them, let my office know when you do and we will come along and collect them up."

"When where they last seen?"

"The night of his arrest, but we have information that they are all together again, we just missed them this morning. I have had the area cordoned off, so as to prevent any further disturbance. My sergeant has all the details, along with their names and photographs. Any information is to be passed directly to this office, and I expect updates of progress every couple of hours." He turned to the soldiers. "You are to assist him in any way. This is our top priority, the emperor's visit commences in a few days. We need this sorted before then. You have your assignment, go now."

Both soldiers saluted, and were about to leave when they realised that Izsak was still stood in front of the Colonel. He cleared his throat, then spoke, "We need to discuss terms."

"You will get the same terms you always get from us."

"With respect, that is for one man. Here you are asking me to track eleven."

"If you think we are paying you eleven separate fees, forget it. Never going to happen."

"It is only fair, eleven people. Eleven fees."

"You will be paid the usual fee, I will add a small bounty for each one you find. That is all, don't press your luck, Izsak."

"And under who's authority am I acting? What power do I have to carry out this job?" Vespian had been waiting for that question. Izsak had been pushing for an appointment as a special investigator with the Rome authorities. It was a position that came with immense power. It was also never going to happen, a Jew would never be appointed to such a sensitive position.

"Forget it, we have had this conversation over and over. You know our answer."

"Surly, under the circumstances, an official capacity would give me the authority to act, should I need to question anyone in relation to this hunt?"

"No, but I'll tell you what I will do. I will clear it with the Jewish council to have you appointed as their special investigator. That will give you the authority you want."

"When I have to deal with my own, yes. It does not do the same for Roman's."

"That's what these two are for. I am not discussing this again. Either take the job, or you can spend the rest of your days as a guest of Rome."

Izsak got the message. Vespian's patience was running out. He nodded to the Colonel, then said, "I only wish to help, it is not for myself I ask these things." He bowed to the Colonel, then left with the soldiers.

After they had left, Vespian had to halt the urge to have his room disinfected. The man's demands were getting more outrageous with each meeting. It may be time to remind Izsak Abraham Sheehan who was actually in charge here.

Looking at the clock on the wall, he decided it was time for lunch. Making a snap decision, he told his sergeant to call his driver. Stepping outside, it was only a short wait before his car pulled up, getting in he told his driver to take him to the Hilton Hotel.

On arrival he saw his man across the road, sat drinking in the coffee house. He gave no indication of recognition, entered the hotel and went straight up to the reception area.

"Good afternoon, Colonel," the woman said. "What can I do for you?"

"George Ambrose, please."

The receptionist reached for the phone, and dialled the room. She let it ring for several moments, then informed the Colonel, "I'm sorry, there's on answer."

"No problem, he wasn't expecting me."

One of the other members of the reception staff behind the desk spoke, "You're looking for Mr Ambrose?" he said.

"Yes, I don't suppose either of you know where he might be?"

"I don't. In fact, come to think of it I have not seen him for a couple of days. Certainly not since Sunday afternoon."

"Really? And you have no idea where he may have gone?"

"None."

"That is worrying, may I see his room?"

"Of course, one moment." The man went to get the key, then took Vespian up to the room. The hotel employee unlocked the door then stood to one side to allow Vespian to enter. He looked around the room, opened the wardrobe to see the clothes hanging, the travel bag folded up in the bottom. He began to open drawers looking inside. Nothing. He continued to look around, noticing that his little backpack was nowhere to be seen. No passport, or any other travel documents.

The man was speaking again, "I was going to call the authorities if he had not come back today."

"Why, did you have concerns?"

"Well, he has been missing for two days, and with the release of ..." The man left the sentence hanging.

"With the release of Barabbas you had become concerned?"

"Well, yes."

"How do you know about that?"

"He's George Ambrose." The man simply stated.

"You're a fan?"

"Yes, I was hoping he would sign my copy of his book."

"Which is why you noticed he was missing." Vespian stated matter-of-factly. He took one last look around the room, swore under his breath then spoke, "I think I can safely say that his disappearance has nothing to do with Barabbas." Vespian thanked the man and then left without any further explanation. He was beginning to realise why eleven amateurs had been able to evade the Roman authorities.

George Ambrose.

There was nothing much he could do about it now. The man had given them the slip, there wasn't even any point in speaking to the man watching the hotel. Leaving the hotel, he was struck with a thought. He returned to the reception, asking for the use of a phone.

He dialled the number of the Judean Times, the call was answered within three rings. "Judean times, how can we help?" The voice at the other end announced.

"James Abbott, please."

"One moment." There was silence from the other end, a couple of minutes passed, then, "I am sorry, there is no answer, can anyone else help?"

"Yes, can you put me through to the city desk?"

"One moment." Seconds later, he was connected.

"City desk," a voice said.

"Hi, I'm looking to get hold of James Abbott."

"Sorry, he's not here, out on a job, been gone for a couple of days now. May I ask who's calling?"

"It's not important, I will try another time," Vespian replied, then hung up. He left his hand on the handset, tapping his index finger, deep in thought. Slowly returning to the real world, he left the hotel and crossed the road. He sat next to his man, asking him if he had seen Ambrose.

"He came out for a smoke, Sunday afternoon. Not seen him since then."

"You have not seen sight of him for two days, you didn't think to check?"

"He has to come through those doors, sir, where else can he go?"

"Well, through the kitchens and out the staff entrance for one." The man's face slowly drained of colour. Watching him, the Colonel continued to speak, "Yes, private. He has gone, flew the coop. Probably not long after you watched him having a cigarette. You're no use here now. Report back to the barracks, where I will think of an appropriate reward for your stupidity." He left the man sitting there and crossed back over the road to his driver, who took him back to his office.

Vespian arrived back, requesting an update from his sergeant he was not surprised to discover there had been no further progress. He could sense his promised promotion from the emperor vanishing into the air. He decided to call it a day, he could not do anything further that day. He told his sergeant he could go home, and did the same himself.

The sergeant, Marcus Watched his boss leave. He could sense the frustration, the man was oozing it. Marcus realised this nonsense could cause him some serious problems. He had a good working relationship with this Colonel, one that could be threatened if they failed in the task given them. One could see him spending a good deal of time in a military prison, not to forget the confiscation of everything he had built up over the years. It was vital that the Colonel not be replaced.

Leaving the building, the sergeant headed back into the market place. Everywhere was busy, it was the height of the Passover celebrations and getting through the square was slow going. People got in his way at every step. It took longer than he expected, but he reached his destination. A small, out of the way drinking house. If you did not know it was there, you would never find it. Which is just how the owner, David Heidelberg liked it. Marcus spotted him sat in his usual place, nodded his recognition then ordered a drink and waited.

It was some time before he was invited to join the owner for a drink, after all he was busy man.

"It's been a while, sergeant. What brings you here?"

"Information."

"The followers of Bartholomew."

"Yes, I'm impressed."

"The news is all over the city, Rome is offering rewards for any knowledge of them."

"Do you know anything?"

"I know that Micah is spreading these stories that they have stolen the body, that they are claiming he has risen, that he is the promised Messiah. I also know that he has the Roman army running round in all directions, with no ideas. You are becoming the laughing stock of the city, everyone is saying how these followers have made fools of the mighty Roman Empire."

"That's not good, not good at all."

"Yes, I can see how that would be. Your Colonel's future is hanging by a thread, and as a consequence yours too. If he fails in this, I can't see him being offered the post back in Rome, assuming those rumours are true."

"How do you know about that, even Pilate has no idea of the true reason for Tiberius's visit."

"I have my sources. I was disappointed it had not come from you, I thought we were friends."

"I don't trade in government information, you know that. I am not a traitor to Rome. You know, information about the emperor's movements are classified. So, do you have any useful information about these people?"

"Nothing certain. It is known they have fled the city, the word floating round is that they have split up into smaller groups. That they are travelling to an agreed destination, for what purpose no-one knows."

"Do you know where?"

"Possibly."

"How much?"

"Ten thousand should cover my expenses."

"Agreed."

"What, no haggling? You really are desperate, aren't you?"

"You have no idea," Marcus said. "Payment in the usual fashion?"

"Of course."

"Well, then, tell me."

"They are heading to Rosh Pina Ben Ya'akov, it's a little used airstrip to the north of the Sea of Galilee. The talk is that they have transport, a flight out of the country."

"How the hell have they managed that?"

"You really don't know anything, do you? Not surprising, to be honest. This whole city is enjoying your embarrassment, a large majority have sworn to tell you nothing."

"That's nothing new. So, how have they managed it, and when?"

"The journalist, George Ambrose. He has been working with them for days now. It is his newspaper that is providing the transport. The talk is that within the next twenty-four hours, give or take, they will be gone. Although I doubt we have heard the last from them. They have been given a sacred task, apparently."

Marcus looked visibly surprised and shocked at this information. Whatever he was expecting to learn, this had never figured in his thoughts. He thanked the man, then rushed out of the bar.

David Heidelberg watched the figure of the sergeant disappear out of the door. He remained sat where he was for a couple of minutes, sure that he was not going to return. Satisfied, he stood up and went into his back office.

"Well," he said. "I told him exactly as you wanted, old friend."

"Good. Thank you, and give my love to your parents," Joseph Arimathea said.

It was late when the sergeant got back to the office, he tried to get hold of the Colonel with little success. Pacing the floor, he realised there was nothing he could do until mid-morning. It would just have to wait until then, but he didn't feel happy about it.

Morning arrived, bringing with it the hope that they would at last make some progress. The emperor's visit was only twenty-four hours away. As Vespian was driven to the office, he used the radio in his car to catch up with the tracker.

"I am closing in on them, Colonel," he informed him, with the usual tone of arrogance. "I tracked them to a village, Ma'ale Adumim. From what I have observed, they have now split up. I am concentrating on four of them, it is my opinion that they are all heading for the same destination. My advice, Colonel is that we wait until we have them all there, that way you can pick up all twelve in one swoop."

"Eleven, not twelve."

"All that I have seen indicates there are twelve of them."

"Inform us as soon as you know anything for certain." He handed the radio set back to the driver, settling back in his seat. At least now he had an idea as to George Ambrose's whereabouts. He sighed inwardly. He liked that journalist, and now it looked as though he might have to treat him as an enemy of Rome. He hoped that the man was just following a story, but somehow, he knew that was not going to be the case.

Arriving at the office, he jumped from the jeep and headed up the stairs to his office. When he opened the door, he was taken back to find his sergeant already there pacing back and forth in a state of agitation.

"What is it, what's happened now?"

"Pilate has been asking for you, and I have some news."

"Right, let me deal with our governor first, then you can brief me," he said as he turned on his heels and headed over to Pilates office, giving his sergeant no opportunity to speak.

As he entered, a man stood up, hand outstretched. "Good afternoon, Colonel."

"Mr Watling, this is a pleasant surprise," he replied, shaking his hand. "What brings you here?"

It was Pilate who answered, "Two of their journalists have gone missing. A James Abbott, and George Ambrose. Is that the one I played chess with?"

"Yes, governor."

Derek spoke, "I know that you and George are friends, I was hoping he may have been in touch."

"No, sorry he hasn't. I've not seen him since Sunday morning. When did you last hear from either of them?"

"We had a couple of drinks together Friday night, I've not seen or heard from them since." Derek paused. "James has not reported into the paper for a number of days, which is completely out of character for him. When I couldn't get hold of them, I became concerned. Particularly after Barabbas was released."

"What's he got to do with it?" Pilate asked.

"George was kidnapped by Barabbas. He seemed to believe he was working for us, some kind of undercover operative." Vespian said.

"Was he?"

"Definitely not, governor. I have no idea why they thought that."

"Have you heard from him?" Pilate continued.

"As I said, not since Sunday. I have been rather busy, governor."

"Of, course. This Bartholomew nonsense."

"What's that?" Derek asked.

"You must have heard the rumours?" The Colonel said to him.

"The body disappearing, his having risen from the dead? Yes, I heard them. I assume the council have asked you to assist in recovering the body?" Pilate and Vespian nodded. "An impossible task I would think."

"It has been challenging," Vespian offered. "Anyway, I will see what I can find out about the whereabouts of your reporters."

"Thank you. Obviously, I could be worrying about nothing. They may just have decided to take some father son time together."

"Sorry?" the Colonel asked.

"Yes, James is George's son. I thought you knew?"

"Yes, of course. My apologies, this Bartholomew business, my mind was elsewhere." He lied, glibly. As he said this, the phone in the office began ringing.

Pilate lifted the receiver, spoke briefly, then handed the phone to Derek, saying, "It's your paper, said it was important."

"Thank you," he said, taking the hand set. "What is it…? When…? Well, at least we know where they are." He handed the phone back, speaking as he did so, "I seem to have been wasting your time, gentlemen, I apologise, they have called the paper. As suspected, they are indeed spending some time together, they meant to call earlier but forgot."

"Where are they?" Vespian asked, curiously.

"Taking a walking trip, George has just called to request the company jet pick them up from an airstrip just north of Galilee. Well, at least that has put my mind at rest. Thank you again for your help." Derek shook hands with both men, then left to return to the paper.

"Will there be anything else, governor."

"No, carry on." Vespian left, returning to his own office. He found his sergeant, waiting in an agitated state.

"Ok, sergeant, what is it?"

Marcus quickly related the information from the previous night's meeting. When he had finished, Vespian was silent for a moment, then asked, "Do you trust this information?"

"I have no reason not to. He has never lied to me in the fifteen years or so we have done business."

"O.K. Then we assume he knows what he knows. It ties in with what I have learned in Pilates office." The phone in the outer office was ringing. Marcus stood up and pulled the call through to Vespian's office. He spoke briefly, then hung up.

"The soldiers you sent with the tracker are back. Izsak has gone missing."

"When?"

"They lost him about an hour ago, so they say."

"What else did they have to say?"

"Nothing, just that. They are on their way over now." As he finished speaking the soldiers appeared at the doorway. Vespian waved them in, speaking as they came.

"Tell us exactly what happened." Both of them began speaking at once. "Just one of you speak."

"We did as you asked, sir. We stayed with him, taking him wherever needed. We tracked them to the village of Ma'ale something or other, then up into Jericho. It is here that he said they had separated. He decided to follow the clearer of the tracks. Which we did, until he disappeared."

"It is possible he is following his own path. Show me where you last saw him." All four of them walked over to the wall map, one of the soldiers showed the location of their last sight of the tracker.

"Just here, sir. A couple of miles from Beit Yosef," the soldier said.

"That's one of our abandoned bases, been so for years now. It would be a good place to hide," the sergeant said.

"My thoughts as well, sergeant," Vespian said.

The other soldier spoke, "We checked it, when we looked for Izsak. We found nothing, no signs of any recent visitors."

Vespian stared at the map. Suddenly, after three days of nothing, all this information. Was he being deliberately misled, or was this genuine? He went through it all in his mind.

The information from the sergeant's contact, a person the sergeant trusted.

The visit from Derek Watling.

The disappearance of the tracker in the very area mentioned by the sergeants informant.

Was it genuine? At least one was. The vanishing tracker. This alone seemed to confirm the other information, the flight from the airstrip, and the father and son walking trip in the same region. He needed to make a decision, if this was all true, they would all be gone by the late afternoon of the next day. His sergeant was speaking again.

"What was that?" he asked.

"The airstrip, Rosh Pina. I knew I had read it somewhere. The journalist, Ambrose, he works for the Times?"

"What of it?"

"The flight manifests. They have requested permission to make a landing at that airstrip, tomorrow afternoon, sixteen hundred hours. And judging from the request, it's a plane big enough to pick up twelve passengers."

"If they wanted to make a quiet escape, why would they make a request?" Asked one of the soldiers.

"Because they don't know, they think they are just picking up two passengers," the sergeant said as he passed the papers over to the Colonel. "Ambrose knew they would make the application to land, so he couldn't tell them the truth. He had to make out it was just for him and one other."

"His son," Vespian said. "Let's make our preparations sergeant, I want everything ready to move by Eight hundred hours."

Chapter Fourteen

The Impossible Conversation

George and Izsak had been walking for two hours, heading in the direction that left little doubt in the trackers mind of his final destination. There was no hiding things now.

Izsak had been a constant irritant. His ceaseless talking. The threats, how he was going to make sure George died the same way as Bartholomew, after all he was a man of influence.

"You followers of this dead prophet are all the same. Peace, love, understanding for others," he said. "None of you have the guts to do what is necessary. If you did, I'd already be dead."

George had responded, angrily grabbing the man by his shirt collar and speaking up close to his face, "I may have become one, but don't make the mistake that I am the same. You are a threat to my family, if it is required, I won't hesitate to remove the gun you brought from my back pack and use it. And don't think it would be a quick end. No, one shot in one knee, then leave you here where we stand."

Izsak made a show of bravado, but it was obvious behind his eyes that he was unsure. After this exchange, they continued in relative silence.

Izsak was trying again to convince George of the error of his ways.

"You won't get away, none of you will," he said.

"We'll see," had been George's response.

Izsak had then felt the need to further explain. "You are all going to be caught. They will hand you over to the council inquisitors. They will make you talk, they are well versed in ways to loosen a man's tongue. And you will talk, everyone does in the end. I will make sure I am there to see you all suffer. When they are finished, they will have you all executed, another thing I will take pleasure in watching."

"Maybe, but not today."

"But you have a chance to escape. Let me go, I will speak up for you when the time comes."

"I will, soon."

"A wise decision. I am the best chance you have to save your own skin."

"Don't get excited. I'm not interested in any deals. I will release you when I know it is safe to do so."

"You will be, the inquisitors are very good at their job, everyone tries to avoid them by coming to an understanding."

"You really think I would give these people up?"

"What else can you do? We always win."

"Not this time, not if I have anything to do with it. The people you work for are corrupt, they have no interest in the people and their needs. They only care about protecting their own wealth and positions."

"Of course they do, as does everyone else. No one will care what happens to any of you."

"Have you never thought that there might be a better way to do things? A way in which all benefit, rather than just the few privileged?"

"Fantasy. You either work with them, or get buried in the surge of humanity."

"They pay you well?"

"Very."

"See, your just like them."

"I am a realist. You have no idea how much they despise you all. I couldn't care less one way or the other, the twelve of you are just another job, another pay packet. I've never seen the council this riled up. Micah in particular hates you all, you especially for some reason. He believes the destruction of every last one of you is a mission given to him by God. He has even convinced the Romans that you represent a threat to them, so persuasive that Pilate has appointed Colonel Vespian to hunt you all down. I think he is looking forward to it."

"Perhaps, but Vespian is a soldier. He will do whatever he is commanded to do. He follows orders, that's his job. Micah has no such excuse. He's just a vindictive, evil little bully. Well, I've dealt with bullies before, he's nothing unusual. The only difference is that he hides behind his religious dogma. All so he can do whatever he wants, and claim it is for God." George stopped talking, turning to face Izsak. He turned the little man around and began to untie his wrists. "What makes you think that God approves of what he does, what any of them do? They continue to corrupt themselves, they use the people as a source of income, they bring in laws to oppress them, they allow child slavery to continue – which is as a direct result of their King taxing them all into penury. I'm constantly surprised God has not treated them the same way he did Sodom." George finished speaking, then pushed the tracker away from him saying, "We are finished here."

"You're letting me go?"

"I said I would. Unlike you, I am a man of my word. The others are no more than an hour away from the airstrip, as am I. The nearest village is at least a three hour walk away." George turned and continued on his way.

"You are a fool, George Ambrose."

George ignored him and continued on his way. He knew why the tracker called him a fool, or hoped he did. It could have been that George had agreed when he accused him of being a follower, a believer of this Jesus Joseph Joshua Bartholomew. When he had admitted that, it had taken him by surprise, but he also realised it was the truth. He could not explain when it had happened, it just had.

However, he hoped he had been called a fool for another reason. The nearest village was actually only half an hour's brisk walk away. Izsak would make straight for it, and call Colonel Vespian as soon as he could. Faced with what he was told, the Colonel would have no other choice but believe the information.

George was deep in thought when he heard someone speak to him.

"So, you believe in me?" He turned at the voice. When he recognised him, for some reason he was not surprised. As though he had expected this moment, this meeting with this impossible man.

"Don't get all excited, I only said that to shut him up."

"No, it is the truth. If it was not, you would not be able to see me, or hear me."

"So, finally we meet."

"I thought it was an appropriate time. You have been looking for so long."

"I've been here a week. It's hardly a long time."

"You have been searching for answers a lot longer than that," Joseph replied. "Not particularly for me, or perhaps even my father; but for something to make sense of your life, this world."

"Is that why you are here now? To make sense of it all for me?"

"Answer this for me, why are you here?"

"Don't you know?"

"Of course. I want to know if you do."

"Someone had to do something, why not me? And, it is the right thing to do." George started to walk again, Joseph at his side. "Not the easy thing, but it is right."

"Why? To protect your son, that is understandable. Why the others, you barely know them?"

"They need protecting, they're naïve. I don't pretend to grasp half the things they have told me. One thing I do know, they believe in you. They believe in a better way of doing things."

"And now you too have come to me, through your own son." George shrugged his shoulders. "You must forget everything you think you know, accept what is new. A rebirth."

"Nicodemus said something similar."

"I liked him. He was willing to be open to new ideas."

"And I'm not?"

"You live in a different world to Nicodemus. Your instinct is to question, to analyse everything. Somethings just are."

"Is that a bad thing? To question, rather than just blind obedience?"

"Certainly not. We want you to ask questions. To discover the truth on your own. If we wanted blind obedience, why would we give you the freedom to choose?"

"Freedom of choice, that's worked out well."

"It is what it is."

"Sounds a bit like a get out clause. You can't blame God, after all you made the decision, now live with the consequences."

"Not how I would have put it."

"Why are you here?"

"To save the world. My father in heaven sent me as a sacrifice. To take on the sins of the world, so that you would know his forgiveness in all things."

"That's it?"

"Simply put, yes. Through me, all men are forgiven their transgressions should they ask for it."

"All men? I thought these where your chosen people?"

"All men, Jew and non-Jew in equal measure."

"That was a hell of a sacrifice, incidentally."

"No more than the one you intend to make."

"Really?"

"You are sacrificing yourself in order to keep them safe."

"To protect my son, I think it is worth doing."

"As did I, to protect and save my father's children, here on earth," Joseph answered back. "There is no greater sacrifice you can make. To lay down your life to preserve those we love. My father loves you all so much that he sent me to save you. All you have to do is accept the truth of that."

"Simple as that, acceptance without question?"

"No, I told you. Questioning things is good. It's how you learn, how you come to the truth of anything. The acceptance my father means, is of yourself. Of who you are, and of others as they are. Go on living your life, as it feels right to you. It is that simple, try to live a normal life, and be happy with whatever God gives you, good and bad."

"Just like that?"

"I never said it was easy. I said it was simple."

"Why does it all have to be so damned hard?"

"How else will you learn? To grow as a person? You learn, gain strength through adversity. It is that very hardship that makes you stronger, able to face seemingly unsurmountable problems. Without that gift, the freedom to choose, no-one would grow in their understanding. It is when you fail that you learn the most. Not just of your own infinite capabilities, but of God's love also. His all-encompassing, perfect compassion for you all."

"So he sent you to remind us all?"

"Yes. I am not here for the righteous, those that have already accepted these things. I am here for the sinner, the ungodly. To offer them the chance of redemption. Repentance and forgiveness, an opportunity to spend eternity with my father, in his kingdom."

"Do you think they will take you up on your offer?"

"Some will. Your son, and the others will be instrumental in calling them to me. Not all will hear, but those that do will receive peace.

"It's like a farmer, sowing his seeds in the field. Some may land on rocky ground, where it will fall away and die. Some will land on fertile land, and so take root and grow strong."

"Nice analogy," George responded.

"Thank you, I'm quite good at them."

George gave a chuckle, saying, "So God has a sense of humour?"

"You doubt it?"

"Looking at the world, it is difficult to see."

"No, it really isn't. This world is full of madness, just take a look at some of the leaders you have selected to govern over you."

"What about those people that don't hear, or refuse to listen, are they going to be summarily condemned to the fires of hell?"

"God does not send anyone to hell."

"Come on, nobody?" George said, turning to face Joseph.

"My father condemns no-one. They make the choice, by rejecting our love for them. By making choices in behaviour. I have another analogy for you. Here we are, walking along when a fork in the road appears. It is clearly signposted. The right path leads to God, the left takes you away from his love. You understand the consequences, yet you still choose the left-hand path. God has provided you with all the data you need to make an informed decision, yet you still walk down the left path. How is that God's fault?

"As to those who never hear his word, it is not God's nature to be unfair. His love is perfect. He is perfect in his holiness. God is loving and patient, he is not going to make anyone perish. It is his intention that you come to know Him freely."

"And the evil that men do, that's all due to His freedom of choice gift?"

"See, already your understanding has grown because you ask questions. In the end though, love will override the knowledge of evil. Bad things happen, but they pass. Love lasts forever."

"And the wars declared in his name?"

"Nothing to do with Him. All your own work. Sadly, war is something you have become very accomplished at."

"I know."

George did not respond any further, he had arrived at the airstrip. Looking around, he could no longer see the physical form of Jesus, as he now called him; but he could sense him, everywhere. There was a peacefulness, one that he had not known in many years.

The sun was low in the evening sky, a light breeze floated across the desert landscape. It was a beautiful day.

It was only just four in the afternoon, he had made good time, arriving with half an hour to spare. As he looked down at the few buildings, the old control tower, the ground staff and baggage area. There were three hangers, all long empty now. Only the letter 'A' had survived from the arrivals sign. The departures signage had done slightly better over the years, with the first letter and the last four still present.

There were other things he could see. The four army trucks parked on the runway, the soldiers strategically placed around the airstrip; And there, stood in the doorway, under what remained of the sign for passport control was Colonel Vespian. They looked at each other from their vantage points. George sensed the soldiers behind him, he started to walk down into the airport before they reached him. They stayed with him as he progressed. No force was used, none was required. He had long ago accepted his fate.

"I privately hoped you would not come," Vespian told him. "And the others?"

"Gone, some two hours ago. They were picked up on the shores of Galilee."

"The helicopter I saw fly past?"

"Probably."

"Where?"

"No idea. Truly, I never asked and they never told me."

"I believe you, it would have been stupid to have done so. Shall we sit? I have an excellent single malt." Vespian turned and entered the building. A table and chairs had been set up, and as promised two glasses and a bottle of twenty-five-year-old Tullibardine whiskey stood on the table. They sat opposite each other, Vespian poured them both a measure, handing one over to George.

"You do, I'm sure, understand the position I am now in?"

"I do. And I am sorry for that. But I had to do whatever I could, to protect my son."

"Well, thank you for that at least. I understand, I had no idea he was your son."

"Don't take it personally, few people do. He did not want others thinking he only got the job because of me. He wanted to prove himself in his own right. Plus, with the work I was doing at the time, it was safer."

"Why the others?"

"They are good people. They haven't done anything wrong."

"Actually, according to the council they have broken several laws."

George poured them both another measure of whiskey, replying, "And we all know how trustworthy and honest they are."

"Maybe, but you don't get to make those decisions."

"It's not a decision, it is common knowledge. You know how corrupt they are."

"I do, but again that is not my problem. I work for the Roman Empire, for Tiberius and I answer to him and Governor Pilate only. The council have no bearing on what I do."

"Other than when they make their demands."

"My orders still come from the governor, not from the council. I am a soldier, that is my profession. I follow the order given to me by my superiors."

"You don't have to like it."

"I never said I did. I find most of the councils' hierarchy beneath contempt."

"So, why do it?"

"You seem to be missing the point. I am senior officer in the Roman services, it is my job. I don't have the same luxuries you have. I don't get to make the choices. I just follow the orders I am given."

"I disagree, but I understand you are caught between the two."

"Hurrah for you," Vespian stated vehemently. "Do you really not know where they have gone?"

"Honestly, no idea."

"Well, that's that then."

"Really?" George said, astonished.

"No, of course not," the Colonel said, anger rising. "I am under instructions to hand you over to the inquisitors. I think the list of charges the council intend to bring against you currently stands at thirty-six. They include sedition, espionage, aiding and abetting to name a few."

"I'm impressed."

"You seem very calm about it."

"Not really, I just don't care."

"You think I won't give you to them?"

"I have no idea. You're an honourable man, or try to be, as much as you can in the service of Rome."

"Well, I'm not going to. I have other orders where you are concerned. You have been charged under Roman law."

"Ah, so you are here to hand down Rome's justice?"

"Yes, sorry. Nothing I can do about that."

"So, I'm to be shot?"

"That's the command I have been given. Executed for crimes against the continued security of Rome. I take no pleasure in it, I like you. I thought, over time, we had become friends."

"I like you, even if you do work for the lunatics that hold power back in Rome."

"You seem curiously calm, all things as they are."

"I have a different perspective on things these days."

Vespian looked across the table, sudden understanding dawning. "Oh, my god,"

"Which one?" George retorted.

"You've become one of them. You, of all people. The cynical journalist that views everything with suspicion, you have fallen under their spell."

"You cannot deny what you have seen with your own eyes."

"Meaning?"

"I have seen him, twice."

"Who? Seen who?" Even as he asked the question, he knew the answer.

"Him, Jesus Joseph Joshua Bartholomew, to give you his full name."

"Not you as well, this ridiculous nonsense again."

"Again?"

"Yes, you are at least the fourth person to make these crazy claims."

"Fourth? In my line of work that would be enough verification for us to run the story."

"No matter how ludicrous? Dead men do not come back to life."

"You have no idea what you are dealing with. There is a power coming that will sweep the old ways to one side. And there is nothing you can do about."

"Wrong, I have been instructed to find them all, wherever they may go. By order of the emperor himself, my last command before I return to Rome as the new head of the praetorian guard. I will take great pleasure in doing so. They have all been an embarrassment to Rome, to the governor and have caused me a great deal of problems."

"You can try, but you will fail. You can hunt them all down, but that won't stop the truth coming out."

"The truth? I find that is dependent on one's point of view. As far as I am concerned, they are troublemakers, a scourge on the world that I will enjoy removing. No matter how long it takes."

"You're wrong. This new religion, this Christianity as they are calling it will spread across the world, you can't stop it." George paused as he heard the approach of an aircraft. "I don't suppose you are going to let me get on that plane?"

"No. But, I will allow them to fly you home. Back to your family," having said this, Vespian stood and indicated to one of the soldiers that it was time. "I am sorry about this, really I am." As he walked away, George called him.

"I have known you for, what, four or five years?"

"That makes no difference. I have my job to do."

"No, I just realised, I don't know your first name."

"Paul, my friends call me Paul."

Sources

1. Application Study Bible, New Living Transliation. Tyndale House Publishers Ltd, Carol Stream, Illinois, 2007.
2. CICERO; Pro Rabiro 3.10. Translated by H D Hodge. Leob Classical Library, Cambridge, Mass; Harvard University Press, 1927.
3. The Crucifixion of Jesus: A Forensic Inquiry, M. Evans & Company. Frederick T Zugibe, 2nd edition,
4. A Doctor at Calvary: The Passion of our Lord Jesus Christ by a Surgeon, Allegro Editions. Pierre Barbet M.D., 2014

Ingram Content Group UK Ltd.
Milton Keynes UK
UKHW022032120323
418425UK00007B/120